When we found the things floating in the darkness between stars, we should have been more afraid.

Here is what we thought we knew: at the extreme edge of our system, just past the distant ring of ice and dust that marks the blast radius of our own sun's kindling—the accretion disc—life was waiting for us. Alien life forms the size of humpback whales floated in the black. Encrusted with rock and ice, they looked like nothing so much as a mad child's drawing of a cuttlefish. The first two we found sported tentacled limbs floating motionless in space and eyes larger than a man placed in a ring around a cavernous mouth.

Seriously, we should have known better.

QUANTUM ZOO

**EDITED BY
D.J. GELNER &
J.M. NEY-GRIMM**

QUANTUM ZOO. Copyright © 2014 by Orion's Comet LLC.

Orion's Comet LLC publishes this work under a limited, non-exclusive license, obtained from the authors. Rights obtained by Orion's Comet LLC reserved to Orion's Comet LLC for the term of the license.
This is a work of fiction. Names, characters, businesses, places, events and incidents are either the products of the author's imagination or used in a fictitious manner. Any resemblance to actual persons, living or dead, or actual events is purely coincidental.

"A King in Exile" Copyright © 2014 by Bridget McKenna
"Echoes of Earth" Copyright © 2014 by D.J. Gelner
"Bestiarum" Copyright © 2014 by Sarah Stegall
"Ignoble Deeds" Copyright © 2014 by A.C. Smyth
"At Home in the Stars" Copyright © 2014 by S.E. Batt
"The Most Dangerous Lies" Copyright © 2014 by Ken Furie
"Playing Man" Copyright © 2014 by Scott Dyson
"You'll Be So Happy, My Dear" Copyright © 2014 by John Hindmarsh
"Skipdrive" Copyright © 2014 by Morgan Johnson
"Demon Rising" Copyright © 2014 by R.S. McCoy
"Your Day at the Zoo" Copyright © 2014 by Frances Stewart
"Serpent's Foe" Copyright © 2014 by J.M. Ney-Grimm

Cover and book design by J.M. Ney-Grimm
Cover design copyright © 2014 J.M. Ney-Grimm
Cover art:
  "Whale and Diver" copyright © 2014 by Philcold / Dreamstime
  "Starry Sky and Cassiopeia" copyright © 2014 by Silvertiger / Dreamstime
  "Blue Water" copyright © 2014 by Firelia / Dreamstime

ISBN 13: 978-1-939417-06-0
ISBN10: 1939417066

To all of the dreamers out there:
You *can* do it.

Table of Contents

A King in Exile 1
Bridget McKenna

Echoes of Earth 19
D.J. Gelner

Bestiarum 41
Sarah Stegall

Ignoble Deeds 65
A.C. Smyth

At Home in the Stars 85
S.E. Batt

The Most Dangerous Lies 107
Ken Furie

Playing Man 129
Scott Dyson

You'll Be So Happy, My Dear 149
John Hindmarsh

Skipdrive 155
Morgan Johnson

Demon Rising 197
R.S. McCoy

Your Day at the Zoo 211
Frances Stewart

Serpent's Foe 215
J.M. Ney-Grimm

A King in Exile
Bridget McKenna

LADY PENELOPE SMYTHE-EVERTON is dead. In point of fact she succumbed more than seven years ago to a chronic illness that had distressed and weakened her for some time, but until today when my train pulled away from Ashford station in Kent, I had never truly felt it in my heart. Now I can feel nothing else.

I am, I believe, the one person who can truly be said to have known Penelope—and I intend no offence by this familiarity—but despite the disparity of our social stations she was my dearest friend and I believe I was hers. So it is that I take it upon myself to set down the record of the extraordinary events of her life as they relate to the magnificent creature who went to his own grave today, still mourning his mistress to his final, laboured breath. I know how fantastic these words may seem, and I may never show them to another living being, but I know I must write them.

Penelope Smythe-Everton was the only daughter of Sir Anthony Smythe-Everton and his wife, Lady Eugenia. Two sons had died in infancy, but a third survived to plague them. Penelope came late in their lives, as these matters are reckoned, and as soon as she began to walk, talk, and wreak havoc about the household it was evident that this was the child they had been waiting for.

When Penelope was six years old, and her brother Richard nineteen, Sir Anthony tired of reading about the wonders of the world from deep in the interior of a leather chair at his club. He announced his intention to take his family on a voyage round the world. Lady Eugenia, uncertain about the wisdom of this plan, but willing to risk it for her beloved husband's sake, packed their trunks and made the arrangements.

They were not to return for four years, or three of them were not, at least. Richard put his foot down after six months of sailing on tramp steamers, and trekking through unfamiliar terrain, and wandering farther and farther from the London society that was his by right of birth. He sailed home to live with his maternal grandmother. His parents were, by this time, delighted to see him go.

It is probably not necessary to point out that Penelope was not reared in quite the same manner as most young Englishwomen of her generation; indeed, at her father's insistence, she was raised to be a self-sufficient human being, exposed to the ideas and customs of a dozen exotic cultures, and thus rendered quite unfit for society. Lady Eugenie used often to bewail this fact, to which Sir Anthony was wont to reply, "Then perhaps she will emigrate to America, where a lack of social graces seems to *be* a sort of social grace."

Though Penelope's education was exhaustive and wide-ranging, it managed somehow to skip right over such niceties as fancy needlework or the rendering of floral arrangements in water-colour. She could, however, stitch up a laceration like a surgeon and depict wild animals with her pens and pencils in startling detail, often from far closer range than she ever let on to her mother. She learnt to ride like a man and to shoot, though she never took to killing her fellow-creatures, preferring to befriend living things of one toothy kind or another in whatever remote part of the globe her family's travels took them. Sir Anthony's wanderlust tended to return most years with the coming of spring, and they would be off for one of the shrinking number of places they had not yet been.

I didn't know Penelope as a child, though I often used to wish I had; I made the family's acquaintance some years later through the firm of Breffny, Blythe, & Warrington, where I had recently become the most junior of solicitors. I was sent to the Smythe-Everton household in Belgrave Square on an errand for a more senior man, and was received at the door by Sir Anthony himself, a breach of etiquette that would have had a proper Englishman fainting dead away on the doorstep, but then I was not an Englishman, proper or otherwise.

"You must be young Mr Maguire!" boomed Sir Anthony in a hearty and quite uncivilised voice. "Come in, lad, and have a whiskey with me!" We became fast friends that day, and within the week he had transferred all his legal affairs into my keeping.

I stayed to dinner at Sir Anthony and Lady Eugenia's insistence, and my first sight of seventeen-year-old Penelope was a streak of dirt-smeared white as she ran in from the garden and upstairs to make herself presentable. When she came down again she wore a pale green dress that matched her eyes, and her light brown hair was pulled up in a loose knot from which little curls escaped to brush against her neck. I couldn't breathe for a good five seconds, but I like to think I recovered before anyone noticed my predicament. "Our daughter, Penelope," her father informed me, "though we call her Penny. Mr John Maguire."

Penny smiled and held out a small, sunburnt hand. My heart thumped painfully, and I muttered something I hoped acceptable about being pleased to meet her before reluctantly releasing it.

My occupation, and therefore my social status, was not mentioned, but my accent was a clear enough indication of my origins, and I could feel the gulf between us, though I must admit the Smythe-Evertons didn't pay it any mind. Dinner was a casual affair, served by a housekeeper and a single maid with whom the family kept up a lively conversation as the meal was served and eaten. I'd never seen anything remotely like it, or not since I'd left Ireland, anyway.

By the end of the evening I was totally and hopelessly in love with Penelope, a condition from which I have never recovered. My social position, or lack thereof, required that I never mention it. Over time we went from being "Mr Maguire" and "Miss Smythe-Everton" to the familiar intimacy of first names.

The following year Sir Anthony was taken with a longing to see some dark and seldom visited region of South America south of the great wide Amazon down which they had journeyed on a previous voyage before I had met them. Leaving in the early spring meant being conveniently absent for the height of the London social season and the endless succession of sporting events, parties, balls, and concerts that consumed upper-class English life until August.

The whole point of the season, after all, was to find husbands for daughters, and no young man of social consequence would have dared consider Penelope as a wife, no matter how much he might appreciate her unstudied loveliness or be secretly bewitched by her wild spirit. The family's fortunes were respectable without being extraordinary, and lacking a great deal of fortune indeed a wife like Sir Anthony and Lady Eugenia's odd and outspoken daughter would do a young man of blood and connections no good at all, and quite possibly a great deal of harm.

For Penelope's part, she found the young men boring and the older ones to be looking for well-moneyed wives to pay their debts. The legal and social restraints that marriage placed on women, at least in England, were not suited to her, or she to them. Her grandmother had insisted she be presented at the Court of St James the previous year, but no-one could force staunchly proper London society to invite Sir Anthony's shockingly improper daughter to meet their sons, or at least not more than once. If Penelope were ever to marry, it would have to be to a different kind of man than she would meet in London. "Next year's trip," Sir Anthony told me in confidence, "will be to America." But first they would journey once more to the far corners of the world.

I was on the docks that day in March to watch their ship depart and receive last-minute instructions as to the overseeing of Sir Anthony's affairs while the family were abroad. Penelope waved at me from the railing as the ship moved away. I waved back, sorry as always to see her receding from my sight. "I'll write!" she called to me. "See you in the autumn, John!"

In fact, she would be back before summer, a virulent jungle fever having taken both her parents' lives, and another life—the strangest I have ever known—having been placed in her care.

I had planned to visit the house in Belgrave Square a few days after Penelope returned to extend my condolences at the passing of her parents, but before I could do so she sent a messenger to my office, asking me to call on her.

She met me in the parlour. She was dressed in black, but she would have seemed pale in any colour, still weakened as she would be all her life from the illness which had struck down Sir Anthony and Lady Eugenia, and still subdued by sorrow.

There was so much I wanted to say, but the only words I could manage were little more than the formalised expressions of comfort she might have heard from anyone. I touched her arm cautiously, then withdrew my hand, helpless to do or say anything meaningful and ruefully aware of my inadequacy. Penelope rescued me from my discomfiture. "Come with me to the drawing-room," she said. "There's something I'd like to show you."

"What do you think of him?" she asked, having led me by the hand to a place near the drawing-room fire where a small, naked, green reptile lay squirming in a tangled nest of blankets on the hearth.

I withdrew my hand from hers before I could betray the consternation her intimacy produced. "He?"

"At a guess." She knelt down by the little creature and pulled me down beside her. "Isn't he the most beautiful thing you've ever seen?"

An unfair question, I thought, looking at her out of the corner of my eye, not at the least because this scaly infant would certainly be regarded by any civilised person as a reptilian nightmare. "Very nearly," I admitted. "But what is he?"

"I'm not sure. I'm still looking through father's natural histories, but I haven't come across anything remotely like him."

Penelope had been given an egg, she told me, big as a bread-bin, by a tribe of natives deep in the interior of the South American continent. These same people had nursed her through the fever that had cost her parents' lives, and after their deaths had performed funeral rites for them with all appropriate local custom. Then, as Penelope was leaving with the other members of their party to rendezvous with their ship at the nearest river-port, they gave her a gift to show their sorrow at her leaving and their hopes for her return. The eggs were exceedingly rare, they informed her, hazardous to acquire, and remarkably good eating.

When she felt movement inside the leathery covering, she wrapped the egg in layers of cloth and kept it close to the heat of her body for the remainder of the voyage home. It had hatched only this morning, and she had sent a messenger to summon me to the house.

The creature was no larger than a skinny hen, and resembled one markedly save for the absence of feathers and the rich green of his skin, over which was a sprinkling of paler spots not unlike the markings of a fawn. His skull was over-large, with huge golden eyes. His hind legs were stout, with birdlike feet, but in place of wings were two ridiculously small forelimbs, too tiny even to convey food from his two-fingered claws to his enormous pink-lined mouth, which it now opened and shut in an obvious appeal for nourishment. He had never taken his gaze from her face.

"What do you suppose he eats?" she asked me.

I regarded the razor-sharp teeth that gnashed against one another as he opened and closed his mouth with a sound like dozens of little needles rubbing together. "Meat," I ventured. Penelope herself was a vegetarian, but it was certain her young charge was not.

"I shall send for some," she replied, and a short time later I was helping her drop bits of finely minced raw beef into the little fellow's gaping mouth. He gulped them ravenously, vocalising his pleasure with soft grunts and squeals while gazing at her in what I imagined was adoration.

In days to come the beastly infant would follow his mistress about the house like a toddling child. He adopted a curious running gait with his head held back atop his curving neck and his heavy tail straight out behind for balance, over-sized chicken feet striking the ground toes first, far more graceful than any description of mine could convey. His natural predilection for hunting was evident in the way he would crouch down on his haunches, swivel his head, and fix his eyes on any moving object, and he had signalled his graduation from chopped meat by smashing through a lath-and-wire cage in the kitchen and claiming one of the chickens that had been intended for Sunday's supper.

Surely no employer save Penelope would have been able to avert the *en masse* resignation of household staff that very nearly followed that scene of horror, and from then on Agnes, the housekeeper, ordered a steadily increasing number of chickens.

"He needs a name," Penelope said to me one afternoon over tea. Since the hatching I had been visiting almost daily, at her assistance, and the duties outlined for me in Sir Anthony's will of looking after his daughter's legal and financial interests had expanded to include the giving of guidance and advice in reptilian affairs. I could scarcely complain if it brought me more often into Penelope's company, and I was forced to admit that I was growing fond of the little terror who was seldom out of the shadow of her skirts.

"Well he's very regal, isn't he?" I mused, watching the subject of our conversation following the flight of a housefly with rapt concentration. "Victoria would never do, though she's a predator, right enough. How about Albert?"

"You haven't an ounce of respect for the crown, John," Penelope chided, shaking her head, but her lips turned up in a smile, and her eyes twinkled. "You're so incorrigibly Irish."

"I might have to act like an Englishman to earn my living, but that doesn't make me one," I replied, returning her smile.

"Well, you needn't put on an act for me," she assured me, "it's one of my favourite things about you. No, not Victoria, nor Albert either. Keep trying, though."

"We might try another language, then. Let's see ... The Greek for 'king' is *tyrannos*."

"Too ponderous."

"The Latin," I suggested, "is *rex*."

"That's it!" Penelope laughed with delight. "I had a dog named Rex when I was little. Even he wasn't as faithful a creature as my little beast. Rex it is."

Rex's jaws closed upon the hapless fly with a loud snap.

Richard—now *Sir* Richard Smythe-Everton—was never a frequent visitor to the house in Belgrave Square, preferring to keep a safe distance from his sister's unorthodox habits, but fortune occasionally frowned upon her in the form of a dutiful visit laden with disapproving remarks and seemingly endless and pointed conversation about social propriety and some people's lack thereof. Penelope was certain that it was an inborn talent for malice that caused these visits to occur at the most inopportune moments, but it may have been attributable only to bad luck that his final visit chanced to occur on the afternoon I accompanied her—driven in Penelope's carriage by Jim, Agnes' husband—to the Crystal Palace at Sydenham.

On the grounds surrounding the palace, itself a large and impressive edifice of sparkling glass, an artificial lake held three artificial islands featuring life-sized replicas of prehistoric plants and animals rendered by the celebrated sculptor Benjamin Waterhouse Hawkins. We walked around the park, while Penelope gazed intently at the rhinoceros-like Iguanadon with legs like mighty tree trunks, the Dicynodon, a sort of tortoise built large, with protruding tusks, and other examples of long-extinct reptilian life, soberly arrayed in sombre colours of dun and greyish-green.

"They're so stodgy," Penelope remarked. "Tedious, in fact."

"Like plump English gentlemen after consuming too much Christmas goose," I agreed. "One wonders how they managed to move faster than a sedate walk."

"I'll admit I entertained the idea that Rex might be related to these dinosaurians," she sighed, "but reptiles are cold-blooded, sluggish by the nature of their metabolisms. He isn't anything like them, is he?"

"No," I agreed with a smile, remembering the little monster chasing Bernadette the parlour maid and her dinner up two flights of stairs from the kitchen. His playing—near constant during his brief waking hours—was enthusiastic, energetic, and usually pursued at break-neck speed. "Your Rex is a beast unto himself."

"*Our* Rex," Penelope corrected me, slipping an arm through mine. "You've been almost as much a parent to him as I have."

I turned my head to study a model of a Plesiosaurus, half-submerged in the lake. By the time I turned back again I had regained most of my composure. "Perhaps we should be getting back," I said. "You told Agnes to expect us for tea."

As the carriage turned from Grosvenor Crescent onto Belgrave Square we were greeted by the sight of Sir Richard running towards us, hat in hand, trousers in tatters. Rex was a few steps behind in full-out bipedal gallop, jaws open, and behind him were Agnes and Bernadette in mad pursuit.

The horses reared up and shrieked in terror as Rex ran past us. As Jim fought to control them, Penelope and I leaped from the cab and joined the chase. Rex was clearly gaining on Sir Richard now, toothy mouth snapping hungrily inches from his backside. "Rex, no!" Penelope cried, and the little creature stopped and wheeled at the sound of her voice, and trotted back the way he had come, docile as a pet hound. She gathered him up in her arms, not without difficulty, as he was already considerably larger than when he had hatched, and hurried into the house.

Sir Richard turned a corner and was gone, pursued now only by his own carriage and driver.

"We haven't heard the last of this," Penelope assured me when at last our tea was served. I was certain she was right. The house in Belgrave Square was actually Sir Richard's property, having come down from his maternal grandfather. He let his sister live there rent-free while he occupied a grander house in Mayfair, but today's incident would almost surely mark the end of that arrangement.

Penelope had inherited, along with other properties and business interests that would provide a more than comfortable living, a large country estate near Ashford, in Kent. It had originally been the Smythe-Evertons' summer home, summer being an unthinkable season to pass in London for any but out-and-out commoners, but except for a caretaker and his wife who lived on the grounds, it had been largely unoccupied these past thirteen years.

"It will take some work," she acknowledged when I mentioned the possibility, "But I think you're right." She patted Rex's scaly head. "After all, we've no idea how large he's going to get."

I travelled to Kent immediately and arranged for a compound to be built adjoining the main house of Willowbridge, the Smythe-Everton estate, and for large trees to be planted both inside and outside the perimeter fence, which would be constructed of heavy wrought-iron, more than twenty feet high, and sunk half as many feet again into the ground. The house was conveniently distant from neighbors on three sides, and the adjoining estate on the fourth side was unoccupied. The Belgrave Square staff would accompany Penelope to Kent, and a groundskeeper and herdsman would be hired to complete the household, a discreet supply of fresh meat being essential.

Sir Richard sent a message through his solicitors, asking his sister to vacate the premises within the month, and to take her pet crocodile with her. I was able to persuade him to extend the date considerably by assuring him that she would be taking up residence nearly fifty miles away and had no intention of returning to live in London. He did not pay another call, which relieved his sister greatly.

The year after Penelope took possession of Willowbridge, the compound was enlarged again, and then again the year following. When Rex was four years old his knee towered above my head, and while I am not a tall man, I know no man so tall that he would not have seemed an infant next to that immense animal. His skull was as long as my entire body, and his teeth were the size of carving-knives. His skin was thicker than boot leather, green shading into yellow-green—the infant mottling long gone now—with patches of brilliant scarlet surrounding his eyes, and scarlet streaks on his body and tail.

His forelimbs were still disproportionately tiny, less than three feet long from shoulder to tip of claw, but his bearing was more kingly than ever as he grew to his maturity, and his appetite was now equal to a live steer every third day, the piled bones of which littered one corner of the enclosure. Like an overgrown house-cat, he would rub contentedly against the trees and shred their bark into ribbons by sharpening his claws. He spent most of his time sleeping, curled in a ball inside his nest of branches and bracken, muscles twitching spasmodically in unknowable reptilian dreams.

I made it a point to take the early train to Ashford on every Saturday I was not occupied with other business, and always caught the latest train back that same evening so as to avoid any suggestion of impropriety. It was a long journey, with a carriage ride of several miles from Ashford station to Willowbridge and back with Jim, but I treasured the hours spent with Penelope, and the next visit was always uppermost in my mind during the dreary London weekdays.

We would stroll the perimeter of the compound on fine days while Penelope sketched Rex in every mood and from every angle, and pay visits inside the fence on days he was not being fed. Penelope never grew accustomed to the sight of him ripping another animal to pieces, and once I had witnessed the sight I was never certain he would recognize us as friends when the predator's blood lust was upon him.

On the weekend before Christmas, nearly five years after Penelope had vacated her brother's house, I came from London with gifts for the household. A rain like icy needles had been falling for days, and streams were overflowing their beds, making the trip from the station a chancy one. After dinner, Penelope and I sat by the fire in the drawing-room, sipping port and listening to the rain blow against the north side of the house. Thunder and lightning came steadily nearer and closer together as the storm gathered strength above us. I put another log on the fire, trying to delay the inevitable moment of my departure.

A flash of lightning mimicked an instant of daylight through the tall windows, and a deafening crash followed it by only a fraction of a second, followed in turn by a roar of what might have been rage or terror from the nearby compound. We started, then smiled at one another. Rex had always disliked thunderstorms. "You should stay the night," Penelope said, rising and crossing to the far side of the room. She shivered in the draft near the window and coughed, drawing her shawl closer about her shoulders.

"Are you all right?" I asked.

"Yes, I'm fine," she replied, but I'd felt for some time that she had grown weaker since her illness, and tired more easily.

Bernadette entered the room silently and began to draw the drapes. Rain pounded against the panes, and another crash of thunder shook the house. The windows secured, Bernadette made a curtsey to us and left the room.

"I don't think it's safe to take the carriage to Ashford. Agnes has already lit the fire in the east guest room," she continued, sensing my argument before I had a chance to put it into words. "I won't take no for an answer."

She turned to face me, colour rising in her cheeks. "We've never spoken of it, John ..." she began, but before she could complete the thought there came a shout from outside and a moment later Jasper, the groundskeeper, burst through the sitting room doors, soaked to the skin, dripping rain onto the fine hardwood floor. "He's got out!" he gasped, face white and eyes large with fear. Neither of us had to ask who he meant.

Jim lit lanterns and ran outside, following the huge, deep footprints until the rain filled them completely. Penelope looked around fearfully, straining to see beyond the lantern's light. "Where can he be?" she cried.

The terrified bellowing of a large animal left no doubt where he was, perhaps a quarter-mile to the east, not far from the boundary to the nearest estate, which had recently been taken over by new tenants. I took Penelope's hand and we ran in that direction, Jasper and Jim panting behind us.

Flashes from the sky illuminated a scene of primal horror as we broke through the hedgerow and reached the meadow. Rex stood with one massive foot on a struggling cow, torrents of rain slashing down on them both. His head shot forwards and down, ripping out a deep, yard-long chunk of flesh and twisting it away from the twitching carcase with a toss of his head that sent blood and meat flying in all directions. My stomach threatened to revolt at the overwhelming stench of death.

To the accompaniment of another lightning-flash he threw his head back and bolted the chunk of meat. Blood flowed from his jaws, and rain washed it down the front and sides of his body in black rivulets. When the thunder faded I heard dogs barking, coming closer, and men shouting. Rex answered their shouts with a bellow that vibrated the air around us. His hot breath pressed against our faces, even through the icy rain.

"We have to get him out of here!" Penelope turned to me, but I shook my head. "We can't get near him when he's like this," I protested.

Rex bent down his head and took another bone-scraping bite of his victim. His eyes glowed like fire in the lantern-light, the slit pupils—like cat's eyes out of some nightmare—contracting and dilating again as his gaze moved from the lantern-shine to the blackness beyond, from which the shouts came again, closer now.

Penelope took a step towards him. I reached for her, but she shook off my hand with a backwards look that froze me in my tracks. "Rex!" she called, shouting to be heard over the rain and thunder. "It's me, Rex!"

The beast turned, cocking his gigantic head at the sound of his mistress' voice. Soaked and shivering, Penelope walked forwards, hand outstretched.

He shuddered and turned one glowing eye on her, blood dripping from dagger fangs. The breath roared in and out of his lungs with a sound like a labouring locomotive. His arms twitched impotently, and a deep rumbling rose up from his throat and was forced out through his jaws as he raised his snout to the sky in a howl of defiance. She stood silhouetted against his bulk by the lantern's light, so small and helpless against his size, his power. He took a ground-jarring step nearer, another.

I started towards them, cold with fear. Then he bent down and touched her outstretched hand, briefly, with his nose. She turned and walked away, and he followed, flanked by Jasper and Jim.

Running footsteps crashed through the darkness behind me. I spun and ran towards them, holding up my lantern to blind the newcomers to any movement in the darkness beyond me. "Over here!" I cried. "Something's killed a cow!"

Three men—strangers—came through the hedgerow and stopped short at the savaged carcase, lanterns high. *"Christ!"* one exclaimed, staggering back. "What could've done *that?*"

"I think it was some kind of lion," I provided. "It ran off over there!" I pointed in the opposite direction to the one taken by Penelope and Rex. Never mind the sheer impossibility of my claim, the devastated body of the cow and my obvious and unfeigned terror were evidence enough for them. The men took off in the direction I'd indicated, leaving me trembling with relief. When I could no longer hear their voices I turned and walked back towards Willowbridge, wet and miserably cold. The rain blew through every layer of clothing, soaking me to the skin.

Jasper was nailing boards over the rent in the compound fence when I reached it. "You should take her inside, Mr Maguire," he said, nodding his head towards a sheltered corner of the compound. "She don't look good, and she won't listen to me 'n' Jim."

I opened the gate and went inside to find Rex curled up in his nest, twitching in his sleep, blood still pooled between the ridges of his hide. Penelope sat beside him, stroking his flank. Chills shook her. She seemed not to notice.

I pulled her to her feet, and she collapsed against me, unable to stand. I carried her into the house, shouting for Agnes and Bernadette.

Soon she was in her bed, piled with coverings. A fire raged in the fireplace, and still she shivered uncontrollably despite the heat and an ounce of brandy I'd managed to get into her. Jim had gone for the doctor, but with little hope he'd be back before the storm abated. I had changed into a set of Jim's dry clothes and taken a coverlet from the guest room. Agnes made no protest when I pulled a chair closer to Penelope's bed and settled into it, but wished me good night and closed the door behind her as she left, making me promise to call her immediately there was any change.

I realised I had dozed when her voice awoke me, calling my name. I threw off my coverlet and bent over her. "I'm here, Penny," I told her, but she gave no sign of hearing. I touched her cheek. Her skin was on fire, and her shivering was deep and awful. I picked up the covers and crept into bed beside her and took her in my arms.

—∞—

Sunlight streamed into the room through the eastern windows. I looked down to see Penelope sleeping in the crook of my arm. My heart nearly burst, and I was afraid she'd wake to the pounding it made, but I allowed myself a moment with my cheek against hers, breathing in the scent of her skin. A tear squeezed out from between my eyelids, and I pulled away, but not before it had fallen onto her neck. She sighed, and I withdrew my arm slowly from beneath her and left her bed.

The doctor came that morning, and every day for four weeks after. I sent word to London that I was unavoidably detained. Christmas went forgotten, and New Year's Day, and the whole of January, as we nursed her around the clock. The sickness had settled in her weakened lungs, and coughing racked her day and night, sapping her strength. I spent many more nights in the chair by her bed, watching her sleep, before we were certain she would recover. When she was well enough to sit up for meals and laugh at my jokes, I returned to London.

My visits to Willowbridge were less frequent after that, partly because of the demands of my practice, and partly because the longer I spent with Penelope the more afraid I grew that I would betray my feelings. I went to pains to avoid the casual intimacies she had often allowed me innocently enough, and kept a certain distance, both physical and emotional, between us. There was nothing innocent in my love and desire for her, and nothing in me that would benefit a lady of gentle birth. It was better left unspoken, or so I thought.

Penelope had often dreamed of seeing America, perhaps even settling there eventually, but it was plain that as long as Rex lived her travels were over. "I hate keeping him captive," she told me one day as we walked around the perimeter of the compound, "but he's out of his world, wherever or whenever that might be, and there's no place for him in this one." We had read reports over the years of the remains of similar creatures found on the barren plains of North America, in strata more than sixty million years old. Five thousand miles away, scientific feuds and shooting wars had been fought over rights to the bones of Rex's gargantuan cousins from another age.

He might very well be the last of his kind, we knew, but Penelope would never allow a suggestion that she might make his existence public, or make him subject to scientific study and scrutiny. Even his bones were to be sacrosanct, buried deep in an unmarked grave at Willowbridge when his life was over. She made me swear to honour that wish should Rex survive her. "He's a king," she said. "Let him live in the dignity that befits a king. I can at least give him that."

And so Penelope abandoned her dreams of faraway places and dedicated the rest of her life to making her strange friend as happy as possible, though that was not such a long time, as it happened.

A few years after the Christmas week incident, Penelope asked me to draw up her will. "You're not yet thirty!" I protested, but she only smiled and touched my hand. We both knew her health was not good; she was thinner and more delicate than before her latest illness—though she seemed as lovely as ever to me. She had never regained full strength, and was even more prone to fevers and coughs.

Her fingers burned against my hand. "I'll just go get a pen and some paper," I said, turning away.

She was dead within the month.

∞

Agnes sent a message summoning me to Willowbridge from London. There being no train leaving for several hours yet, I hired a carriage and paid well for speed. When I arrived Penelope was asleep, her face flushed and her breathing difficult. I wiped away my tears and reached a hand out to cover hers. "I'm here, Penny," I whispered, leaning over her.

"Just like before," she murmured. "Come hold me again, John." Her eyes opened and she watched my face. "You thought I never knew." She held out her arms to me.

I was still holding her when her breathing slowed and ceased.

Rex lived another seven years, bewildered and confused every day of it, always listening for a certain voice, always searching for one who never came. I continued to oversee the financial affairs of the estate, but visited seldom. We had been friends of a sort, he and I, but it was her he missed, and I could not replace her.

There was another reason as well: when I walked through the house at Willowbridge, it seemed almost that I might meet Penelope round the next corner, or hear her laugh from another room. It was hard to leave that feeling and go back to London, so I made it a point to stay in London most of the time.

∞

I went back for the last time only yesterday, in response to a telegram that said "He is dying." There was nothing I could do, but I had to witness what was, more than anyone living save myself could know, the end of an era.

He seemed old and frail, ribs showing under the sagging skin of his sides. The once-bright eyes were rheumy, half-closed, the fires of intelligence nearly extinguished. I watched him from beyond the fence for a few minutes, then asked Jasper to let me in the gate. I sat down beside him where he lay in his favourite corner, deep in a nest like that of a giant bird. I laid a hand on his flank and he raised his head and turned one eye upon me, then seemed to realize I was not she. A sharp, wheezing breath exploded from his nostrils, but he suffered me to stroke him and murmur words of compassion and fellow-feeling.

"It's been a long exile, old boy," I told him. "Such a cruel thing to be out of your time, born into a world that can never understand you."

A great golden eye blinked and looked on me with unmistakable sorrow. "I miss her too," I told him. He sighed deeply and fell into the sleep from which he would not awaken. I stayed by his side a while longer, as though he might still be able to sense my presence. "I think perhaps we were all three born out of our time," I said.

When I arrive in London this evening I will go directly to my office and make arrangements for the upkeep of Willowbridge and the future livelihood of Penny's faithful staff. Tomorrow morning I will tender my resignation to the firm of Breffny, Blythe, & Warrington and, as soon as possible, take ship for America.

It's fitting, I think, for such a bold and audacious land to have been ruled, many millions of years ago, by giants like the one we buried today. Such a country would surely have had a place in it for someone like my darling Penny. Perhaps it will have a place for me as well.

Echoes of Earth
D.J. Gelner

DAY 86

I CALLED THEM STINGERS.

They had a different word for them, to be sure, but it was a word that I had no hope of pronouncing. It was to be expected given that, best I could tell, the squeals and whines that passed for "language" around these parts were little more than confirmation of whatever asinine thoughts these things sent each other telepathically.

Unfortunately, the octopi (that's what I called the awful purple creatures) and I weren't "on the same wavelength," so I had no idea whether the long tentacles tipped with sinister barbs had any other purpose than to scare the ever-living shit out of me.

Most of the adults seemed to enjoy just that; they'd shoot a gangly limb through the force field, right at my forehead, and stop less than an inch before they sucked out my brains or (maybe more mercifully) put me out of my misery already.

The kids weren't quite as kind, though for some reason they targeted the fleshy part of my butt and laughed gleefully as the stinger entered, released some kind of fluid into the wound, and retracted.

For a good day or two after that, my ass felt like it had been gouged by the worst kind of hornet you could imagine.

It had been exactly eighty-six days since my life had emptied. That was the way I thought of it, you see; a life utterly drained of meaning, devoid of purpose.

At least, I *thought* it had been eighty-six days. When they weren't jamming needles or teeth or whatever the stingers were into my ass, some of them tried to keep things as "normal" as possible for me.

The result was a small room, maybe twenty feet by twenty feet, segregated into four climates: desert, jungle, arctic, and a tiny shorefront of beach, which is, unsurprisingly, where I spent most of my time. The lights brightened and dimmed to approximate my day and night, and though it sure seemed like twelve hours of light and twelve hours of darkness, time dragged like an anvil to the extent that it could have well been six or three hours of "daylight," and an equivalent amount of night.

I counted each cycle since, against my wife's better judgment, and somewhat ironically because of several recent muggings in our area, I decided to go for a late-night run through the neighborhood, all the better to wrestle with all of the now-unimportant thoughts that raced through my head: "What if Jennings hates my presentation tomorrow?" "If I get fired, how will I pay for Sarah's braces?" "How will I face my family, my friends, hell, the *neighbors?*"

It's not like we lived in some secluded wooded area, either; we were firmly planted in the suburbs, surrounded by streetlights, sidewalks, and those very nosy neighbors with whom I was preoccupied as some classic rock song or another (maybe Zeppelin, probably some of their earlier stuff) blared through my headphones.

I stepped awkwardly off of a curb and must've yelled a dozen different curses into the sky. I wonder if my cries were enough to entice the busy-body Kipsmillers or Chandrasekhars to open a curtain or widen the blinds enough to witness what happened next.

As I took a seat on the curb, the prematurely dew-soaked grass seeping through my gym shorts and into my boxers all the while, I looked upward to find what first appeared to be a star, then a planet racing toward me. What was once one solid, bright light soon separated into three, then six, then over a dozen distinct orbs within seconds, so fast that my mind couldn't begin to comprehend the series of events.

Before I could even mouth another curse of astonishment, the only way I can describe it is that I felt "warmth" in my head. Not necessarily that my brain was boiling, or anything like that, but almost like it was vibrating incredibly quickly, and being goaded to race.

As the sensation leaked down to the back of my head and neck, the rest of my muscles tensed. A sharp whine rattled my brain. The distinct scent of warm biscuits followed.

Then I blacked out.

And woke up here, amid all of the imitation foliage and cacti they could manage—all the better to disguise the alloy walls. Malleable enough for my overgrown nails to dig into, to tear hash marks into the wall to help measure the days. Strong enough that when I tried taking larger scoops out of it, or hitting it with my fist, I was rewarded only with a damn-near broken hand.

That's not to say that all of the walls were made out of the strange metal; the fourth wall was a transparent force field of crackling, pure energy, a background hum that served as the soundtrack to my solitary confinement. Obviously the force field was one-way as it failed to keep those *miserable* pranksters' stingers away from my backside.

It was enough to drive a man crazy, day-after-day, bits of your soul leaking out by the hour. It's too easy to forget in here; forget where I'm from, who I am.

When I couldn't remember my wife's name today, I finally couldn't take it anymore. I decided to start filling in the edges and margins of my already-full runner's journal of times and distances with my experiences here, to chronicle the madness that goes on, the terrible aliens that pass by. My only accomplice is the "Willowbrook Country Club" golf pencil I had carried with me, now worn down to a nub.

It's obviously been horrible for *days* before this, mind you—the coterie of repulsive creatures dressed up in hideously garish garb who paraded through, snapping pictures and otherwise gawking at me in my rapidly-tattering workout attire.

When not avoiding the stingers, I spent my days pacing through all four climates, happy to feel something different, something other than the crippling loneliness and the sharp piercing of the stingers into my flesh.

To pass the time, I would single out patrons and mercilessly make fun of them, teeth gritted into a smile all the while. There was one atrociously-attired reptilian fellow who shook the habitat with each step, towering above me in height and strength, but a relative intellectual lightweight by all other measures, as far as I could tell. He swilled deep draughts of drink out of a fluorescent can adorned with all manner of crazy symbols, each swallow punctuated with a combination burp/roar that shook the habitat.

Worse still was the smell—imagine if a pig hadn't ever been bathed, then rolled up in a damp carpet and left in a chilly basement in an old folks' home. Unfortunately, the force field allowed those wondrous miracles of olfactory offenses to enter, but not leave. Thus baked in the hot "sunlight" of the desert and ocean, my life, quite literally, stank.

Anyway, this saurian guy swilled the drink, then burped, swilled and burped, swilled and burped.

I would point at him and smile, "Man, you're one *ugly* mother, aren't you? You reek of *shit*—ever tried brushing your teeth, or, God forbid, flossing? Some simple steps toward proper oral hygiene can go a long wa—"

As if to interrupt my diatribe, his awful claw penetrated through the force field, nails covered in dripping slime, which, of course, seemed to be the root of his hygienic problems, and cascaded down in liberal streams toward the desert below.

I pulled my shirt over my nose and ran toward the pockets of goo festering in the sand, eager to bury them so as not to be tormented any longer by the awful stench.

As I dug my nails into the coarse beach, the idiot creature out a roar that I figured represented "absolute giddiness." He tapped his equally-awful companion (I would say "wife," but my revulsion at the thought that something would actually *mate* with this thing was too much to bear) squarely in the midsection and pointed directly at me.

After a few more snickers, they both started launching streams of the foul liquid into the terrarium, each one going farther and farther than the previous one.

My mouth hung slack—I was absolutely astonished.

It was a mistake.

A torrent of the sludge entered my gaping maw—some of it flowed right onto my tongue before racing directly down my gullet, uninvited.

If the stench was bad, the taste was far worse—I began to retch uncontrollably. It seemed like every meal of bland "paste" I had been given since my imprisonment evacuated onto the ground, desperately trying to void me of this awful, alien substance that no human was ever meant to ingest.

Unfortunately for me, that's not the full extent of my abuse—just one story. I have many more. The time they withheld the paste for a couple of day-night cycles before some creatures entered the habitat and started whipping six-inch-long grubs at me, presumably for my enjoyment. There were the baths, which were essentially hose-downs with brackish water with a tinge of something particularly foul added. Off-putting for reasons I can't fully explain beyond the strangeness of the smell the water gave off when finished, almost like shoe polish.

The worst, bar none, were the jellyfish. Pleasant enough looking, damned near majestic for my money. These things floated in, a big brain encased in a constantly-changing swirl of colors, with tentacles that were far more delicate than the ones the octupus-like creatures sported—and most importantly, without a stinger.

Then it started: the sharp, piercing cry of a child. The room got incredibly hot, then incredibly cold. The walls crumbled down and a cadre of awful beasts thundered into my habitat, content to each grab onto a limb and quarter me for their amusement.

Part of me was blissful, happy to finally be released from my abject torture, to just sink away into the comforting void of oblivion.

Just as I felt my arm wrench out of my socket, everything went quiet.

I came to on the floor of the habitat, walls up once more, arms and legs spread wide, jellyfish creatures chortling at the one-way hallucination they had induced.

Instead of going absolutely nuts on them, of running into the force field repeatedly, hoping for nothing more than to burst through the barrier and strangle the life out of a jellyfish—hell, *any* creature that dared to view me for its amusement, I just yawned.

As I said before, my life was empty.

I could only chuckle and give them an imaginary cap-tip.

Well played, jellyfish ... I thought.

That little stunt earned the jellyfish a stern rebuke from one of the octopus creatures, clad in some ridiculous blue uniform.

For its trouble, the octopus soon found itself surrounded by the jellyfish, who again swirled with color and put the octopus through who-knows-*what* kind of fresh hell. It shook and convulsed as a white foam bubbled up to its beak, and five of its eyes rolled back in their sockets.

Then, just as suddenly, the jellyfish squared its even, hollow head at me, and released the octopus, still-heaving, from its misery.

As it struggled back onto its tentacles and got its bearings, I tip-toed up to the force field and frowned.

I tapped on the wall of energy several times, and the octopus turned to face me.

I cupped my hands around my mouth and yelled.

"WHERE THE HELL HAVE YOU BEEN ALL THIS TIME?!"

It narrowed its eyes.

I shrugged, as nonchalantly as I could.

It shot out a tentacle toward me, stinger bared, ending maybe a half-inch from my forehead.

Normally, you might think that my eyes went wide with fear, or I would flinch or cower or show some other display of abject terror.

Instead, I welcomed it.

Unfortunately, this octopus was just as cowardly as all of the others. It held the stinger there for a second, saw my eyes narrow, a glare leveled on it, daring it to finish the job.

It shook its head, and scurried out of the observation room.

It hasn't been back since.

DAY 102

What an amazing two weeks it's been!

First, a little bit of excitement! A day or two after my last missive, I heard deep rumbles and growls from the cage next to mine. Dozens of octopi rushed through the observation room for two or three days, whining their crazy whirs and squeals at one another, pointing to the doorway that led into the chamber next to mine.

I waited for the door to the observation room to open—the alloy from which the walls are hewn is semi-reflective, so I hoped to catch a glimpse of whatever it was that caused such a ruckus.

Boy did I ever.

It was a fearsome creature, maybe thirty feet tall. A lustrous, brindle coat covered its hide entirely. Large fangs protruded from a surprisingly simian face and gnashed at the octopi, who swung large cattle prod-like devices at it to keep the thing subdued.

One of the octopi got overly aggressive while trying to hit what I could only call a "space ape." The octopus's tentacles brushed against the back of the monkey's shoulder, the arc of electricity at the end of the stick crackling ominously all the while.

Before it could connect, though, the ape turned and grasped two or three of the octopus's tentacles in its teeth and tore them off, stingers and all.

I like this space ape already ... I thought.

The other big surprise came a few days later. Spurred on by a gaggle of what appeared to be younger octopi, probably on some damned field trip, and the glee-inducing roars of the space ape next door, I felt a little bit of mischief was in order.

I stood in my habitat, back toward the force field, stretching and acting as nonchalantly as possible. Occasionally, I'd bend over to touch my toes; I did everything but stick a sign that read "sting me" on my back.

One of the slimy little cephalopods took me up on my offer—he shot out a tentacle, stinger bared, headed directly toward my swaying butt cheek.

I sidestepped the offensive. I fell to a knee and reached for the exposed appendage, slowed only by the goo that sloughed off of the tentacle in small buckets.

I cleared my mind, not wishing to dwell on what I was about to do.

They drove you to this point, I reminded myself.

Before I could chicken out, I bared my teeth and sunk them through the slime and into the meaty part of the octopus's tentacle.

That elicited a scream from the little punk. It tore its stinger away and jabbed it wildly around the room for a moment. I dove behind a nearby cactus and felt a rush of air followed by the slick of plasm as it desperately tried to make me pay for my misdeed.

Fortunately, one of the larger octopi slid into the observation deck, clad in his boring blue outfit, and pointed at something next to the force field. Before the little one could respond, one of the larger one's tentacles cracked across its face like a whip, causing some of the goo to pool around what I imagined was a pretty rough gash.

My mouth swung open, not at the open and violent rebuke of a younger creature, but rather with the savagery of this newfound "tool" in the octopus's arsenal. Had I known that these things were capable of *that*, I likely wouldn't have dared risk a lash to the back, or worse, my face or chest.

It also helped me put the pieces together as to exactly why the space ape was beginning to growl with increasing frequency.

To its credit, the younger octopus stood there and took it like a champ. Soon after, another large octopus came by, whined at the younger one, and herded all of the little ones out of the observation deck.

I thought the uniformed octopus would take its frustration out on the space ape.

Much to my chagrin, it turned its grotesque face toward me and stared, beak opened as if chiding me, even though I couldn't hear a single sound coming from its mouth.

It glared at me again, as if expecting a response.

"I ... uh ... it had it coming?" was all I could muster.

This caused the uniformed octopus's purple skin to turn a greenish, almost aquamarine hue. Its beak barked out more silent commands, though this time the occasional "squeak" would leak out of its torrent of invective.

Just when I thought it would stare at me *again*, it instead lurched out of the room on its tentacles, though in the opposite direction of the space ape.

I sighed. My legs wobbled and my head swam as I sat down on the warm desert sand, knees bent, eyes wide and unblinking.

I thought about the near-atrocity I had almost brought upon myself, just by giving into my base, primal urges. Even if I was a prisoner, even if I was being kept against my will, tormented, no, outright *tortured* for what seemed to be months, weren't these creatures still intelligent life? They could build a spaceship to go out and collect specimens, or at the very least, construct this oddest of space zoos, and here I was, biting a child and causing a ruckus.

But from deep within, a more sinister part of my brain *liked* what I had done. There's only so much a man can take—so much pain before he snaps. And while it was disconcerting to think that I had broken past the point of no return, even this dare-I-say "evil" feeling that now sparked inside of me felt preferable to the crushing emptiness of only but a few days before.

The door on the right side of the room opened again and snapped me out of my daydream. The uniformed octopus returned, though grasped firmly in his tentacles was a sight so achingly familiar, yet now so alien that I rubbed my eyes, gritty sand in them be damned, to make sure I hadn't gone *completely* insane, or was imagining things.

It was a human woman.

And she was beautiful.

Now, granted, I was ecstatic to see a familiar face, any familiar face, among the multitude of circus sideshow freaks that had paraded through to watch me over the previous weeks. But that still couldn't hide the olive skin, the high cheekbones and hazel eyes that burned with halogen intensity toward the octopus.

She wriggled to free herself from the uniformed octopus's grasp while she shouted what I imagine was a wonderfully intoxicating stream of insults in a language that I didn't recognize, but sounded vaguely Russian.

Even if I couldn't understand her, I knew we'd get along famously.

He pushed her toward my cell. The force field flashed with energy as she plunged through and staggered toward the sand, her legs unable to hold her.

I bolted to my feet and lunged out to catch her, but only succeeded in cushioning her fall.

I looked up to see the uniformed octopus launch into *another* unintelligible lecture, punctuated by several clicks and squeaks before it turned and left the room in a huff.

The woman slowly rose to her feet. She swayed a bit; I imagine it was pretty traumatic being pushed through whatever the hell that force field was made of. As I jumped to my feet to catch her, she raised a hand back at me and mumbled another few unintelligible words as she walked off her daze.

I stood there, mouth agape, for a good minute or two. All I had wanted for weeks was the chance to speak with someone again, to communicate with something outside of this damned journal.

Now that she was here, though, I didn't even know if she could understand me.

"English?" I asked.

She turned to face me, face still trembling a bit, though I gather more with anger at the octopus than fear.

"Do you speak English?" I asked again. This time, I punctuated my question with a smile.

She shook her head and raised her pointer finger next to her thumb, "Little."

I thought for a moment; even the act of formulating a thought to speak seemed oddly foreign after over a hundred days of relative silence.

I jabbed my thumb toward my chest. "Bill. My name is Bill. Yours?"

Her eyes went wide as she shook her head—not, I hoped, at what must've been my revolting appearance.

I pointed at her this time and asked again, "Name? Your name?"

She nodded with understanding, "Sanatha."

"Samantha?" I asked.

"No ... San ... ath ... a. Sanatha."

I waited in silence for several moments.

"Samantha?"

(Ain't I a stinker?)

She rolled her eyes and threw her hands in the air. Just as she was about to turn away, I placed a filthy hand on her shoulder and smiled.

"Joke! Joke!" I pointed at her, "Sanatha."

She looked at me, quizzically.

"Joke—ha ha ha ha ha," I rubbed my non-existent belly and boomed out each syllable.

"Joke ..." she replied. She thought for a moment. "Bad joke."

"Yes! Bad joke!" I smiled and stuck out my hand, "Nice to meet you, Sanatha."

She responded with a string of unpronounceable syllables that may have been telling me to go screw myself, though judging by her forced grin, I hoped that wasn't the case.

She ended the minor tirade by pointing to the observation deck, which had just been repopulated by a garishly-attired small octopus, and threw up her hands.

"Yep—aliens," I said. "Aliens—prison. Do you know prison? Or ... zoo?"

She brightened at the word, "K'ee—zoo!" She walked over toward the force field, grinning all the while. She tapped on the "glass" and waved at the little octopus, who was swilling down some awful concoction, and startled him with a string of more words.

The octopus's middle set of eyes narrowed. He raised a tentacle as the sticker slowly slid out from its sheath.

"No! No—Sanatha, *we're* the animals!" I bounded toward her, arms outstretched, willing her to understand. "We're the—"

The octopus's arm shot out at her. I leaped in front of it and turned, hoping it would get the fleshy part of my butt.

Instead, it lodged firmly in the small of my back.

I howled with pain as the poison drained into the muscles surrounding my vertebrae. With less tissue to absorb it, the burning pain radiated out from my spine, jolting my limbs with evil electricity.

My howl morphed into a loud, sucking wail, then a staccato series of yelps as the little monster finally retracted the barb.

Sanatha stood there, mouth hanging, eyes wide. She rushed over to me and asked a half-dozen questions that I couldn't understand even if they had been spoken in perfect English before she turned to face the miserable little alien gremlin and started to (best I could tell) read him the riot act.

The little bastard must've understood—he shot out another tentacle, whip-like and lean toward her lithe midsection.

I wanted to shout, to reach out, to pull her down behind me once more, anything to keep this innocent young woman from feeling the searing pain that kept me doubled-over, debilitated, and useless once more. She waited to receive the stinger, eyes wider than dinner plates as it sailed through the air, one of the most awful constructs ever crafted by what I was increasingly coming to believe was a sadistic God.

At the last moment, her eyes narrowed as she spun away. The barb sailed by her harmlessly as she twirled back toward it and shot out two surprisingly agile hands to grip the terrorizing appendage.

Maybe she's not a fan of calamari; for whatever reason, instead of sinking her teeth into the tentacle, she dug into the slippery skin with her nails and gave it a healthy, sharp pull at a funny angle.

CRACK!

I would've winced had I heard the sound on Earth:

Bone shattering.

Once I looked up to find Sanatha smirking, unharmed, it was music to my ears.

The octopus's appendage leaked that same, odd purple goo that had been my "prize" for biting one mere minutes before.

I reveled in the octopus's shrieks, laughing and smiling like an idiot, all pain washed away from my back, if only momentarily. The stupid larger octopus in the blue uniform came into the room, cracked this other kid on the face with its tentacle, and stared at us once more. As I struggled to turn my head toward it, I can only describe its body language as "aggressive."

I thought for sure that Sanatha would get the same treatment that I had before: some kind of alien tirade, followed by the blue-uniformed octopus bringing in *another* exotically-beautiful, ass-kicking woman with which to placate us.

Instead, it wasted no time in shooting its own tentacle out, aimed right toward Sanatha's forehead. Again, I was powerless as the stinger hurtled through the air, eager to take away my partner in crime after only a few minutes.

As I braced myself for the inevitable, I cringed.

Sanatha remained unmoved. She stared it down, right up until it was about to scramble her brain, resolute all the while.

It stopped, a mere fraction of an inch from its target.

The uniformed octopus let the point hover over her forehead for several moments, its purpose clear:

Here, we *are in charge!*

Once more, it retracted the tentacle, and headed through the door to the left, presumably to join its comrades in doing battle with the space ape.

I exhaled, though my heart would continue to thunder into my ribcage for hours afterward.

Sanatha stood in place, staring down her now-imaginary foe, forehead quaking, eyes trembling, lip firmly within grasp of her teeth.

Tears started to stream down her cheeks, and though I wanted to rush over and console her more than anything in the world, *she* shook her head and rushed over to *me*.

She motioned for me to turn over, so that my back faced the ceiling. She sucked in a tight lungful of air.

"That bad, huh?" I croaked.

She took off toward the arctic area and returned with handfuls of snow. She knelt and started to rub them in the wound. It didn't feel like it was bleeding, but the poison from that ornery little prick seemed especially potent; my back felt simultaneously ablaze and dead.

After several more trips to get snow, she sat and tucked her calves under her thighs. She turned me back over and placed my head in her lap, face up, and stroked my hair, her soft hands trying to knead through months of caked-in grime with each stroke.

I closed my eyes. With each long, lingering caress, it was as if her fingers reached through the long mass of tangled hair directly into my mind, calming it, and returning it to some semblance of normal.

I sank deeper into her lap. Waves of relaxation crashed over me, slowly wearing away the crags of insanity borne me by this awful collection of creatures.

As my wits slowly came back, she began to hum what sounded like the most beautiful tune in the universe. Even though I had never heard the song before, its familiarity amid a cacophony of utterly alien sights, sounds, and smells tethered me back to Earth—back to *home*, I should say.

The pain in my back subsided and my mind went mercifully blank. Eventually, Sanatha's gentle coos turned to lyrics, her breathy voice sweet, yet reassuring, perhaps as much for her intoxicating beauty and capability as much as anything else.

"Na na wada, na na ee-ah, na na wadah … haaay …"

At that moment, I couldn't think of a better place to be.

DAY 109

After a day or two, the burning sensation subsided from my back, and I felt as good as new. I attributed the rapid improvement to Sanatha's treatment plan, which consisted of rubbing snow on the spot and singing me lullabies in that wonderful language of hers. It was amazing how a tongue that probably would've seemed so distant, so foreign back on Earth would be welcome as the most soothing, familiar sound possible in this hellhole of the galaxy.

Once I was mobile, we started to go for long walks around the terrarium. Though the space itself wasn't terribly large, we'd circle through all four habitats a number of times, shivering through the arctic, then welcoming the warm blast of desert air before we'd laugh and jump in the ocean.

It didn't matter that we could barely understand one another, though it eventually came out that she was from a village in Georgia near the Caucasus Mountains. We simply toured the habitat, grateful for one another's company.

Sometimes, we'd search for shells or rocks in the short stretch of beach for hours at a time. They were rare finds—the sand was an odd mixture of coarse and silty soil, and was obviously of a different origin than Earth.

But when we found an intriguing piece of something to break up the monotony, the smile on Sanatha's face was enough to fill me with joy, and bring me back into a present that I could at least tolerate, if not necessarily relish.

To be honest, I was amazed at Sanatha's attitude through those first few days. She always did her best to look on the bright side of things, to keep me in good spirits, even through all of the leering creatures that paraded through the observation deck.

That is until one night. After the observation deck closed and the lights dimmed, we lay on the beach next to one another, gazing up at the "night sky," which consisted of twinkling specks of light projected off of the ceiling by some kind of cut-rate hologram.

Sanatha sighed. She pointed toward the ceiling, eager to tell me the Georgian names for the various constellations.

Only, as I had found out months before, the pin-pricks were arranged haphazardly, or at least in an unfamiliar pattern for someone on Earth.

Her half-smile rapidly faded, her face drained of its usually impeccable olive coloring. She squinted at the display on the ceiling and pointed around the room, eager to find something, anything familiar in the night sky.

I simply shook my head—in all of their infinite wisdom and technology, with the ability to zip from star to star, collecting animals to be brought to this place to be leered at, poked, prodded, and pushed to their breaking point, they hadn't even cared enough to make the stars appear as they would from home.

Sanatha brought her hands up to her face. She choked out a sob, then another and raised a forearm to cover her eyes.

I was devastated.

"Hey, now—don't do that ..." I sat up, "... don't ..." I placed an outstretched hand on her shoulder.

Her crying intensified.

"It's okay—it's all going to be okay." I scooted over toward her and scooped her up in my arms. I brought her in close to me, her warm breath working through short, choppy sobs as she worked her arms around my neck and buried her head in my shoulder.

I brought my hand to the back of her head, caressing her silky hair as she had done for me those several nights before. I pulled her tight, *willing* her the notion that everything would be okay.

She sniffed and pulled away from me enough that my hands rested naturally on her shoulders. Her saucer-like green eyes found my own, brighter than any fake stars these damned things could project onto the ceiling; far more real.

I hoped against hope that she found *something,* in mine. Even if only pain. Anything to assure her that over the course of only a few days, she had given my life meaning once more.

Her gaze penetrated my own, her eyes glossy with tears.

She stopped.

My eyes went wide.

In a rush, she brought her trembling lips in toward mine, meeting in a long, slow, tender kiss.

Any thoughts of my family were cast aside; I pulled her in closer, the kiss deeper, our tongues darting and swirling as our mutual lust manifested.

She took my lip in her teeth and gently tugged on it, playfully beckoning me toward her as she lay on the silty sand.

I ran a hand up her thigh and she shot her head backward; she let out a sharp gasp of pleasure as we rolled around on the phony beach, beneath a canopy of false stars in an utterly constructed habitat, our passion the only truth to be found.

DAY 112

The day started innocently enough; I awoke with Sanatha in my arms, the forced lapping of the waves barely audible beneath the developing cacophony of alien sounds coming from the observation deck.

I lay there, steadying my breath so as not to wake her, content to stare at her angelic face, smile seemingly omnipresent.

I squinted through the commotion—initially, I thought it was another field trip of young octopi causing a ruckus for us and the guards alike.

But the octopi that were out there were full grown, and adorned in outlandish outfits that changed colors as they caught the light. They were accompanied by all manner of other species, some of which were familiar, but most of whom I had never seen before, crazy creatures that defy analogies to animals that an Earthling might recognize.

Each one of these aliens wore shiny adornments, even the ones that went unclothed. Some of them pointed at us, though, thankfully, the jellyfish didn't seem to take much heed.

By and large, they ignored us—there were no tentacles to dodge, no foul, dripping projectiles of slime to ruin our day, at least in its first five minutes.

Sanatha yawned, and I looked down to find her clasping both hands on top of one another on top of my chest, large eyes gazing up at me.

"Good morning," I said.

"Good ... morning," she imitated me.

Sleep well? I asked with only my eyes.

She nodded.

We got up and started wandering the habitat, as per usual. I pointed at the observation deck, and Sanatha simply shook her head and laughed.

I couldn't believe it—in all of my hatred for these things, in all of my deranged madness directed toward them, I had forgotten to really *look* at them—and what a sight it was! These ridiculous creatures, preening around in outrageous getups, discussing who-knows-*what* kinds of ridiculous alien business deals about asteroid mining (or species kidnapping)—whatever the case, to an external observer, the whole situation seemed absolutely surreal.

We slowly made our way toward the spot that usually housed our meal of tan gruel, only to find that one of the uniformed octopi hadn't managed to deliver it.

That's odd ... I thought. As awful as they could be, the octopi were generally prompt, and not prone to shirking responsibility.

We lingered on the left side of the enclosure. Several of the blue-clad octopi emerged from the space ape's habitat. I tilted my head and smiled, eager to hear the punishment that my overgrown comrade in arms would deal out to our horrible captors on this wonderful morning.

The space ape's room was silent.

I craned my head for a view into its room, but received a jolt from the force field for my troubles.

Curiously, the guards who had slid through the door clicked and shrieked to one another, not with panic, but with an expression that I can only describe as "calm delight." As their top and middle sets of eyes turned toward us, I could've sworn that somehow their beaks curved up into knowing smiles.

The hours passed. We continued to roam the terrain, hand-in-hand.

"Something's not right," I kept repeating. I would list my concerns to Sanatha, who would smile, nod, eye the creatures on the observation deck suspiciously, then peck me with a kiss.

At dusk, as we sat on the beach and gazed at one another, we were jolted out of our reverie by a horrific series of squeals, which must have passed as "music" to these beasts. We both cringed; the doors to the space ape's habitat opened and the motley collection of aliens paraded inside, leaving us blissfully alone once more.

I sighed. Maybe it had been some kind of gala, or something that even I couldn't begin to comprehend. After all, for as much as I tried to discredit these things, *they* were the ones who had figured out how to get to Earth, kidnap us, and bring us here—not the other way around.

Sanatha ran a hand through my straggly bangs and turned my face toward hers. She smiled and shook her head as she patted me lightly on the cheek.

"You were right—nothing to worry about," I said. I brought my lips to hers and kissed her deeply.

Just as her hands started roaming in the right direction, a low, draining noise filled the room. I tilted my head just enough to catch a glimpse of the tell-tale glow and crackle of the force field fading away.

Sanatha's eyes narrowed, her lips drawn taut as I pulled away and pointed desperately at our chance for escape. Her expression brightened. We both scampered to our feet and bolted toward the door on the right side of the observation deck.

I grasped her hand. We remained step-for-step with one another, each stride growing larger as we reached that tantalizing portal—toward what, we didn't know, but hopefully we could find some way to—

A half-dozen octopi slithered through the doors, tentacles bared, clutching their cattle-prod like devices in another one of their appendages.

I threw myself in front of Sanatha as she turned. She refused to let go, and nearly pulled my arm out of my socket as she flew, full-speed, toward the only other available door:

The door to the space ape's habitat.

It was our only desperate hope. Our bare feet slid through the trail of slime on the floor, but we kept our balance, tugging on each other to stay upright, our only chance of survival.

As we reached the doors, the first stinger plunged into my shoulder and released its poison. I cried out with pain, then redoubled my screams as two barbs plunged into Sanatha's flexed midsection.

"You bastards!" I yelled as I fell to my knees, close enough to touch the door. I reached my arm out for it, hopeful to trigger a motion sensor and get even a glimpse of freedom, or whatever awaited us inside.

My shoulder began to seize up. With my last ounce of strength, I pounced on Sanatha, shielding her from whatever these awful creatures had in mind.

The doors opened.

It didn't matter.

Assembled inside were huge tables of varying sizes, with aliens gathered around each one, shoveling food into their faces.

On a large table at the front of the room sat a charred, dark brown pile of meat. The smell of burnt hair and the carbon-like odor of overcooked flesh was overpowering. Three octopi stood next to the mound of muscle and fat, carving off large chunks with laser tools. One of them threw the steaks onto plates that were passed around the room, to various species clutching polished alloy utensils in their respective appendages.

As my gaze turned upward, I knew what I'd find, but somehow even my mental picture didn't prepare me to see it myself:

At the top of the heap of flesh, face twisted into an angry grimace, teeth bared and eyes still open, was the unmistakable visage of the space ape.

Far more troubling, he had been skinned.

And cooked.

The awful stench of singed simian flesh pervaded the room as the octopi continued to slice off large servings of meat.

I barely felt the next couple of stingers, even as the large fire pits lit up on either side of the room. I mustered a chuckle at just how mistaken I had been, though ultimately right that we were there for these aliens' "entertainment."

We weren't animals in a zoo.

We were lobsters in a tank ... waiting to be eaten.

I twisted my head toward Sanatha, her eyes still set with grim determination that *somehow* we would get out of this.

I shook my head.

I knew better.

I willed my hand out with all my might until my quaking fingers grasped something that felt like her thin digits and desperately intertwined them.

She nodded, even as I licked my lips and opened my mouth to croak out the only thing I knew she wanted to hear.

"Na na wada, na na ee-ah, na na wadah ... haaay ..."

She mustered a thin smile, and could barely open her mouth, but she bravely joined in on the second verse, "Na na wada, na na ee-ah, na na wadah ... haaay ..."

"Na na wada, na na ee-ah, na na wadah ... haaay ..."

As we finished, the sick whine of the cattle prod-devices whirring to life caused us to shudder. We caught each other's eyes and smiled. My mind focused on grasping that moment for all of eternity, even as I felt a sharp shock and everything went to black.

Bestiarum
Sarah Stegall

"THE CHILDREN ARE HERE," Eight announced. It stood in Thimet's office with that peculiar stillness of the not-quite-human.

Thimet wiped her hand through the hologram projected before her. The noisy newscast cut off in mid-report; the projection disappeared. "How many today?" she asked.

The synthagen, its blue skin gleaming in the dim light, turned to face her. "Six males and five females. Average age is ten point one Earth years."

"A lively age group. Let them into the Anteroom."

"Yes, Zookeeper." Eight's response was as neutral as a computer's despite its humanoid (if androgynous) appearance. It turned, the solid wall behind it dissolved into mist, and it walked through. The wall reformed behind it.

Thimet felt a little thrill of anticipation. She never tired of the tours, of the children. She wondered how much longer she would be able to enjoy them. The newscast had disturbed her; with the final failure of the life support system in Pod 4, the lifeship was down to seventy percent of its original capacity. Thimet thought of the families being evacuated to other Pods, and wondered when Command would finally decide to shut down her bestiarum and move a bunch of refugee families into the animal exhibits.

Focus on the tour, she thought. One thing at a time.

Thimet made her way down the corridor, noting the dying float light at the intersection of one passage. As she approached the end of the corridor, the wall dissolved, reforming behind her as she stepped into the Anteroom.

Accustomed to her dim, quiet office, Thimet flinched at the light and noise, as shouting children dressed in every color of the spectrum ran and jumped around the ten-meter diameter space.

"*Silence!*" Eight's amplified voice boomed in the enclosed space. Children cried out, then crouched down with their hands over their ears. One girl began to cry.

"Thank you, Eight," Thimet said dryly. "Go prepare the exhibits."

Turning to the cowering children, Thimet put her kindest smile on her face. "Namasté!"

The children put their palms together and bowed, uttering a ragged chorus of "Namasté!"

A tall bronze-skinned woman wearing the silver braid of Pod 91 stepped forward, hands together in greeting. "I am Cysteinyl," she said. "I am Mentor to these children today. We have scheduled a field trip tour."

"Cysteinyl?"

"Of the Fifth generation," the woman said proudly.

They grow up so fast, Thimet thought. She herself was of the Third Generation from Earth, and yet here was a woman young enough to be her own granddaughter, teaching the next generation. Thimet felt very old for a moment.

She put her hands together and bowed to the children. "I am Zookeeper Thimet. Have any of you ever seen animals before?"

A short girl with almond eyes said, "We were at the Aquarium last tenday. And at the Arboretum the tenday before that."

"Silly. The Arboretum is for plants, not animals," said a boy with the facial tattoos of Pod 33. His name tag read *Tek*. Thimet remembered that the Sixth Generation was named for genes. *Tyrosine kinase*: TEK. She felt old again.

"These are the rules: Do not run. Stay with your group. Do not throw things at the exhibits. Do not damage the animals."

"But they are not *real* animals, are they?" A small brown-skinned female at the very back spoke up. Her hair was trying to escape from two pigtails and her tag read *Olah*. "How can we hurt them?"

"They are very old, and very fragile. Like Eight, they are synthetic genetic forms, or synthagens. They look and feel real, and you can touch them, but they are only biological copies. What's more, we do not have facilities here on the Ship to replace them if they were broken. Some of them are over five hundred Earth years old. That is longer than two human lifetimes."

Olah's eyes got round and big. "Five hundred years?"

"They were created on Earth," Thimet said. "Before the Ship even launched."

"They must be the oldest things in the Ship," one boy said.

"That cannot be," Tek said. "The Ship itself is older than anything in it."

"Not true," said Mentor Cysteinyl. "The genome base stored in the Ship's outer skin is older than the Ship itself, and some of the fossils are millions of years old. But that is covered in Chapter Seven, which we have not yet studied. Line up, please." She clapped her hands.

Obediently, the students assembled into a more or less straight line. When they were ready, Thimet brushed her hands together and flicked her fingers in the Open gesture.

Part of the wall to her left faded into mist and then dissolved, and the smell of old dust and machinery drifted out. One girl held her nose; Thimet stepped past her to the head of the line.

"Remember," she said. "No running! And stay together."

Inside the first chamber, the float lights had been dimmed to allow better viewing of the exhibits. Doorways on either side misted open and two large, tawny animals padded into the room. One paced back and forth along the wall, and the other began circling the group. Two or three of the children gave muffled shrieks.

"Do not be alarmed," Thimet said. "Remember, they are not real. The large one with the mane is a 'lion.' The one with the stripes was called a 'tiger.'" The lion swung his head back and forth, snuffling.

"Both of them are in the genus *Panthera*," Mentor Cysteinyl added pedantically.

"Why are their teeth pointed?" one boy said. His eyes shone in the dim light from the globes floating overhead.

"They were carnivores," Thimet said. "It means they ate other animals."

A chorus of "Ewwww" greeted this. The lion chuffed and two children stepped back, fear in their eyes.

"I do not believe such a thing ever happened," said a stout boy in a blue jumpsuit. His name tag read *Urad*. "Really, *eating* other animals? No one would do that."

"Our ancestors on Earth ate animals every day," Thimet said. "When we reach landfall, we may someday eat meat again."

The children looked embarrassed. Urad turned a little green. "Do these animals ... eat people?"

Thimet shook her head. "They do not eat at all, of course. That is the only reason we can maintain them."

The children exchanged looks of revulsion. Thimet rested a hand on the medallion under her shirt, the gold disk of Authority that only a Zookeeper could wear. Who would wear it after her? Who in this entire Ship cared about its animal heritage, the last remnants of dead Earth?

In her mind's eye, the lifeship—a collection of bunched pods grouped along a central structure, each equipped to house 1,000 families—looked like a cluster of grapes. She thought of the 'grapes' turning black, one by one, as the long voyage through space took its toll on systems and machinery. And the ship still had at least two hundred years to go before it reached its destination. At Thimet's age, one hundred and twenty-nine, she didn't expect to see it, but she could do her part to make sure the animals of Earth were preserved.

Seeing the children so afraid of the animals, she wondered why anyone would bother.

Olah, the girl with the untidy pigtails, stepped close to the tiger and stared at it. The tiger, triggered by a proximity detector, stopped pacing and stared back at her. Its lips pulled back in a programmed snarl. The children all took one step back, except for the girl. She held out her hand.

"Step away, Olah," the Mentor said.

"I only want it to smell me," Olah said.

Urad snickered. "It cannot smell you anyway. It is not real."

The boy's smugness annoyed Thimet. "It was, once. All of the animals in our exhibits are bioengineered replicas of actual specimens, grown on a base of latticed DNA from the originals. This tiger actually died in a zoo in China one hundred years before Launch."

"Come," said Mentor Cysteinyl. "We must progress to the next exhibit." The children trooped after her through the archway to the next chamber.

Olah lingered, staring at the tiger, then crossing to stare at the lion. Thimet crouched down by her. "Do you have any questions?"

"When do they sleep? Did they eat each other? What kind of sounds did they make? Do they get lonely in here? Is there more than one of each kind?"

Thimet smiled. "Lions used to sleep in the daytime and hunt at night, while tigers hunted in the daytime and slept at night," she said. "They might have fought over a kill, but they did not eat one another. As for the sounds they made—"

She brushed her palms together to activate the sensors, then moved her fingers in a quick pattern. Suddenly the room filled with a savage roar. Thimet watched the girl closely: she did not shrink back, but rather looked around the room with wonder-wide eyes.

"What is it saying?"

Thimet explained about territory and dominance, while the girl watched the lion pace. Olah looked at her solemnly. "They are all dead, are they not? All of the lions and tigers?" There was a world of mourning in her voice.

Thimet felt sudden tears, a stab of grief she had not felt in decades. "Yes," she said. "When the Dust Cloud swallowed the Sun, it would have been too cold on Earth for them to live." She gestured at the enclosure. "Most of the lions and many of the tigers lived in India or Africa, which were warm climates. They would have died when the Earth grew too cold. That is why we brought copies of them, to save them."

"And the other Ships? They had animals, too?"

Thimet shrugged. "They were supposed to. We do not know if any Ship but ours survived Launch. You know the Dust Cloud made it impossible to communicate with them."

Olah looked down at her slate, made a small gesture. It shut itself off and shrank to palm size. "Will we bring them back, when we get to Second Home?"

Thimet smiled. "Second Home? Is that what they call it now?"

Olah stared. "What do you call it?"

"When I was a little girl like you, over a hundred years ago, my friends and I called it Waterhome, because the atmospheric analysis said it had water in its atmosphere. Before that, people called it Gamma Ophiuchi-beta. That is a long name, is it not?"

Out of the corner of her eye, Thimet caught a flash of movement. A brown blur shot between the girl and Thimet, into the shadow of the tiger.

"What was that?" Olah asked.

"N-nothing," Thimet said, gesturing in her palm for Eight. "I suppose one of the animals escaped from its exhibit."

"Escaped? How can they *escape*?"

Eight stepped into the room. "I am here, Zookeeper."

Thimet turned her back on the girl and addressed Eight. "How did it get out?" she hissed.

"I warned you about it, Zookeeper," Eight said. "It is dangerous to keep it. It is too clever."

"Find it, and put it back!" Thimet turned to Olah. "Shall we join the others?"

"But I want to see the—"

"Your mentor will be unhappy," Thimet said, and caught her hand. "Come along."

Olah came along reluctantly, looking behind her.

The rest of the group was in the Hall of Domestics, which Thimet thought of privately as the Petting Zoo. The children gingerly approached the barnyard collection, dodging chickens and wary of the grunting pig in its pen. Mentor Cysteinyl began a lecture on the raising of livestock; Thimet tuned her out, watching Olah. The goat, the calf, and the lamb fascinated the girl. Thimet found herself moved by the girl's endless curiosity.

"Can I touch one of them?"

"Yes, carefully."

Gently, the girl put out a hand and rested it on the head of the goat, which *baa*-ed at her. She snatched her hand away, but then, fascinated, put it back. She stroked the synthagen and a smile broke out on her face.

"It feels warm," she said.

"Yes," Thimet said. "They had warm blood, like we do."

Olah carefully petted each of the animals, especially the calf, which licked her hand and made her laugh.

"There are many more animals to see," Thimet said. "Do you have more questions?"

Olah shook her head, and now Thimet saw tears in the girl's eyes. "Are you sick? Is something wrong?" Thimet felt a tide of rising panic. Despite years guiding children through the zoo exhibits, she had never gotten used to childish tears. "Did something frighten you? You know that the animals here cannot harm you, they—"

"I know," Olah said in a small voice. "They are not *real*. You told us many times." Her head jerked up, and now Thimet saw that what she had taken for sorrow was anger. Blue eyes snapped fire behind tears as Olah lashed out with the contempt only the young can summon. "You show us these things, made by people, and talk as if they were real. But real animals were not made, they *grew*. All of this is a *lie*."

"You know why we cannot keep real, living animals in the Ship," Thimet said, choosing her words carefully. "You know why we must wait until we are on a planet again, with water and resources. There is not enough air and water and food in the Ship to support non-humans." She did not say, but both of them knew, that for the same reason the number of humans was strictly limited.

Olah looked at her feet and shrugged. "I know. But it is still a lie."

"Why is that bad?" Thimet asked.

Olah twisted her hands together, then looked up at Thimet. "Because we will forget them."

At that, something in Thimet warmed, and hope flowered.

Maybe this was the one, she thought. But caution warred with hope, and she said nothing. Yet.

Thimet turned walls to mist as she led the tour from the fake forest to an artificial riverbank (where an otter synthagen slid into a stream), to a rocky tundra (where a white Arctic fox watched them from a granite outcropping).

Olah tried to touch each one, her hands eager. She crouched down to stare into their eyes. She even put her head on the chest of a pygmy horse to try to hear its heartbeat. Throughout, the girl kept up a barrage of questions, observations, and comments.

Finally, the Mentor called for a rest period. The children sat down in a ring around her. "Zookeeper," Mentor Cysteinyl called. "Anpep has a question about bears."

Thimet found herself surrounded by the class, a dozen questions launched at her at once. Laughing, she answered each one.

Urad asked an unexpected question: "What does your name mean?"

"Thimet oligopeptidase is an enzyme," Thimet said.

"You are named for an enyzme?" Tek's mouth fell open. "But that means you are *Third Generation!*"

"Commenting on age is a breach of the Sociability Code," Mentor Cysteinyl said gravely.

Tek ducked his head. "Apologies," he mumbled.

Thimet was spared the indignity of a reply as Eight arrived with juice and wafers for the children.

When Thimet raised a questioning eyebrow, the synthagen shook its head. Thimet felt a chill; Eight had not located their escaped animal.

Mentor Cysteinyl clapped her hands. "Rest period is over. We will proceed. Zookeeper, where shall we go next?"

"Where would you like to go?"

Anpep spoke up first. "Can we see the ice place again?"

"I want to see more birds!"

"Dragons!" A thin boy in a blue turban shouted. "I want to see dragons!"

"I cannot show you that which did not exist," Thimet said.

"Can we see a dinosaur?"

"Dinosaurs? No, we have no synthagen dinosaurs," she explained to Tek. "How about a woolly mammoth?"

"When we get to the planet, can I have a horse?" Hadha asked.

"I want to ride a whale!" cried another boy.

"Where is Olah?" the mentor said suddenly.

Everyone looked around. The girl with the untidy pigtails was gone.

"Eight? Where did she go?" Thimet demanded.

The synthagen turned its body in a complete circle. "I do not know, Zookeeper. She was here forty-seven seconds ago."

"Go find her," Thimet said. The synthagen marched off, and Thimet turned back to Mentor Cysteinyl. "Do not fear, Eight will find her. She probably returned to the Petting Z—Hall of Domestics," she said. "Can you lead the children to the next exhibit? I will go back and search."

"Of course," Mentor Cysteinyl said. Thimet heard the annoyance under her voice. The woman clapped her hands and assembled the others.

"Next, we will visit a marsh," the Mentor said, consulting her slate. "Tek, lead the way, please."

Thimet hurried back through the exhibits, carefully searching each one. Where had the child gone? And why? Children had wandered off before, but most were too intimidated to go very far. She went all the way back to the first hall, and there was Olah, huddled on the floor between the lion and the tiger. Both of them were lying down, watching her.

"Olah," Thimet called sharply. "You were told not to lag be—" Olah turned, and Thimet stopped when she saw the girl's hand. "You are bleeding!"

She almost fell to Olah's side, striking her palm on the floor in an emergency signal to Eight. "What happened? Did you fall?"

"It was the animal. The one that you said escaped." Olah's eyes filled with tears. "I was only petting it. I only wanted to touch. I thought you said they could not hurt us."

Oh, no. Thimet's stomach did a slow roll. "Let us go to my office so I can tend to this." She looked closely; the girl's finger had a small cut which welled blood slowly.

Not a serious bite, Thimet thought with relief. A real tiger or lion could have taken her hand off. But how had this happened?

Eight appeared in the doorway. "Zookeeper, I am here."

"Bring her to the office," Thimet said. Eight scooped the girl up easily and followed Thimet through the Anteroom, into the office. The girl sniffled but said nothing, looking around her. Thimet directed the synthagen to place the girl in a chair.

The synthagen straightened. "Zookeeper, she has been bitten." He looked at her very straight. "There is only one thing that could have done that."

"I know," Thimet said. She passed a palm over the wall and a cupboard opened, revealing a small medikit. "Find it."

Eight turned on its heel and left. Thimet sat in a chair facing the girl. "Let me see."

"Will it hurt?" Olah curled her hand protectively.

"I must wash it," Thimet said. She coaxed the girl into letting her clean and disinfect the wound, and sprayed skin-seal on it. "There, that will do until you see a physician." She began to return her supplies to the medikit. She chose her next words very carefully. "You are in a lot of trouble. You realize that, yes?"

"Yes," Olah said in a small voice. "I was only—"

"I must fill out reports. Your family may be very angry with me for allowing this to happen. They may even insist that Command close the Zoo."

Olah's eyes went wide. "What would happen to the animals?"

Thimet bloomed inside; the girl's first thought had been for the creatures in the exhibits. "We would put them on standby mode, of course. Like going to sleep." She did not say that most of them, old and fragile as the synthagens were, would never wake again.

Olah blinked. "You did not ask me what animal bit me," she said.

"I do not need to ask," Thimet said. "I already know. There is only one thing that could have bitten you."

Eight entered the office, and this time it held a small brown-furred creature in its arms. "I found it, Zookeeper," it announced unnecessarily. "As I predicted, it had somehow opened the cupboard."

"That is it!" Olah cried. She dashed over to the synthagen "That is the animal that bit me. Why did it do that?"

The fur-ball curled back into Eight, alarmed.

"Stop," Thimet cried. "You are frightening it. Step back."

Olah stopped and put her hand behind her back, confused. "*Frightening* it?"

Eight turned to Thimet. "Shall I put it away?"

"Away?" Olah's eyes grew round. "You will not ... punish it?"

"No." Thimet closed her eyes. *But Command will punish me.* "We should—"

"It ate my wafer cake," Olah said.

Thimet's eyes snapped open. "You *fed it?*"

Olah quailed. "Um. I did not mean to hurt it."

"It ate from your hand?"

"I ... yes, Zookeeper." The girl looked down at her feet. "I am sorry."

Thimet realized she had been holding her breath, and slowly let it out. *This was extraordinary.* "Tell me."

"It came to me. It looked hungry. I ... I did not mean any harm." The girl was on the edge of tears.

"Olah, listen to me. Answer carefully. Did you do anything to call the rabbit to you?"

"No. I was looking for it, and there it was, in back of some bushes. It looked at me and I held out my wafer and it came and took it in its hands. Or ... paws. And then I wanted to pet it and it tried to get away so I tried to catch it and it bit me." This came out in a nervous rush.

It came and took it in its hands. Thimet bit her lip. Should she trust this girl with the truth? It was madness to think she could trust this girl.

But it had come to her.

"Olah," she said slowly. "This animal is called a *rabbit*. Do you like it?"

"Oh! Yes, I do! Rabbit. Rabbit." She stared at the rabbit, which stared back at her.

"And the other animals?" Thimet pressed.

"They are wonderful! Even the ones with sharp teeth. I only wish—" The girl stopped, flushing.

"What do you wish?"

"I ... I wish they were real."

That decided Thimet. She stepped over to the synthagen and took the rabbit out of its arms. "Eight, secure the door."

"Is this wise, Zookeeper? She is—"

"The door."

"Yes, Zookeeper."

She knelt down level with Olah and held out the animal. If the girl flinched or looked away, or acted frightened ...

Olah reached out eagerly but carefully, taking the rabbit out of her hands. "Oh! It is so soft! And it is warm! And its ears wiggle!" She laughed.

Thimet tensed, prepared for the rabbit to make a break for it, but the animal snuggled into the girl's arm. "Olah, I will tell you a secret. The rabbit is real."

Olah gasped and looked down at the small animal huddled in her arms. "*Real?*"

"It is. She is a real, live rabbit. Not a synthagen. She bit you because I am the only human being she has ever known. You scared her."

"Why do you hide her here? Why do you not show her to everyone? Does she make noise? What else does she eat? Are there more?" The rabbit's nose twitched, but it made no move to get away.

Thimet held up a hand. "One question at a time, Olah! The most important thing to know is that she is a secret. She is the *only* living animal on the entire Ship, and if Command found out about her they would put her to sleep."

Olah stared at her in shock. "Sleep? You mean *kill* her?"

Thimet nodded, sober now. "I am afraid so. Command is afraid that even one animal requires more oxygen, food and water and heat and other resources, than we can spare."

And they might be right, Thimet's conscience whispered. She turned away from that thought.

Olah drew one hand slowly down one of the rabbit's ears. "How did she come here? Are there others?"

"I defrosted one of the rabbit embryos from Section M," Thimet said. "I will tell you later how I brought it to term in a lab, but she has been here with me, in this room, for nearly three years now."

Olah stroked the rabbit. Then she glanced up, meeting Thimet's eyes with a hard question. "*Why* did you do this?"

Eight turned from the door, one hand at its ear, where it had been listening to the Exhibit sensors. "Zookeeper, Mentor Cysteinyl is looking for you, and for Olah. Their tour is complete."

"Have them meet us in the Anteroom," Thimet said, standing.

When the synthagen had gone, Thimet said, "You must tell no one about this, you understand, Olah? You asked why I have kept this one animal alive. I do it for the same reason my predecessor, the Zookeeper that I replaced, and the one before him and the one before her, kept one living animal in secret. Because you are right, Olah—we must not forget. We must never forget that they are alive, and real, and they are not playthings. And some day, when we have reached Waterhome, or whatever we call the planet we eventually live on, we will need them again, to build an ecosystem. And to keep us ... humble."

It was probably more than the girl could grasp, thought Thimet. But it had been so long since she had had anyone to talk to about this, anyone who might appreciate the problem. Would this one understand?

"Olah, do you know there is only one Zookeeper in every generation?"

Olah stroked the rabbit, looking puzzled. "No."

Thimet looked into her eyes. She had only met this girl a few hours before, but her heart told her this was the one she had been waiting for. "Think about what you have seen and learned today. The Zookeeper is responsible for all the animals, real and not real. The Zookeeper is the one who helps us all *remember*. I think it is important that we remember."

"Yes." Reluctantly, Olah said, "I will not tell anyone about her."

"The others are waiting."

"May I come see her again?"

"Perhaps." Thimet passed one hand across the wall, finger-keyed a code, and a panel opened. Olah watched, fascinated. Inside the wall was a cupboard containing a bed of hay and a water bowl. At Thimet's direction, the girl placed the rabbit inside; it immediately scuttled into a corner and huddled into a ball. Thimet passed her hand across the panel and it closed, merging seamlessly, secretly into the wall. "The rabbit is a secret. She escaped today, somehow. It must not happen again."

Thimet could see the girl had more questions, but Olah said nothing more.

Eight misted open the door to the Anteroom. On the other side, the students were filing out of the exhibits corridor, an angry Mentor at their head. She came over quickly, staring at Olah.

"What has happened?" the Mentor demanded. "Why is her hand bandaged?"

"I cut it on a rock," Olah said quickly. "There was a shiny rock. I tried to pick it up. It cut me." Olah held out her hand. "See, Zookeeper Thimet took care of me. It does not hurt anymore."

The Mentor glared at Thimet. "There should be nothing dangerous in the exhibits," she said. "I shall report this."

"Of course." Thimet spoke calmly, but her mind was awhirl. The girl had lied to hide the living animal—Thimet was both proud and appalled. "Of course, I shall also be making a report. Possibly the Education Committee will be asking why she was allowed to wander away from the group."

The Mentor paled, then turned abruptly. "Come, students. We must return to the classroom."

The children, who had been staring at this tense scene, suddenly scrambled into a formation roughly resembling a line, and followed their Mentor out of the door. Just before the door misted shut, Olah looked back over her shoulder at Thimet. Their eyes met, but neither said anything.

What have I done? Thimet wondered.

―∞―

The chime of her annunciator woke Thimet the next shiftmorn. Groping her way to wakefulness, she touched the responder. "Who is it?"

"Doctor Prominin," came the answer. "May I see you?"

Thimet blinked. "I did not call for a physician. I am well."

"This is in regard to the girl Olah."

"I will meet you in my office." Thimet felt cold beads of sweat along her brow as she dressed hurriedly. Had the girl told about the rabbit? But if so, why was a physician, and not Security, at her door?

The physician waiting in her office was tall, gray haired, with dark skin like her own but the blue eyes and half-shaved head of Pod 5. He held out a slate. "I am investigating an incident that took place here yestershift. A child was injured."

Thimet's stomach did a slow roll. So this was it. The girl had talked. "How may I assist?"

"I am trying determine what pathogen infected Olah during her visit."

Thimet blinked. "*Infected?* Are you certain?"

Doctor Prominin consulted his slate. "Olah, a minor, visited this facility at 1125 hours Ship time yestershift, did she not?"

"Yes, as best I can remember. Eight would know—"

"And at that time did you conduct a personal tour?"

"I did. We—"

"During the course of this personal tour, did she touch any of the exhibits?"

"Yes, they are encouraged to do so in the Hall of Domesti—"

"Do you recall Olah cutting herself on any projections or surfaces?"

"She said she cut her hand on a shiny rock. I believe she mistook a piece of broken glass—"

"Did one of the exhibits bite her?"

"*Bite* her? What are you talking about?"

"Olah was bitten on the finger."

Thimet forced her voice to remain calm. "The animal synthagens in the exhibits cannot bite the visitors." On this point she could speak honestly, since the rabbit was not an exhibit. "They are programmed—"

"Then how did Olah get this?" Doctor Prominin held up his slate, and Thimet gasped. In the image, the girl's finger had swollen to almost twice normal size, with the red/yellow smear of the bite mark standing out starkly. "That is an infected animal bite. I had to search the medical databases to find it, since no one has seen anything like this since Launch."

"I do not know what to say," she said honestly. "You know as well as I do that children cut themselves all the time, and do not practice good hygiene."

The physician nodded, looking tired. Thimet wondered how long he had been up treating his patient with her mysterious infection. "Nevertheless, my duty is clear. I have a med-scanner," the physician said. "I must sweep your office to locate whatever pathogen has infected Olah, and eliminate it."

"Of course." Thimet racked her memory for a list of diseases that might be transmissible between rabbit and human. Tularemia? Rabies? Plague? But the rabbit was the only living mammal in the zoo other than herself. What possible disease could it have carried? She watched the doctor scan her desk, her storage cubes, her wall panels.

Thimet felt her face growing hot, then cold. She wanted to push the physician away from the wall panels, to shout, "No!" and have him go away. She wondered if she could get Eight to throw him out of her office. Anything to keep him away from—

The physician's scanner beeped when it came to her hidden wall panel. "What is this?" he said sharply. "Code override," he said, giving a priority password. The panel began to mist open.

Thimet's stomach clenched, and more cold sweat popped on her brow. There was no way she could explain the rabbit.

The physician stepped to one side as Thimet opened her mouth, prepared to apologize, to bluster, perhaps to cringe—but the cupboard behind the panel was empty. Thimet's mouth remained open in shock. "Ah ..."

Doctor Prominin waved a hand. "Why is there dried grass and water in this cupboard?"

"I ... ah. Um." Thimet could not take her eyes away from the empty cupboard. *Where was the rabbit? How had it escaped again?* She shook herself. "I am preparing a vivarium. That is an enclosure for raising laboratory animals, used back on Earth. I thought that the students—"

The physician waved his scanner, and the panel closed. "My scan is negative for unknown microbes. Do you object to my scanning the exhibits?"

"Not at all." Thimet made hand gestures, and Eight entered the office. "Eight, please escort the doctor through the entire exhibit. Assist him in any way."

"Yes, Zookeeper." As Doctor Prominin turned to follow him, Thimet sent him a silent message with hand-gestures over the scanner in her palm: *do not let him find the rabbit.*

The scanner in her hand told her where Eight and the physician were, so Thimet slipped along behind the exhibits in a maintenance corridor, looking everywhere. The rabbit was not in any of her usual haunts. Dodging the slow progress of the physician sweeping through the exhibits, she searched every one: the rabbit was nowhere to be found.

She returned to her office, flushed and breathless, just as Eight led the physician back into it.

"I do not understand," Doctor Prominin said, frowning into his scanner. "There are one or two ancient pathogens, but nothing we have not seen before. And not the one that infected the girl. Most puzzling." He looked up, bowed stiffly. "Thank you for your time."

As soon as he left, Eight turned to Thimet. "You did not find it." It was not a question. "Has it escaped into the Ship?"

"Ancestors forbid," Thimet breathed. She closed her eyes, appalled at the idea of an animal set loose in the crowded corridors of the Ship. "Where could it be? How could it have opened the cupboard?"

Eight ran a palm over the surface of the panel. "It was opened from the outside," it said.

Thimet's eyes flew open. "From the *outside*? But who—?"

And then she knew.

Thimet took the corridor to the central plaza of the pod, then boarded an interpod transport. As it sped along, she fought the disorientation and dizziness that went along with the transition between gravity zones by staring at the darkened portals they occasionally passed. Too many pods had died since they had left Earth. The Ship, like its hundreds of sisters, had been constructed in haste, a desperate attempt to get humans off of Earth before the interstellar dust cloud swallowing the Sun could cut the energy reaching Earth by half, turning it into an ice ball.

There had not been the luxury of testing or redundancy, and maintenance could only do so much without replacements. No machine on Earth had lasted two hundred years, much less the five hundred years required of their journey. Thimet knew this, knew that some failures and deaths were inevitable. After all, that was why the Ship had been built as a collection of pods, so that one or two or a dozen failures would not doom the entire Ship. But it still made her sad to see so many pods dark and silent and cold, their human populations scattered among other, crowded pods.

As the transport slid to a stop on its rusting rails, she stepped off into the featureless gray airlock common to all the pods. Inside, Pod 33 was a busy, hurrying mob of workers in coveralls walking home from work or market with bags and tool boxes. She closed her eyes for a moment, recalling Olah's address, and turned left.

She entered a residential section, and had to flatten herself against one wall as a half dozen children raced past in pursuit of a brightly colored ball. The sounds of vids and games floated out of open windows as she passed apartment doors painted in every color of the rainbow. Finally she came to one in mint green. She placed her hand on the doorplate and heard it announcing her name.

The woman who opened the door had been crying; her black face was shiny with tears. "Why are you here?" she said.

"Let her in, Hepsin." A tall woman with silver eyes and hair stepped up behind her. "Come in, Zookeeper. Olah has been asking for you."

Hepsin swung the door open, but glared at Thimet as she entered. "What did you do to my daughter?"

The silver haired woman put her hands together. "Namasté. I am Dynein. This is my sister, Hepsin. Please excuse her, we are quite distraught."

"Namasté," Thimet said. "I am worried about Olah. I do not know how she came to be infected." She felt very guilty telling a lie, and fought the impulse to confess everything to these two worried women. "This has never happened before." That much, at least, was true.

"That place you run, with animals in it. It is filthy. It should be shut down." Hepsin turned and walked out of the room.

"Come, I will take you to Olah," said Dynein. She led Thimet through a central room decorated in hand-woven cloths and pillows, with rooms opening out of every side. The central back room was Olah's. "Here she is. Olah, here is the Zookeeper."

Thimet quailed at the sight of the small body in the bed, the braids a hopeless tangle, Olah's face flushed. On the coverlet, her bandaged hand looked large, as though she were wearing several gloves. She turned when Thimet came in. "Zookeeper!"

"Do not rise," Thimet said hastily, gesturing for the girl to lie back. "I am sorry to hear that you are hurt."

Olah raised her hand. "I am better than I was this morning." The girl looked past Thimet. "Aunt Dy, may I have some water?"

"Of course." Dynein went out and closed the door.

As soon as she was gone, Olah shoved herself up against the pillows. "Quick! Look under my bed!"

"Olah, you should lie down. I am so sorry this happ—"

Olah waved her bandaged hand. "Do not worry about me. The medicines they gave me are already making the swelling go down." The girl leaned forward conspiratorially. "I know why you are here. Look under the bed!"

Thimet bent down to look under the low bed. Like most on the Ship, it was fastened to the wall to swing down as needed. The gap below it was no higher than the width of Thimet's hand, and dark. At first she could see nothing other than a stray book, then her eyes adjusted.

She shot to her feet. "Olah! What have you done?"

"I sneaked out last night," Olah said. Her tone was unapologetic. "What you said. You said they would kill her. It was not right. It was not really her fault she bit me. I should not have scared her."

"How did you get her out of her cupboard?" Thimet bent down again. There, crowded in a ball of fur in the dark corner under the bed, was the rabbit. It looked back at her; it was not shivering in fear. In fact, the rabbit's nose twitched in the signal that told Thimet it was curious. "How can you expect to hide her?"

"That is what I need you for," Olah said eagerly. "Yestershift evening, I snuck out when my mother and aunt were asleep. I asked the Door of the Zoo to let me back in because I forgot something. I saw the finger gestures you used to open the cupboard. I ... I took Fred and put her in my lunch sack. She was very quiet, and she did not bite me. She likes me!"

"This was very unwise—"

"You must help me! My aunt will be back in a moment. I will open the ceiling vent, but I need you to put Fred in there."

Despite her shock, Thimet smiled inwardly. *Fred? Olah had named the rabbit Fred?* "What must I do?"

"Help me up." While Thimet lifted her, Olah held up her good hand and made a few large, exaggerated hand gestures. The vent above her bed swung down silently. "That is how I got out last night. Mother and Hepsin do not know about it. Put Fred in there."

Thimet knelt swiftly and snatched the rabbit out from under the bed. Fred struggled a moment but, recognizing her scent, did not bite. Without letting herself think, Thimet thrust the rabbit into the overhead vent. It swung silently shut just as Dynein de-misted the door and walked in with a cup of water. Thimet made her face calm, despite her thudding heart. What had the girl done?

What I would have done, Thimet thought.

"One more minute, please," Olah was asking her aunt. "Just let me talk to Zookeeper a little longer."

Dynein looked at Thimet. "The physician told us an hour ago that the infection is yielding to treatment, but she is still feverish and should rest."

"I will go—"

"No, please!" Olah held out her good hand. "Please. Let her stay just a moment. I ... I have some questions for my class report."

Reluctantly, Dynein nodded and left again. Thimet spun back to Olah. "This is impossible," she hissed. "You cannot lie to your family. I will not allow it."

"Then they will shut down the Zoo," Olah said firmly. "I know it. You said they would."

Her voice was firm, her gaze unflinching. To Thimet, she seemed older than the little girl who had giggled at a goat yestershift.

"We must keep the Zoo safe."

We.

Thimet slowly sat on the edge of the bed; it sagged a little under their combined weight. "You are truly getting better?"

Olah held up her hand. "Soon I will be up. I will keep Fred here and take care of her."

"I cannot let you do that—"

"You have no choice." Now Olah's voice held no compromise.

She has found her mission, thought Thimet. "It seems that I do not," she said. "If your mother catches Fred—"

"She will not," Olah said. "But I need you to bring food for Fred until I am up again."

Thimet nodded. "I can do that. And after you are well, Eight can bring you food for Fred. But are you sure you want to do this?"

Olah looked back at her. "We have to remember them. We cannot let our people forget."

Thimet smiled inside herself. Without knowing the words of the Oath, the girl had nearly recited it. It was the final indication Thimet needed.

She reached inside her tunic and pulled on the golden chain that hung there. She lifted it over her head, and the medallion on the end winked in the light. She turned it so that Olah could see the double helix that twined across its surface.

Olah gasped. "A Command Authority!"

Thimet nodded. "One of the five Authorities handed out at Launch," she said. "But it will not be legal, or activated, until planet fall." She pressed it into Olah's good hand. "Only a Zookeeper may wear it."

Olah stared at the gold disk in her hand. "A ... a Zookeeper?"

"For now, it is only symbolic." She smiled a little. "Like the synthagens, it is only a reminder of the power and grace of living things. But when we reach our destination, the Zookeeper will be charged with powering up the laboratories, opening the freezers, unlocking the genomes stored in the databases. Olah, in your lifetime this Ship will come to journey's end. I will not live that long. But the Zookeeper who replaces me will."

Olah looked up at her, then at the ceiling vent where the rabbit, sole non-human animal on the Ship, lay quietly in the darkness. "You want me to be the next Zookeeper?"

Thimet smiled and rose. "Olah, I believe you already are." She turned to the door. "Keep that medallion out of sight. You will need it when you are older. And when you are healed, come to the Zoo. There is much for you to learn."

As she walked back towards the transport station, Thimet felt younger than she had in years.

Ignoble Deeds
A.C. Smyth

It is, alas, chiefly the evil emotions that are able to leave their photographs on surrounding scenes and objects and whoever heard of a place haunted by a noble deed, or of beautiful and lovely ghosts revisiting the glimpses of the moon? —Algernon H. Blackwood

"I'LL NOT BE GONE LONG, MUM. I promise. Just a few days. Three or four."

You can hang on. It's important.

Lila sat by the hospice bed, her thumb absently stroking the parchment skin on the back of her mother's hand. Her mum had been vital, energetic, dropping hints about men and weddings and grandchildren. Then almost overnight, it seemed, she had become this husk of a person propped up on a mountain of pillows. That she might die seemed inconceivable. That she *would* die was inevitable.

I'm not ready to lose her yet.

"Do you have to go, Lila? Will you come straight back?" Her mother had been a teacher, able to reduce a class of rowdy children to silence with one perfectly-pitched sentence. Now her voice had the quaver of the very old or very sick. It broke Lila's heart.

The lump formed in Lila's throat again, that feeling of having swallowed a snooker ball whole. She tried to swallow it, but the ache turned into pain and she couldn't shake it.

"Here, let me plump those pillows for you." If she were doing something, she might be able to fight the feeling; her mum might not see the tears in her eyes. "They'll take good care of you."

They know I'll have plenty to say if they don't.

"And I've brought a new bottle of squash, and magazines, and those fruit sweets you like when your mouth gets dry from the meds. Aunt Zoe says she'll pop in too, so you'll have a visitor. And Father Timothy normally comes in at the weekends, doesn't he?"

Her mother's head barely moved, but Lila had seen the negation.

"Doesn't he come any more?"

"I told him not to. You know why."

Lila sighed. Her mother was wrong, but she'd never convince her otherwise. "But he was such a comfort to you after Dad died."

It had been hard. Lila had only been thirteen, and the pension from his work didn't cover their needs. But they'd pulled together. They'd always been close, she and her mum. Her dad had seen to that.

"It's important that I go. But I'll only be a few days. And I'll have something marvellous to tell you when I get back."

"Is it about your dad?" It was almost uncanny how she knew.

Lila considered a moment. She didn't want to tell her mother what she was up to. But she had always been a lousy liar.

"Yes, Mum. It's about Dad. I'll phone you, okay? Promise."

∞

Lila camped outside the gates for two nights to be sure of being among the first visitors. Wrapped in her blankets, with her supplies of food and water, she felt like a kid queuing for front row at a rock concert. Her dad had died here. There was something she needed to do.

"Is there any particular reason you chose this location for the park?" That was the historian. Edward, his name was. Suitably old-fashioned for a historian. They'd chatted in the queue, and he'd been surprisingly good company. Him, and Urijah the ghost hunter, and the rest. They'd only allowed eight in. The others had been sent away with free tickets and a serious case of disappointment.

Caleb Johnson, the park owner, laughed. The sound was brittle, rehearsed. On the basis of his ten minute presentation, Lila had already decided she didn't like him, or his pinstriped suit, but she'd been trying to give him the benefit of the doubt up till the phony laugh.

"Spook Zoo, they're calling it. I suppose you've heard that? Spook Zoo." He chuckled, shaking his head and wiping his mouth with an oversized cotton handkerchief. An affectation. Lila ground her teeth and hated on him even harder. His set-up wasn't the only reason they called it that.

"The land was available," he said with what was clearly meant to be a nonchalant shrug. "After zoos were banned in the international accord of '34, the sites were offered for redevelopment. But where the amount of landscaping required was a problem for most developers, it was an asset to us. We feel we've kept the original character of the zoo. The enclosures where monkeys and apes once swung have become our haunted forest. The savannahs where elephants and giraffes roamed have become stately homes and castles. And so on."

"What became of the animals when the old zoos were closed?" asked a woman in a jacket covered in migraine-inducing black and white zig-zags. She'd kept herself to herself in the queue. Lila didn't even know her name.

Johnson frowned. "Well, now, this isn't my area of expertise. But I believe that DNA was taken from any surviving creatures."

"They were preserved?"

"Indeed. And used in digizoos, so the holograms and 3D images you see there are accurate representations of actual animals."

Johnson spotted another raised hand, this time a very young girl in her mid- to late-teens. "Yes, the young lady over there."

"Why did it take so long to get up and running?"

Feet shuffled. The problems Johnson and his team had encountered had been well documented. One could hardly log in to news feeds without hearing a report on another accident, how the consortium was in financial difficulty, how the safety inspectors were requiring two layers of fencing, each using separate circuitry and backup generators, to ensure the ghosts would be contained in the event of a power outage. Fears of the zombie apocalypse had been replaced by fears of a ghost invasion, at least in the park's immediate area. Property prices had dropped like a stone, and residents demanded compensation.

Lila could see Johnson trying to work out how to dodge the question, and failing.

"The Paliakis fields were designed for a different purpose. It was only by chance that their effect on the, ah, lingering deceased was discovered. And you have to remember that nothing like this has been done before. We have broken new ground, technologically, legally and ethically. Each area has had its issues."

Off to one side, Lila could see one of the park's PR people looking worried, and making a subtle 'don't go there' movement with her finger.

Johnson acknowledged it with a raise of his eyebrow. "And that's all I'm able to say on the matter, I'm afraid. Shall we continue? There is so much I'd like to show you, and so little time."

∞

Johnson showed them the containers in which the ghosts were stored for their journey to the park. They reminded Lila of the capsules supermarkets had used in their pneumatic cash systems before cash had been done away with in most countries in the '20s.

"None of this would have been possible without the Paliakis box," Johnson explained, displaying one of the contraptions. "These both attract and entrap the spirits, enabling them to be brought to their final destination. We have made the ghosts' surroundings as close to their original environment as possible, within our limitations, of course."

"Does the transfer cause them any distress?" That was Urijah, the ghost hunter. Lila supposed a park like this would be a godsend to him. No more traipsing around the world, spending nights in draughty old houses. Plenty of ghosts to spot, all in one place, rounded up and corralled for the curious to peer at. Or maybe what he valued was the thrill of the chase. Maybe this would take all the fun out of it.

Johnson gave that sharp laugh again. God, but Lila despised the man. "It's hard to see what sort of distress they might experience. They *are* dead, after all. Hard to imagine anything bothering you once you'd passed away. I doubt they even know they've been moved."

"Could they escape? Try to return to the place they originally haunted?"

"The capsules have been tested to extremes of temperature and pressure. There is no chance of them escaping."

"Not from there, maybe. But the compounds? What if they try to return to where they came from?"

Johnson waved a hand as if the question was too trivial to consider, but the ghost hunter pressed on.

"They were bound to the places they frequented by whatever held them to earth. A trauma. Whatever. What holds them here?"

"That's easy enough to answer. They are held by the Paliakis fields—the same fields used for the capsules in which we transport the ghosts, but much larger. It appears to visitors as if they can wander freely through the castles and prisons and mausoleums, but visitors actually pass through a series of these fields. These are impenetrable to the spirits, but imperceptible to those of us still on, ah, the mortal plane. An exhibit with none of the wire and safety glass to which previous generations of zoo visitors were accustomed."

"We can go *into* the exhibits?" Urijah could barely contain his glee.

Sold, to the man in the pink tie.

"Certainly. Explore the historic buildings at the same time as you watch for spectres." Johnson beamed. "You will find few places here to be off-limits."

"Is there any danger? If you go into the exhibits with them, I mean?" Zebra Woman looked almost as pale as her white stripes at the prospect.

"If you stick to the paved routes you will remain outside the Paliakis containers. Then you will be guaranteed never to come into direct contact. Of course, if you do so, we can't guarantee you'll see much. The ghosts will come and go as they did in their previous abodes. Although they are drawn somewhat to the fields, so we expect everyone will have at least a few sightings during their visit."

So, she could get through these fields, but a ghost couldn't. That could be a problem.

"Now, if you'd like to come with me, I'll show you something no visitor is likely to see again."

They trooped after him, silently falling into ranks and filing through a door which swooshed open as he approached it. He led them along corridors as sterile as a hospital, steel grey walls seeming to close in on them as they walked. She'd never been claustrophobic in the slightest until her mother had started having all those tests. Endless grey corridors and the smell of disinfectant and bleach had taken their toll. The damp heat of sweat broke out on her skin.

The room to which he led them held row upon row of aluminium racks, which in turn held row upon row of the little capsules. Somewhere along the way they'd lost PR woman. Maybe she thought Johnson had weathered all the more dangerous questions successfully.

Johnson gave another of his flamboyant arm flourishes, encompassing the containers. "These, ladies and gentlemen, hold the specimens we have not yet released into their new environments."

Specimens? Seriously? Like they were grown in a petri dish, or something?

"So not all the ghosts are out yet? Why's that?" Urijah's disappointment was obvious as he scanned the capsules arrayed on the shelves. He'd clearly been looking forward to filling a good many pages in his spook hunter's notebook. With dozens of them still in their capsules, here in cold storage, or whatever it was, he might be at risk of not getting enough for his boy-scout badge. Lila couldn't find it in her to feel sorry for him.

"Oh, not all these capsules are occupied. Most, but not all. No. We have spares in case we get notified of an interesting case, which we might want to acquire for exhibition. If a Roman legion marches through someone's cellar every night, do we want all of them, or just a soldier or two? But we don't know how they would react. Would it even be possible to separate one off, or would we lose all of them? So much we don't yet understand, you see?"

They saw. Or at least Lila saw. That this man was meddling with things without understanding, interfering without compassion. But without him and his research what Lila planned would have been impossible.

"I thought I'd give you a treat, you who queued for so long and so patiently. I'm going to release a new specimen into the park today, and you will all accompany me." Johnson had the air of Father Christmas bestowing largesse on a crowd of children. "Now, which to choose?" He dragged his fingers along one of the racks. Whatever he thought, he wasn't fooling anyone. He knew exactly which capsule he was going to pick.

Lila sighed at the farce—he really was a very tedious little man—and looked for names on the containers. Some had them, printed in capital letters in chinagraph pencil. She had expected barcodes, computerised labels—something more advanced than handwriting, at any rate.

"How do you know who's who?"

Johnson paused and smiled at her. "We have names on the capsules if we've been able to discover them, see? If not, they are labelled by time period and their planned release area." He indicated coloured stickers on the sides as he spoke. "This one is Elizabethan, and will be released into our castle-slash-manor house exhibit. This one is World War II, and will be placed in our urban environment. We had to decide whether to separate by era or setting, and decided that since some haunted houses have ghosts from many historical periods, they would in all likelihood co-exist quite happily."

"Is World War II as late as you go? Do you have any recent ghosts?"

"We have one from 1968, and another from 1976. Both as yet unreleased. They are the most recent we have. Don't want to risk anyone coming eyeball to eyeball with granny, now, do we?" He chuckled at his own joke, and picked out a capsule that to the uneducated eye was just like all the others. One red sticker, one orange. "Ah, here we are. A lady who used to haunt a pub in Oxford. She's an ideal candidate for our urban environment. We have a pub in that enclosure, so I'm sure she'll feel quite at home."

He wasn't here then. Not even close. He'd died in 2029, when Lila was thirteen. It was possible, of course, that Johnson had caught him already and released him somewhere else, wanting to be sure that no recent ghosts contaminated his precious park. If that was the case, Lila might never find him. For now, she had to assume that he was still here, somewhere.

Lila cast one last look over the racks before she left. She'd need a capsule for what she planned to do, but Johnson was last out, ushering them from the room so no one got the chance to linger. Or acquire a container to hold a ghost. Once outside, Johnson wormed his way to the head of the line again, leading them in a stream of bodies like a mother duck with her ducklings. He raised the container over his head, like a tour guide with their umbrella.

"Shall we go, ladies and gentlemen?"

∞

Before they went into the park proper, Johnson gave them their final briefing.

"Remember, you can pass through the Paliakis fields with no trouble. The boundaries are all clearly marked. The exhibits cannot pass through the fields, so if you don't want to get close, stay outside the marked areas and they cannot approach you. The fields attract them, so even if you remain on the paths, you should catch glimpses of them from time to time. But for a more authentic experience, you can enter the buildings, forests, mines, and so on, and watch them in their natural environment. Please don't attempt to touch, feed, or speak to the specimens. We are still researching how they react to interactions with the living, but for now we ask that you please observe our rules."

Lila found the changes a little disorientating, but could still recognise the paths she had wandered as a child. That over there had been the brown bears. That had been the sea lions. Did they have aquatic ghosts?

People who had died by drowning, maybe? The underwater viewing area looked to have been transformed into caves and mines—plenty of dead miners and potholers, evidently. She mapped the area in her mind. The tigers had been across the main thoroughfare from the savannah area where Johnson had said the castle and manor house were now located. If she'd got the layout right, he was going to lead her pretty much where she needed to be.

The dribble of ducklings wound their way around a menacing-looking forest. In a spot where several paths met, which Lila vaguely remembered had held an ice-cream stall, a double red line showed where Paliakis fields enclosed a circle about three metres across. In the centre of the circle stood a gallows. They all slowed as they registered what it was, then stopped to watch the rope swaying gently, although there was no breeze. A shiver ran down Lila's back.

Wonder if the rope always swings. Whatever, that's creepy as heck.

Zebra Woman had paled again, and Lila began to wonder what the hell she was doing there. Fear of ghosts: don't go near the spook zoo. Comprende?

"Is the—" Zebra's voice cracked, and she swallowed, tried again. "Is the ... ghost— Is it in there?"

Johnson grinned. "Three ghosts, my dear. Three. All hanged, and all protested their innocence until the bitter end. Marvellous, isn't it? We can stay here and see if one of them shows up, if you'd like?"

Zebra shuddered. "Can we just go?"

Some of the others looked like they would prefer to stay and see if they could watch a hanging, and might have done so, had a release not been in the offing. Up along the cemetery they went, with its suitably macabre mausoleum garnering fascinated glances from Urijah. *He'd be in there like a shot.*

Johnson stopped by the double red lines that delineated the manor house exhibit.

"I'd like to invite you all in to observe the release of this specimen. Since some of you," Lila could have sworn he gave Zebra a sharp look, "may not be keen to cross into the compound itself, I shall conduct the release near the boundary. If this release follows the same pattern as previous ones, the spirit will investigate the fence nearby and then proceed to the rest of the enclosure. If you wish to follow it, you may, since I intend to make this the point at which I leave you to explore for yourselves. There will be staff nearby at all times, should you have any further questions."

"Just one more thing," Edward the historian chimed in. "You say we can cross the barrier, but will we feel anything?"

Will it hurt, you mean.

"Some people report a tingling of the skin. A very few feel slightly faint on first crossing the field, but that fades in a few seconds. To be honest, I've always put that one down to nerves, myself. If you'd like to follow me."

Johnson stepped smartly over the two red lines and stood beaming on the other side.

"See. Nothing to it." He waited for those who were going to cross to follow him, then took the container in both hands. "This is how it opens. It's designed so it can't be opened by accident. Fingers placed just so, push the tabs in and—" He twisted the top of the container and it split roughly two-thirds of the way up. "There. Do you see it?"

A faint, white blur skittered from the container, towards the two red lines, bumping along the periphery of the enclosure like a fish trying to swim through the glass of an aquarium.

A young man leapt forward. Toby, Lila thought his name was. He'd talked in the queue, but without really sharing much about himself beyond his name. She'd never got a feel for why he wanted to be here so badly.

He drew a crucifix from beneath his t-shirt, and brandished it in the direction of the blur, which had resolved into the figure of a young woman dressed all in white.

"Go into the light, daughter," he said, his voice taking on the resonance of the pulpit. "It is not right that you should be captive here for the entertainment of others. Go towards the light, and meet your redeemer."

You should really feel old when the priests started looking young. Or the evangelists, whatever he was. Something pretty damn religious, anyway.

A siren wailed.

Lila dragged her gaze from Toby, standing by the ghost, arms raised as if to bless her, and towards Johnson. He held a small electronic device in his hands. A tiny light on one end flashed red. Seconds later security guards arrived, pinning Toby's arms to his sides.

The white lady faded, but whether she had chosen to make herself invisible, or whether she had indeed passed over for good, Lila had no way of knowing.

"Please drop the cross, young man," Johnson said mildly. Lila noticed that to draw the device he had needed to toss one end of the container to the ground, where it nestled in the grass. "We won't harm you, but I need you to put the cross down."

He addressed the guards. "Take him to my office. Make sure he has no other religious paraphernalia on him—holy water, incense, anything of that sort. Oh, and stop by marketing, and tell them that religious objects need to be added to the list of things guests are not allowed to bring into the park. I told them we should do a background check before we let people in, but no. 'Too intrusive' they said. 'People won't go along with it,' they said. If he's cost us a prime specimen, I'll see him in court for it."

Lila's throat tightened. They were very close to her father. What range did an exorcism have? Was that even an exorcism, or just an attempt at one by a deluded dreamer? Were his ministrations only directed at that one ghost he could see, or could all within a certain area have been affected and shuttled off into the 'light'? One interfering idiot could have ruined all her plans.

On the other hand …

She stooped to pick up the piece of the container, turning it thoughtfully in her hands. When she looked up, Johnson was watching her, a frown creasing his forehead.

"Can I have it?" The words burst from Lila's lips. "As a souvenir, I mean."

The frown on Johnson's face deepened.

"I wouldn't sell it or anything. I'll sign something to that effect if you want me to. Only I'm—" She grasped for a good reason to keep the capsule. "I'm a journalist, and your people said we couldn't take any pictures in here. If I can put up shots of the container, of me holding it, at least that would be something." She gave Johnson what she hoped was her most endearing smile.

"The design of the containers is secret. None go beyond this park, unless to retrieve a specimen and bring it back here."

"I understand that. I can send it back once I've done my article. I wouldn't try to break it open or find out how it worked or anything." Swallowing hard, she ramped the smile up another notch, forced her eyes to moisten. She could easily have puked right there on the grass. If there was one thing she'd never done in her life it was turn on the cutesy, wide-eyed act, and here she was, using it like a pro. Still, needs must.

"Miss, ah ..."

"Muchamore. Lila Muchamore." She watched Johnson's face, wondering if the unusual surname would trigger a reaction. Not a flicker. Thank goodness for that. "Mr Johnson, it would mean the world for my career. I'm already intending to give you a good write-up."

"Well, I—"

"—and I assume you'd not want any mention to reach the outside of the security breach we just witnessed."

When negotiation doesn't work, send in the artillery. That incident with Toby would be an embarrassment to Johnson if word got out. Could stir up another hornets' nest with the church, too.

Johnson nodded curtly, lips pressed into a line as fine as his pinstripes, and handed over the top half of the container. "Sent straight back. No tampering."

Her smile was genuine. "Thank you *so* much."

Here's your ride home, Dad. Sorry it isn't more comfortable, but dead men can't be too picky.

They dispersed then, some towards the castle-cum-house, some to the other exhibits. Lila returned to the gallows. She wanted to be sure she was alone for the next part, but she wasn't surprised, or indeed upset, when she was joined by Urijah.

"Really something, isn't it?" he asked, as the pair of them watched the rope swinging.

Almost as if someone was on the end of it.

Lila shivered. "Not my thing really, I don't think. A bit macabre."

"I can understand that. A journalist, you said?"

"Uh. Yes, that's right. Freelance, you know. I'll do a write-up and see where I can sell it. Maybe sell it direct." The last thing she needed was for him to ask where she worked. There were so few actual publications these days. Pay-to-read had taken off in the last decade or so, and most journalists were in that market now. Some had become celebrities, after a fashion.

"Good market to be in." He jerked a thumb at the rope. "Reckon we'll see anything?"

"No clue. Not sure I want to, if I'm honest."

"Ah, come on. You can't come here and only see the incredible disappearing woman." He chuckled. "He could have got that effect with a lump of dry ice in the container or something. Holograms. Smoke and mirrors."

He was bound to be sceptical, she imagined. "Yeah, but that bumping along the fence it did looked pretty hard to fake."

Urijah shrugged. "I suppose. Do you think your gadget could call them?"

She looked at him quizzically. "Call them?"

"Yeah. He said they were attracted to the fields. That was how they lured them into the jar. Reckon putting it by the rope might call one?"

It would be a test, if nothing else. The area enclosed by the lines was quite small, and those fields might be interference, of a sort, but at least she'd have some idea if it was likely to attract her father to the capsule.

"I'm not sure we should. What if they think we're trying to steal one?"

He laughed, the corners of his eyes crinkling. "Why would anyone steal a ghost? Not like you're going to want someone being hanged in your bedroom every night, is it? And if you're returning the capsule, you couldn't even put it on your bookshelf for a trophy. Go on. Give it a try." He grinned. "I double dog dare ya."

She couldn't help but grin back. "I never could resist a dare."

Lila stepped over the double red lines. She unscrewed the top of the capsule and laid the two pieces on the wooden platform out of which the gallows reared. Rather more hastily than she'd intended, she retreated to where Urijah stood.

"Now what?"

"We wait, I guess. Here, ghostie. Come on out." He whistled softly between his teeth.

Lila blinked. She was imagining things. No way would it have worked that quickly. She shot a glance at the man beside her. Had he set her up somehow? But no, Urijah was watching, open-mouthed, a look of awe on his face that she didn't think he could have faked.

A figure mounted the platform. He wore a torn and stained shirt that had once been white, and his hands were bound behind his back. He paced up and down as if looking for something, growing more and more agitated, while his wrists grew raw and bloody as he tried to free them from the rope which bound them.

This is sick. I don't want to be a part of it.

She turned away. People had campaigned against zoos, citing the indignity of them, arguing that animals should not be confined. Others held that they protected species which might die off in the wild. The two sides were permanently at loggerheads, and yet people had kept taking their kids to them, watching the monkeys swing and the bears prowl and the penguins waddle while putting the ethics carefully to the backs of their minds.

She couldn't believe that this wouldn't cause the same sort of uproar. These were people for heaven's sake, albeit people who had died years, maybe centuries ago. While there was any doubt—any!—that they had no awareness, how could this ever be justified? Maybe the guy with the cross had the right idea. She fought back a sob.

"You okay?" The ghost had disappeared, and Urijah had finally noticed her distress.

"I'm just— I'm just not handling this very well."

"Gotcha. You want me to stick around?"

"If you don't mind, I think I'd sooner be on my own." He was sweet. Her mother would like him. But there was no way she could explain to him what she was planning.

"Fair enough. Hey, I'll be at the mines, if you want company later."

"Sure. Thanks."

She reclaimed the capsule, screwing the parts back together. It was time. The tigers had been off to her right when she'd been a child. At school—children still went to school then—she had been something of a star. The other children's parents had normal jobs; to have a father who was a zookeeper was exotic and exciting. Up till the point when the tiger he had known from a cub—that he had roughhoused with, and fed from a bottle when its mother couldn't feed it—turned on him and all but ripped his head from his shoulders.

A freak accident, they'd called it. Privately, the zoo suggested that he had grown complacent. That his familiarity with the creature had led him to treat it as more of a pet and less of a wild animal. He'd never have done that. Her father had his faults, many of them, but he knew his animals. He loved them, but it was a love tempered with respect and a more than healthy dose of fear. The tiger had been shot, later.

That wasn't the event that started the zoo ban bandwagon rolling; there had been other deaths among the keepers over the years, there and at other zoos. It contributed, but it wasn't the cause. But before the zoo was closed down a few years later, she and her mother heard rumours that he'd been seen. People watching the tigers had seen a man come into the cage and watch them. Just watch. Sometimes wiping his face as if he were crying. Some days, more people stood at the toughened glass in the hopes of seeing the phantom keeper than were there to watch the tigers.

She passed where the pile of flowers had been left by well-wishers outside the tiger enclosure, and stepped over the double red line. The old tiger enclosure now held a hospital-sanatorium-lunatic asylum sort of building, in the haphazardly multipurpose manner this spook zoo had adopted.

She crouched where it had happened, as close as she could judge.

"Hey, Dad. You still here?"

The ghosts couldn't cross the red lines, Johnson had said, yet he had carried the white lady into the mansion exhibit in the container, so that must negate the restrictions. So if she could only get her dad into the container—if he was even still here, now that his beloved tiger cage was a mockery of a hospital—then she *should* be able to get him out.

Oh, the container? Yes, Mr. Johnson lent it to me. You can check with him, if you like. I'll wait.

"Dad?"

Was that a rustle of the grass, or was it her imagination? The hair stood up on the back of her neck, and goosebumps rose on her skin.

"Dad?"

Beer and tobacco.

He had persisted in smoking hand-rolled cigarettes even when the governments of the world had taxed them to the point they were worth their weight in—well, not gold, but they were as expensive as all heck all the same. An occasional treat, to be enjoyed in the same way a good Cuban cigar had once been, usually with a pint or two of craft beer.

Ginger and raw meat.

However well he washed, he somehow managed to smell of the meat they fed the animals. The zoo had suggested that might be why the tiger attacked him; it could smell the blood on him. Ginger biscuits from the staff room.

He was there. She could sense him, smell him.

She could see him, backing away, his hands up to fend something off. His eyes were wide, his face frozen in an expression of terror. Surely he'd *want* to get into the container, if only to escape the tiger. To escape dying over and over and over again.

"Dad? Come towards the field, Dad. The tiger won't hurt you anymore. You'll be safe in here. Mum still thinks about you. I still think about you. We don't want you in a zoo, Dad. Come to the container, and I can take you away."

Take you away from all the dead people.

Her mouth became dry, and her palms became moist.

How the hell does that even work?

"Dad? Dad, come to the container. I can take you away, Dad."

Come towards the light. Jeez, I sound like the priest. How do you know if you've caught a ghost in one of these gadgets? Does it flash, or feel heavier, or what?

She just caught the movement: a mistiness going into the capsule, like the white lady in reverse. She'd got him! Recapping the container, she straightened, breathing hard as if she'd been running. Her pulse raced, and her heart thumped against her ribcage. She had him. She was certain she had him.

All the way out of the park, Lila was convinced she'd be confronted. After all, when Johnson had given her leave to take one of the flasks, he hadn't expected it to be occupied. If they searched her, could they tell it wasn't empty? Although she hadn't stolen one of theirs—not really. She had just removed one they had inherited with the property. One she had as much right to as they did, if anyone could be said to *own* a ghost.

She could have sworn she didn't breathe until she was free and clear.

Purchasing a return ferry ticket was the next part of her plan, though she fretted at the delay that kept her from her mother's bedside. But this was the part that would set her mother's mind at rest. The part of which Lila had dreamed. The part where her father found his final resting place.

Lila stood on the deck, seagulls wheeling overhead, salt water on her lips. She held the flask in one hand while she called the hospice. Please let her mother still be alive. Please, please, please.

"Hello. This is Lila Muchamore. I'd like to enquire after Mrs Sophie Muchamore, in room 12." Her palms sweated as she waited. "I see. Can you tell her I'll be in tomorrow?" She nodded, forgetting the person on the other end couldn't see her. "Of course. I understand. Yes, if she needs morphine then go ahead."

Morphine. That means it's close, doesn't it? Really close.

Her chest ached when she terminated the call.

This was all for you, Mum. It was always for you.

Lila had never been much for religion. Her mother now, she was a different story.

"I don't want to die, Lila," she had said, her liver-spotted hand mopping spittle from her mouth with her lace-edged hankerchief. "He might be there. I swore to spend eternity with him, and I couldn't bear that."

Lila wasn't well up on the wording of the marriage ceremony, but she was pretty sure spending eternity with a drunken wife-beater wasn't part of the terms and conditions.

"If he's there when I pass, I don't know what I'll do. Can't exactly turn around at the Pearly Gates and come back, now, can I?" A bitter laugh turned to a cough that threatened to rip her chest apart.

"He's hardly going to be in heaven, Mum," she had said. "Bastard like him wouldn't get *there*. The tiger only did what the rest of us wanted to do."

Ripped his bloody head off. Score one for the tiger.

"But what if I get sent to—you know—the *other place*?" Her voice was scarcely a whisper. "What if he's there?"

"You've not done anything to get sent below. Don't be ridiculous."

"I've hated. I've wished him dead. I've wished him rotting in hell. Father Timothy says you get sent to hell for even thinking bad things."

Lila shook the memories away, and held the capsule out into the wind and the sea spray. For a moment she saw the hanged man again, doomed to pace the gallows platform, looking for his family forever. Could she do this? She had pitied the hanged man, but maybe he had raped, or murdered. Maybe he *deserved it*. Maybe it had been his victims who had damned him to an eternity of torment.

"You ready to spend the rest of time at the bottom of the sea, Dad? Everyone thought you were a hero, but you were just a sad woman-hating bastard, weren't you?"

Trapped within the container forever. No escape. No release. No priest to send him peacefully into the beyond. Just forever, and the walls of the container, and the dark depths of the ocean, where light could not penetrate.

Her mother deserved peace for the days remaining to her. Her mother deserved to enter eternity knowing he wouldn't be there; that he'd *never* be there.

She let go, and the capsule disappeared beneath the waves. Lila watched the wake for a moment then turned away, the plaintive shrieking of gulls lingering in her ears.

Her mother had faded while Lila had been away, but she still lived. Lila had almost not gone on her journey, terrified that her mother might die while she was away, might never know the peace of mind Lila hoped to bring her. But her gamble had paid off.

Her mother was drifting now, barely conscious. The nurses assured her she was in no pain; that the morphine had settled her; that it was just a waiting game now.

"She can still hear you, you know. You can talk to her." The nurse in her blue overalls looked too young to be in a hospice ward, her youth a stark contrast in this place of death, however much they tried to sweeten it with flowers and perfumes.

Lila leaned closer and took her mother's frail hand in her own.

"It's safe now, Mum. He can't get you. No matter what, he won't be there. I promise. I saw to it. You can pass on in peace."

And a smile brushed her mother's lips.

At Home in the Stars
S.E. Batt

"I TOLD YOU ALREADY," Alice said. She obviously didn't ball her fists hard enough the last time she said it. "We're not animals, and even if we were, there's absolutely no way we could live in the conditions you've put us in. All you've left us with is a large glass box and a sparse, green field of grass that goes on forever. Somehow."

"Yeah, well," Narlok said, rubbing a three-fingered hand through his green tentacle hair. He was the most well-dressed alien Alice had ever seen, which wasn't admitting much, given he was also the first alien. "They all say that, really."

"I'm not sure what exactly I should be saying right now. Surely the fact that we're talking to you means we're not animals?"

"Depends. What IQ are you again?"

Alice scratched at her head. "I never had it checked, really. Jenny, did you ever have an IQ test?"

"What?" Jenny said, turning around from staring at the endless green field the three of them stood in. "I did, yeah."

"What score did you get?"

Jenny shrugged. "I dunno. Came in to the testing place late."

"Never mind. The point, mister alien, is that we're not some animals that you can stick into a zoo. Human beings have average IQs of around a hundred, you know."

"How adorable," Narlok said, adjusting his necktie. "You do realise that we, the Harrol race, average around the thousand mark? That's why you're in a zoo, and we are the spectators."

"If you really were that smart, you'd realize just how much trouble you'd be in for keeping me in here."

"And if you're as dumb as you look," Narlok said, "Then I have absolutely nothing to worry about."

"You will do when you list us both as 'idiot aliens with puny IQs' in your park guide."

"Actually," Narlok said, drawing a small screen from his pocket and looking at it, "we have you listed on the guide as a 'thin, athletic, black-haired specimen who wears the tribal garments usually worn by more privileged matriarchs of her species.'"

"Ooh," Jenny said, her eyes lighting up with excitement. "What does it say about me?"

"You? 'Brown hair, with minor excessive fat storage and wears shirts advertising movies that went out of fashion ten years ago.'"

Jenny frowned, looking away as she folded her arms over her shirt's design. "On second thought, I think it's high time you left."

"Very well." Narlok pocketed the screen and gave a solemn nod, then turned to face the large, glass box that stood out like a sore thumb in the otherwise-featureless field. He opened a door on its side and closed it behind him, giving a small wave as the floor of the cube sank into the ground.

"That stupid jerk," Alice said, falling to her knees. "I can't believe that happened."

"Me either," Jenny said. "I mean, I got into the worst traffic jam possible, and then halfway there I thought I left the oven on. It's a miracle I even made it."

"Not your IQ test. This." Alice stretched her arms out to their sides, indicating to the seemingly-never-ending grassy plane. "We're stuck here with nothing around us for miles."

"Not true," Jenny said. "We got the glass box."

"Yes, the glass box. The one where all the aliens are going to come up on an elevator-floor and stare at us as we slowly die from either starvation or boredom. I can't believe they made a zoo exhibit for us and failed to put any actual food in here."

"But surely that's a good thing," Jenny said, her voice slightly muffled by the fact she was pressing her face against the glass box, trying to see as much as she could through the descending floor. "Would you rather be here two days and cop it, or spend the next seventy or so years of your life being a tourist attraction?"

"I'd rather be back at home, and not on a gigantic zoo spaceship which is on the mission to abduct as many suckers as it can."

"Well, we can't have that, now, can we?" Jenny said, in the same tone a teacher would use. "We're here now, so we have to make the best of it."

"By dying?"

"No. Wait. Yes. Exactly that. By dying."

Alice rolled her eyes. "I can't wait."

"The way I see it, we're all going to kick the bucket some day. What better place to do it in than a seemingly impossible field, on a *space*ship, *in space*? We could walk in that direction, or that direction, and we won't find a single thing to eat, and nobody could force us to eat anything ever."

Jenny put on a pose that consisted of a big beaming smile and hands on her hips. It would have been inspiring for Alice, if Jenny's pose wasn't accompanied with a robotic, bodiless male voice saying "habitat module activated." A blue wall of light raced across the field; where there once was nothing but grass, suddenly flora and fauna appeared. A flock of birds flew across the blue sky as they sang, unfazed by their sudden appearance. Some squirrels explored a nearby tree, peeking into its nooks and crannies for any nuts to eat. Pears, apples and peaches dangled from branches, accompanying fruits which neither of the two had ever seen until now, but instinctively knew they were delicious. A nearby blackberry bush held so much produce that it looked more like a pile of blackberries had caught a nasty case of leaves.

"Jenny," Alice said. "You opened your big mouth again."

"It would appear that way," Jenny said, looking around. "On the plus side, look at these apples! Now we definitely won't starve."

"I thought you said the objective of the mission we were on was to deliberately get ourselves killed, so that we don't spend the rest of our life as an amusement for aliens."

"Changch off plan," Jenny said, her cheeks like a chipmunk's and a half-eaten apple in her hand. "Now we eat ourfelfes to deff."

"Surely there's a better way we can go about this. Like managing to go back to Earth, for example."

"Iff you haff any ideaff," Jenny said, before swallowing her mouthful, "let me know."

"The best I can think of is that we convince the aliens that run this ship that our current conditions are not ideal for us, and that we should be sent home."

"I don't think that will work," Jenny said, raiding a nearby peach tree. "I mean, check out what they did with this place. We didn't even ask for anything and they've already made the entire place a bounty of food. There's fruits, vegetables, plants ... even that rabbit looks absolutely delicious somehow. Sort of like a fluffy sweet wrapper."

"So what are you saying?"

"What I'm saying is that it's impossible for them to give us a place where our needs aren't met. I even think that they could replicate better conditions than anywhere on Earth."

Alice sighed. For once, her friend was right. They were both stuck on an alien ship, probably thousands upon thousands of miles away from their home, about to embark upon a life of being gawked at through a glass box until the day she died of old age. She felt she was supposed to be sad, but Jenny's last spoken words were bouncing around the inside of her head, as if it hadn't quite done its job yet. But what was that job exactly?

Alice clicked her fingers.

"You know, they probably can," she said.

"Can what?" Jenny said, looking up from trying to find the wrapper on a nearby rabbit, giving it time to escape.

"They can replicate Earth better than on Earth. You know what that means, right?" Alice rubbed her hands together, a devious smile appearing on her face. "It means it's time we got creative."

∞

Narlok didn't think of himself as a monster. It took a lot of mental power, given that he basically swept down onto planets and took specimens, but it helped him sleep at night at least.

One thing that helped him take his mind off of his own morality was a good walk around his own zoo spaceship. It came equipped with everything he ever wanted; plenty of docks for eager visitors, inter-dimensional "cages" that were huge on the inside and compact on the outside, and large laser turrets for shooting down rival zoo spaceships.

In short, he had it pretty much set.

Despite his somewhat capitalistic tendencies, however, he did take very good care of his animals. If not from a kindness perspective, then for the business angle that dead animals didn't make much revenue. He had never managed to catch a human before. Every time he sent someone to do it, they had a fantastic idea that involved corn fields and screwing with the locals' minds. There was also the time where they had the bright idea to chip the new zoo exhibits into a very invasive and personal place, which just left everyone feeling awkward. Now, however, he had got two humans. Both with their dignity still intact, as well.

Of course, now that he had them, he couldn't stop thinking about them. Much like when someone gets a new car and spends the rest of the day straining his neck to look out of the window to the front drive, his mind was obsessed by just watching them. He always had a ravenous interest in studying aliens. He also had a ravenous interest in abducting as many as he could get his tractor beams on, but that was for the lawyers to sort out. Right now, he had an exhibit to check up on.

As he made his way to the human exhibit, he wondered how they were getting on. By now, they would have discovered their habitat populating itself with resources more than sufficient to keep themselves alive for however long they lived. There were no poisonous foods, no vicious animals, and definitely no quicksand pits for them to get stuck in. Yes, he was rather pleased with his environmental modules. They often gave the recipients a better home than home.

This is why, as he took the elevator back up into the glass box and saw one of them lying on the floor, he was very worried.

"What's wrong?" he said, slamming a hand against the door and running in. "What's wrong with her?"

Alice came out from behind the trees. "Thank goodness you're here!" she said. "I was worried she was going to die!"

"Die? Why in space is she dying? I thought the habitat module built the perfect world for you both."

"For a caveman, maybe. This is the bare minimum. In fact, I'd go to say this is much less than minimum. We've come a long way from our club-thwaking days, you know. We've evolved, we've grown, and with it, we've gained additional needs and requirements."

Narlok took in a sharp breath. "I'm really, really sorry about that. We just assumed that this was what humans could live off of."

"Well, you thought wrong. We have to do something fast, or else Jenny will pass away. There has to be something you can do, *right now*."

"This will take something a little more than the habitat module, I'm afraid. It's programmed to replicate real-world scenes, instead of generating individual things. There is, however, something that can." Narlok withdrew a handheld device from his pocket, pressing a few buttons on it. "Alright, it's on the way. In the meantime, we can make a list of all the things you two need to be able to survive. So, what does she need?"

Alice wiped away the tears she forced to well up in her eyes when Narlok got here. "Well, when she's in this state, it's hard to say what she'd need to get back on her feet. I'll have to see if I can get an answer from her." Alice nested Jenny's head in her hands. "Jenny, are you there? Can you hear me? Can you speak?"

"Mm?" Jenny said, rubbing her face. "Oh, Alice. You're here. Where did you go? I thought I ... I was going to die."

"It's alright, Mr. Alien is here now. Just say what you need and we'll see if we can get it made for you."

Jenny put a hand to her forehead. "It's ... it's so hard to think, Alice. My mind ... it's swimming ..."

"Try to build an image in your head. What is it your body needs? What does it crave?"

Jenny squinted her eyes, staring into the blue sky as if it somehow held the answer. "I can see an image ... it's manifesting itself into my mind ... I can see ... I can see ... a mansion."

Alice nodded. "What else do you see?"

"I ... I see the mansion. And it's big. Like, really big. And it has a big garden to go with it. And I can see ... to the side of it ... an outdoor jacuzzi. Yes, that's what my body needs," she said, nodding. "An outdoor jacuzzi."

"Are you getting all this, Narlok?"

"Mansion ... garden ... jacuzzi ..." Narlok said, scribbling on a notepad. "Good grief, I didn't know humans were so high-maintenance for their low IQ levels."

"Would you be able to manifest these things?"

"Definitely. But the problem is, it doesn't appear your friend is recovering any better than when I first arrived. Does she need more?"

"No, that's fine," Jenny said, resting her head back onto the grass. Then, suddenly, after a glare from Alice: "No, wait, I meant no. Ooh, no. My stomach, it's hurting so bad. The pain."

"What else do you need?"

"I need ... a wardrobe crammed full of clothes. And shoes that adapt to any social situation. And a personal catwalk. Oh, and, uh, butlers."

Narlok clicked his mouth. "I'm not sure about the butlers. Those will be very taxing on the asset generator. Are you sure you'll—"

His sentence was cut short by a blood-curdling cry of pain from Jenny, as she rolled around the grass, clutching her stomach as if she had been shot.

"Okay, okay," Narlok said, writing in his notebook with a blur for a hand. "We'll get you the butlers, I promise you."

"Male butlers!"

"Male butlers, got it."

"Male butlers *without shirts on!*"

"Okay."

"And abs I can rappel off of."

"Yes, yes, alright. I've noted it down. Do you feel better?"

Jenny flopped back onto the grass. "Much."

"Is there anything else I can do to help you feel better?"

"Sure. A hot pink sports car with all the best modifications you can slap on it."

"Scratch that," Alice said. "What will really bring her to life is a sensible, normal-coloured car that wouldn't be an absolute disgrace to be seen in by alien tourists. *Right,* Jenny?"

"No," Jenny said. "I'm pretty sure it's not. I'm pretty sure it's a car that would make Barbie go green."

"You'll take the normal car, or I leave you to die."

Jenny sighed. "Fine, fine."

"Is that all?" Narlok said.

Jenny nodded. "Will you be okay making all that?"

"They're relatively low-technology things, so it shouldn't be too hard. The butlers, however, will have to be holographic renditions. I trust this is okay?"

"Depends," Jenny said, sitting up. "Are the rock-hard abs there?"

"They can be."

"Then we are fine."

"The robot should be here at any time now. If you could give him this list with instructions, then he'll make everything for you."

Narlok handed over his notepad and turned to leave, hoping the robot would get there in good time. He was so worried, in fact, that he totally failed to hear the two girls behind him give each other a high five.

As a leader of a country, Jordan thought he had seen it all. This, however, took the biscuit. This was something nobody on the entire *planet* had seen, let alone just him.

He'd had many people stand before him. Presidents and prime ministers. Kings and Queens. Artists and scientists. Today, however, his official office had been breached by an intruder for the first time in its long history, and only because the intruder beamed down directly in front of him and waved a gun that looked like it needed a brain five times the size of his own to even operate. When everyone discovered that the alien was here to talk rather than shoot, the wheels of diplomacy became a little more well-oiled. Calling the SWAT team in would merely harm the potentially only chance humans had to interact with those that dwelled amongst the stars. Didn't stop him having a shaking finger placed on the big red button, however.

"So what you're saying," Jordan said, "is that you abducted two of my citizens?"

The alien rubbed his hands together. "We don't really like to think of it as *abducting*. We like to think of it as ... giving surprise adventures. But yes, two of your ... *tribe's* people are currently on board a large entertainment cruiser in outer space, which is mainly dedicated to being a zoo for creatures all across the universe. Of which your species qualify for, of course. The problem is, every other race we've ever taken from have just shrugged their collective shoulders and said that there were loads more where that came from. This was the first race we've encountered where they actually *miss* the poor things. I think you're the only race out there who has managed to invent the lost poster."

Jordan tapped the end of his glasses against his lips. "So you're saying you're going to just take our citizens?"

"Just those two. That's all we can really ask for. In exchange, we can get your planet on the universal map with the attraction. I understand that you haven't really gotten around to all that space faring stuff yet, so I'm sure the other aliens will be more than happy to visit you with all kinds of technology to sell. For a price, of course."

"I'm sure however steep the price is, it'll be worth it for the tin cans we somehow get up into space. It does sound like a good deal, but ... of course, my mind always goes to the safety of the two citizens that you abducted. I'd just hate to have them suffer so that we can get some decent spaceships."

"Suffer? Oh, no, dear leader. Please understand that a badly-kept animal makes nobody happy, and we wouldn't be able to call ourselves an entertainment cruiser if everyone had a sad look on their face when they left. No, be reassured that your humans are being kept in the best conditions."

"Would it be too much to ask what kind of conditions they're currently living in at this moment?"

"Not at all." The alien tapped commands into a wrist-bound mini computer. "At the current moment, they are dwelling inside a mansion. We were told that a swimming pool was vital to their well-being, so they have one of those as well. Confusingly, we have data to suggest that an all-chocolate diet was *bad* for human health, but one of your subjects was adamant that it's just what she needed. They also have some holograms doing all their housework, every television channel in the universe, and food on demand every time they clap their hands. They've gone on to say that this is the 'bare minimum' that a human needs to have a healthy life, and that we can 'expect more in the future.' Well." The alien gave a smile. "I do hope you're not enraged with the sub-par environment we've given them. It's the best we could do."

Jordan frowned at the desk. "You're saying they get all that?"

"Indeed. All day, every day. And they have access to more resources should they feel their conditions are not right."

"So they can literally ask for anything?"

"Well, not *anything*. If they asked for complete control of the entire ship, we might not be able to grant them that. Then again, if such a small animal requires such a large thing to live, then we're clearly not up to the task for housing them."

"But if they wanted, say ... a never-ending roast dinner, a log fire that never stops crackling, and a pipe that never ends up eventually killing me—er, *them*, you guys can do that?"

The alien frowned. "Apologies. It's just that your level of amazement is on the same level of being astounded when I said I could get you a pile of rocks and some dirt. Yes, of course all of that low-technological stuff is easy to reproduce. Why, do you think they'd like that?"

Jordan never did say if they would. He did, however, slowly stand up from his chair, adjust his tie, and press the intercom button on the table.

"Clear my schedule for the rest of the day," he said. "In fact, bring your family and friends."

"Are you coming to see our zoo?" the alien said. "Very quick of you."

"No. Rather, asking you if you'd like a leader of a country for an exhibit."

"Oh." The alien grinned widely. "Oh, yes, I think that would go down very well."

"Good." Jordan shook the alien's hand. "Because I think so, too."

Alice had never once tried a professional make-up session, foot massage, or nail manicure before. Let alone all three at once.

She didn't have much of an idea as to how computers worked, but she had to admit that these alien robots were very advanced. They had machines that could produce entire things out of thin air—seemingly, at least. They also sported intelligence that probably defeated her own. What she liked most about them, however, was that their computers both knew how to pamper someone, and didn't think twice about indulging requests. She could get very much used to computers after today.

Alice clicked her fingers twice.

The asset generator—which Narlok said would solve every problem that they might have, and was named "Jeeves" on request—was little more than a floating television screen with arms on either side of his head.

Despite his rather simple design, he could produce anything that Alice could ever want. Which was convenient, given that Alice was on the verge of giving up not wanting things for life. The generator even placed down a small, floating cylinder in the middle of the house, which took the brunt of most requests should the asset generator be hovering off somewhere. Even the cylinder gave its own, calming blue glow.

"Yes, Alice?" Jeeves said.

"Can you make me a martini, please? In a crystal-cut glass, if you will."

"As you will."

Jeeves held out one of its hands. A small blue glow appeared within its palm, which formed itself into a glass with a perfect-looking martini within it.

"I hate to say it," Jeeves said, "but my records dictate that too many of these are bad for your health."

Alice took the glass. "I haven't had too many."

"You've had *six*."

"I stand by my original statement. How are you and that cylinder thing faring with our requests?"

"We're doing all right. The power draw from the ship is minimal. We'd have to have a lot more requests to be close to being too much for the ship's power systems to handle. For now, it seems to be holding up the projections and asset generation just fine."

"Excellent. Jenny? How are you doing? Didn't you say you were going to check if the butlers were good enough?"

Jenny came out of a door near Alice, with hair that looked like she had gone through a tornado, and a face to match. "They're fine," she said. "Totally fine."

"Awesome. Well, I think we've seen without a shadow of a doubt that this place is more than suitable for our every day needs. We could make a career out of this gig, you know. Everyone from across the galaxy will come to see us two stuff our faces with truffles and lounge in a jacuzzi all day. And for free."

"This is literally my dream job," Jenny said.

"It's not even a job, really. This has gone into dream living."

"Well," Jeeves said. "I'm glad that we could make the pair of you feel at home. I was worried that this wouldn't be up to scratch as to what humans usually have back on their planet."

"Oh, don't worry." Alice finished off her drink, placing it back onto the computer's hand. "This is definitely satisfactory. Not a single complaint."

A knock came from the front door.

"Jenny?" Alice said. "You didn't make the generator create some picture-perfect pizza delivery guys, did you?"

"Depends." Jenny peered over at the front door like a curious meerkat. "If they're good-looking, I'll gladly take the credit."

"Maybe it's some aliens wanting to have a safari."

"A safari? Oh boy, I'll blow their brains out with some of the cool stuff we have here. We'll be having safaris every ten minutes."

"You wait here." Alice got up from her lounger, leaving the pedicure robots to fend for themselves. "I'm going to check out who it is."

Jenny crossed her arms. "So you want the deliverymen to yourselves, I see."

"If it's ham and cheese, you can have them. I was always a pepperoni girl."

Alice placed her hand on the handle, opened the door, and came face-to-face with her country leader's humble face.

"Hello," Jordan said, raising a briefcase to head height. "Just moving into the neighbourhood."

It's when Jordan pushed past Alice to reveal the large crowd behind him that Alice knew something was horribly wrong. She managed to eek out a "what on earth are you—?" before being taken by the tsunami wave of curious visitors, each one of them stopping in the middle of the room to look around in awe. One of them poked the blue cylinder.

"All right," Alice said, picking herself up off the floor. "Jordan, with all due respect, what exactly is going on here?"

"Well ..." Jordan rubbed the back of his head. "I brought my friends and family. And when they heard where we were going, *they* brought *their* friends and family. Turns out, in the space of about an hour, half the entire country can be notified about a spaceship that will take out the trash for you. I needed SWAT teams to get me to the landing point, and another SWAT team to stop the first one from trying to sneak onto the ship themselves."

"So what you're saying is, you've gatecrashed our home."

"I like to think of it as shared accommodation. Monkeys don't get their own houses in zoos back home."

"Yeah, and they don't get robots that can do their every bidding, either. Hey, you. What are you doing?"

Alice pointed to a man who didn't seem as awestruck as his comrades. While everyone else was still prodding and poking at things (to which the flying computer was very unpleased about, especially when they began prodding him), the lone wolf had picked up a box of chocolates from a nearby table.

"I don't like these chocolates," he said. "These ones have nuts in them."

"Well they're not for *you*," Jenny said, standing beside Alice with insult in her voice. "They're for us."

"Well, Jordan said we're all in this together. So this is mine as well."

"No it isn't," Alice said. "We asked for it, so it's ours."

"Well I don't want it to have nuts in it. I want it to be a selection of white chocolate."

As the man waved the box of chocolates to emphasise his point, a blue beam shot from the cylinder. The box—once sporting a lovely array of nut-based chocolates—slowly morphed into a selection of Belgian-picked white chocolates.

"Ah, that's more like it," the man said, flipping open the box.

"Peter," a woman from the crowd screeched, snatching the box away from the man's hands. "What have I told you about eating chocolates in front of me? I'm diabetic, remember? I can't just sit here and watch my husband stuff his face while I'm left in the cold. If you're going to have that box of chocolates, at least make it suitable for diabetics."

The blue beam appeared again, adding a "suitable for diabetics" sticker to the lid.

"I don't want none of that," Peter said, grabbing at the box. "The diabetic ones taste awful. Turn it back."

"They don't taste any different," the woman insisted, swatting at the blue beam turning the chocolates back to normal. "You're just imagining it. Turn it back."

"Go away, will you? This is my box, so I get to say what they are. Turn them to normal again."

Alice cleared her throat. "I think you'll find they were *mine* before you stole them from me. Turn them back to the nut kind."

"Oi, they were *my* white chocolates. Make them white again. And while we're at it, turn all that crummy wine you have over there to beer. Don't want any of that nasty stuff in my house."

"You dare touch my wine collection as well?"

"Beer is horrible," a female voice from the crowd said. "Why get that bilgewater when you can have champagne?"

"These chairs are too girly," a man said, testing one out. "Make them more suitable for men. In leather, as well."

"Girly?" a woman cried. "They were pretty, not girly. Get rid of that horrible cow-skin thing and make one with flowers on it."

"Please," Jenny called out to the crowd. "Please, don't fight."

"I don't *want* steak for dinner," a woman complained, peeking into the fridge. "I'm a vegetarian. I want salad. Turn the steak into salad."

"Sod your salad," a man grumbled, barging her out of the way. "There's loads of it out there. We're having a roast. Make the rabbit food into a nice chicken please."

"Chicken?" said a third. "If we're having roast, it's not going to be chicken. Some beef, *please*."

"Please, everyone," Jenny tried to raise her voice over the hubbub. "We musn't fight."

"What do you mean the television is too big? This size is tiny. Make it bigger."

"The television is fine," Jenny called out. "Don't fight over it."

"Who made the wallpaper so plain? Make it something out of the sixties, some tie-dye or something. I miss those times."

"Please keep the wallpaper the same," Jenny said, turning it back. "Let's all just calm down and talk about this like civil human be—"

"Who the hell thought it was smart to make these *male* topless butlers? Turn them into female ones. That's more like it."

"Alright, sod *you*," Jenny yelled at the top of her voice, rolling up her sleeves and storming into the crowd.

While everyone descended the spiral of anger and disagreement, the generator in the middle of the room shot blue rays all over the house. It was changing things to one state, changing them back to another state, deleting things, adding things, deleting things that were just added, adding things that had only just been removed, and trying its best to suit everyone's demands all at once while they declared them as loudly as they could at one another.

The lights dimmed for a brief moment.

"Oh dear," Jeeves said. "Everyone, please, stop demanding from the generator. We're drawing far too much power from the ship."

"What happens if we manage to draw too much power?" Alice yelled over the small riot brewing in the main room.

"Well, if it gets too bad, I suppose something drastic could happen, such as—"

There was a sound like the largest light switch in the galaxy being flipped.

Everything went black and silent at the exact same time.

"—a blackout," Alice finished.

A small clicking sound pierced the silence, followed by a brilliant white light. When Alice managed to stop squinting, she could see that Jeeves had turned its television 'face' into a wall of white light.

"Well," it said. "I'm just glad that I don't run off the mains. If I did, then I wouldn't be able to say this; we all need to get out of here as fast as possible. I'll explain everything while we go."

"Why should we—" Alice began.

"*While we go.*"

Jeeves opened the front door, hovering out of it. Nobody was too keen on going anywhere (especially out of the house they only just made their home), but they slowly began moving once they saw Alice and Jenny jog to keep up with the robot.

"Okay, we're going now," Jenny said. "So what's the problem?"

"*That* is."

Alice followed the pointing finger to the glass box; or rather, what was left of it, which was nothing.

"Wait," Alice said. "Where on earth did the glass go?"

"It was never glass, my dear. It was simply a forcefield designed to *look* like glass. Something as simple as glass would be easily shattered by some of the more advanced animals we have in our care."

"So the forcefield is down?"

"Unfortunately, yes. Which is why we're in a hurry."

"To get out and escape from the enclosure? So we can go home?"

"Yes, but not because anyone's in a hurry to leave the enclosure. It's because that every *other* enclosure in the entire ship worked off of the same power source."

"So you're saying all the animals are free?"

"Correct. Including the meat-eating ones."

Alice went white.

"I mean," Jeeves continued with a shrug as it pressed the button on the elevator to go down. "It's not like *I'm* in any danger. Last time I checked, the razor-fanged Guulonk from the Alera Swamps didn't have a taste for flying monitors. I'm only doing this because I know I'd feel utterly awful if I sat back and watched you all get eaten. I mean, there's the profit to be had off selling the footage to the media, but that's not worth all of the therapy."

"So what's the plan, if the power is out?"

"The power's dead, so the teleporter to the planet is out of play." The computer pressed the elevator button again. "The ships in the hanger bay, however, don't need electricity to fly. We'll have to work out how to get the bay doors open. There's probably a manual way of doing it."

"I thought you knew about this ship."

"I do." Jeeves pressed the button firmer. "Just that we've never been in the situation where all of the power died. I don't think the backup systems even had a fair fight. They got knocked out the moment they came online. Poor things."

"So … why is the elevator taking so long to get to the bottom? It's not even moving."

"I don't know," the computer said, slamming a fist on the down button. "It's almost like the bloody thing is broken, or out of power, or needs a reboot or—oh." It put its hands to its monitor. "I really should have thought this out a little better."

"So, we're stuck now?"

"Purely by my own disgust. See, we have this." Jeeves pulled a lever on the side of the control panel. A hatch opened up, a ladder extending itself to the ground floor. "Just … do it while I'm not looking."

Alice frowned. "Why on earth do you have a problem with ladders?"

"Ugh, it's just so … just so *tribal*. It's like watching someone eating a mud pie and roasting maggots and doing their business in pits in the ground."

"Well then," Alice said, placing a foot down on the first rung. "Let me be the first to show you the ways of my tribe."

"Ugh, you're doing it. You're actually … *using the ladder*, like some sort of monkey, or ape, or, or …"

"Or someone who needs to get out of here fast before she gets eaten by a monster she's never even heard of. Come on, brainbox, you don't even need to use the ladder. Let's go."

It took a lot of coercing to get the robot through the hatch, especially given that he was treating the ladder as if it was laced with some kind of deadly disease. Once everyone was down (and the robot had washed his hands), they resumed their escape, running down corridors as they went. A few animals had escaped their enclosure, but they were more scared of the stampede of human beings than anything.

"Uh," said Jenny as they went, watching a small lizard race skitter away into the shadows. "So what kind of creatures will we need to avoid?"

"Hopefully security will be able to contain all the ones with more teeth than intelligence, but there's no harm in being cautious. There is one threat that security won't be able to deal with, however, and that's Narlok. No doubt the logs detected a spike from your containment, and no doubt that he's coming with a vengeance. If he catches us, Heavens knows what he'll do. But don't you worry; I have access to the security in the ship, and it's showing no movement within the next few corridors. In fact ..." He knocked the side of his monitor with a fist. "It's showing nobody moving anywhere. Not even down *this* corridor we're currently doing a sprint down."

"Computer," Jenny said. "One question."

"Yes?"

"Is that security system, perchance, dependent on power to run?"

"Oh." Jeeves sighed. "Blast, I've done it again, haven't I? Well, I'm sure that the speed we left the enclosure at means that it'll be a while before Narlok gets here to—"

The door at the end of the corridor opened.

Narlok stood inside.

He didn't seem too pleased. His face seethed with an expression that would put wrath to shame. His suit was marred by scars and scorch marks. What really put the nail in the "we're definitely in trouble" coffin was that he had appeared to have gotten too close to the exhibits on his way there. Slowly, he reached up to pluck what looked like a leech with teeth from his cheek and flicked it to the floor.

"Pack your bags," he said, with the tone Alice imagined a prison guard might use. "You're leaving."

Final goodbyes are always hard, especially when they carry with them the weight of infinite foot massages once known. That was, however, all that anyone could do, as they gave a weak wave to the huge cruiser that was ascending from the Earth's surface, its path slightly wobbling as the pilot was attacked by yet another nasty from the zoo. Within moments, the spaceship engaged its warp drive and shot off into space, disappearing as quickly as it came.

The waving died down.

Of course, nobody was feeling particularly good. A lot of them watched morosely as the ship fled from sight, depressed that all of their gained bonuses were vanishing at lightspeed with it. One person watched the entire procedure with balled fists and clenched teeth.

"Well," Alice said, giving her best "angry bull trying to be a fluffy sheep" voice. "I think we all learnt something today."

Everyone exchanged worried looks. Jenny nodded with enthusiasm.

Alice began to pace back and forth in front of the crowd like an army general. "When given the chance of lifelong happiness, you all threw it away. Why, do you ask? Because of human greed. Basic, ugly, human greed. We couldn't live together under the same roof without someone having a problem. Could none of you conceive living in separate houses? Of calming down and seeing that, perhaps, we could have sorted this all out with a bit of diplomacy and some good old fashioned human spirit and compassion? Instead, we made ourselves look like idiots to aliens who could *literally materialise chocolate*. Well, what do you all have to say for yourselves?"

The *most* worrying part was that, while everyone still looked very sheepish, Jenny had her hand in the air.

"Excuse me," Jenny said, "but was that it?"

"What do you mean, 'was that it'? Of course that was it. Did you expect me to continue ranting?"

"No, I mean ... was that what we were supposed to learn?"

"Yes. Wait, what did you learn?"

"I learnt that we need to invent holograms *really freaking fast*."

"Great," Alice said, with a sigh. "I can always trust on you to see the reality of the situation. Did anyone *else* learn anything?"

Someone raised his hand.

"Yes, you. What did you learn?"

"I learnt that Jordan gets the best opportunities in life."

"I am the leader," Jordan said. "It comes with the territory."

Someone else raised her hand. "I learnt that Jordan invites the worst kind of people to his 'opportunities,' and I won't be voting for him in the next election."

"Oh, hey, come on," Jordan said, turning to the crowd where the voice came from. "This was *one time*."

A female voice came from the crowd. "I also learnt that people are picky jerks, and that they should all get kicked out next time. Who doesn't like champagne, for goodness sakes?"

"And I learnt," a man said, "that you shouldn't live with a crummy, no-fun vegetarian."

"And I learnt that the man who just spoke is an absolute jerk, and should choke to death on the next slab of steak he'll have."

"And I learnt that, if *someone* had a good taste in chocolate, we'd still be in the ship."

"That's nice. Guess what I just learnt? That your jaw needs breaking."

Alice didn't even try to stop the first fist that flew, let alone the many that followed. She didn't, however, feel *total* crushing disappointment in her race when she saw that Jenny wasn't joining in with the fight. She didn't even look like she was ready to take bets.

"So, what do we do now?" Jenny asked.

"We're moving to Roswell and waiting," Alice said, walking away from the scrum. "I don't think there's any intelligent life left on this rock."

The Most Dangerous Lies
Ken Furie

NOTHING IN HIS EYES marked him as a monster. In fact, women seemed to adore getting lost in his eyes. He had seldom come across a female in all of England who didn't instinctively trust those fawn-like eyes of his.

They had come in handy during his killing spree.

The woman who stood before him, a red-headed treat in her thirties, searched his eyes for danger. Like so many others, she nearly fell into them. She forced her gaze away and beckoned to a group of teenagers, who approached with slow steps.

"Here's our most recent addition to the Crime Hall," Red-Headed Treat said. "This is Jack the Ripper."

Teens of both genders ogled the man. He returned their stares with a slight smile on his lips. Their eyes drifted to the gleaming blade, hanging on the wall of Jack's room. Ten inches of perfectly polished steel, its worn leather handle showed the measured use of a master. Its thin blade tapered into a sadistic downward curve at the point.

"This is Jack's fourth victim," Red-Headed Treat said. She moved her hand in front of her body as if turning a knob.

The tag on her breast pocket read "Lucia." Jack opened his mouth to speak her name.

As if by magic, a living scene blinked into being around Jack, surrounding him in all directions. He cast a quick look at the teens, expecting to see frightened eyes and gasps. Instead they merely nodded along, as if city streets popping into life before their eyes were commonplace.

It was a street that Jack knew very well.

He inhaled sharply, expecting to catch the familiar smells, but he only tasted the sharp medicinal smell of his enclosure. He swiped at a nearby wooden door, but his hand passed through it as if it were air.

The street flickered in broken darkness under a feeble flame from a single gas lantern on the corner. The cobbles swam in mud from a recent downpour. A young woman shivered under the lamp, bone thin and pale as a wraith. The woman stood barefoot. She wore the ragged remains of an evening gown, torn as if it had been dragged behind a horse carriage, and so soiled its original color could not be guessed.

"This is the region of Whitechapel, in London," Lucia said. "You're seeing this slum as it was about two hundred years ago, when it suffered hardship that the world had rarely seen. This poor waif standing before you is a prostitute. She is so spent that no one will take her offer."

The prostitute shook from a coughing fit. Looking to her left, she saw the shadow of an approaching stranger. The frail creature struck a pose, primping her bodice to show cleavage. The man drew near, his overcoat collar turned against the damp. She called to him, but the man did not slow his pace as he passed. She watched him go, gave the man up for lost, and hugged herself.

"It appears she only had two choices. Will she die of disease, or will she starve? Her health is fading."

The prostitute coughed again.

"Her once beautiful face has been eroded by grim worries. She stands shivering and alone in her darkest hour."

Lucia paused for effect.

"But wait!"

The prostitute's face brightened. A man came into view. His slender silhouette cut through the darkness with an affected nobility, the gait of a man brimming with deep-rooted confidence.

The actual Jack watched this image of his London self and poked at it. His hand passed through it. He shook his head slowly, amazed.

"She recognizes him. Yes, it's her friend Jack! She prays every day that her handsome friend will take her away, far from Whitechapel, away from the freezing rain, from the rats, and from the death that stalks her. Jack is here! Is this man the savior she has been hoping for?"

The teenagers watched with mouths open, scarcely breathing.

The projection of Jack smiled at the woman. He moved to her side. His left arm curled around her with an easy familiarity. He pressed his lips to her ear, whispered something, and her face broke into a smile. Her eyes twinkled with budding tears. She snuggled against him and permitted herself to be steered away, toward a thin, black alley.

"She's completely enchanted." Lucia's voice dropped to a low tone. "Her prayers have been answered."

Jack's left arm draped across her shoulders. His right extracted the familiar curved blade from his overcoat, flashing like fire as it caught the pale lamplight. Jack led the woman into the alley, slowly immersing them both in complete darkness.

The students all held their breaths for one heartbeat, and then another.

Amidst the black, so quick they nearly missed it, the blade flashed again as it swept downward in an arc.

Inside the enclosure the scene faded. Jack stared unblinking, astounded.

"That's the first time Jack has seen himself in action," said Lucia, her voice quiet. "Perhaps until now he thought to protest that he wasn't really Jack the Ripper. He was never caught at the time of his crimes. But our dear Jack is now grasping that we just viewed the past. *His* past. That's why I brought you all here for this moment—to see his reaction."

Jack continued to stare at the now-vacant area, shaking his head in wonder. None of this made any sense. He'd awakened in this room hours ago, but he still had no idea what was going on. He was suddenly two hundred years in the future? How absurd.

"Can we talk to him?" asked a girl.

"Yes, Laura, although I can't guarantee he will answer."

"What's your real name?" Laura asked.

Jack looked blankly at the teenager, still bewildered by what he'd just seen.

"His name is Clarence Creeley," Lucia said. "There's no point in playing dumb, Clarence. We already know what we need to know about you."

"Then what do you mean by questioning me?" Jack asked, pleased at the firmness of his response.

"I'm sure there'll be no harm in their questions."

"Is that so? No harm for them, that's certain. Perhaps we should make this more interesting. Well, more interesting for me, as it were. If I answer yours, you answer mine, yes? What do you say, gov'ness? You in the game?"

Lucia nodded, her eyes glinting, her mouth slightly upturned into a smile. "Who goes first?"

She looked at the kids expectantly, but they shifted on their feet—they looked everywhere *but* at Jack.

Jack scanned the faces. He could always tell which girl to choose. Something connected them, showed him his path. He smiled. This girl, regarding him with rounded eyes, trembled ever so slightly, the perfect mix of terror and longing. It was as obvious to him as her nose. And looking at her, he began to feel the same thing.

He smiled, only for her. "Do you have a question, my love? What's your name?"

"I'm Marian."

"Ah, like the fair Maid Marian, Robin Hood's desire."

"Um," she said, looking around at her peers, who merely shrugged. "I guess so."

"A suitable name," said Jack. "And your question?"

"Clarence, why did you do it?"

He grinned. "Ah, I see. You want to climb into my head, have a peep at the clockworks. Very well. What's the usual rot? Sold my soul, withered heart, a lost cause before I was born."

"You sound like you don't believe any of that," said Marian.

Jack sighed. "Daresay it don't matter much what I believe, now that I'm nabbed, 'ey?" He raised a finger to his cheek and scratched. "My turn."

"Go ahead, Clarence," Lucia replied.

"Am I in hell?" he asked.

"You expected hell, Jack the Ripper?"

He thought about it for a moment. "Daresay I didn't expect anything at all, did I? Don't remember dying, however. Just the waking up part."

He probed at his left thigh gingerly, expecting pain.

"That's right, Clarence. We healed your leg infection."

"I thought it would do me in, that leg. My bloodlungs—gone too? And my teeth ..." he slid his tongue across his incisors. "They're back. As if they'd never gone to rot."

She nodded.

"Never felt better in my life. Bit of a twist on me, now that I got nowhere to go."

"Our turn now, Clarence." Lucia motioned to another girl.

She asked, "Did you know your parents?"

Jack raised a brow and took a breath. "You're still asking the same bleedin' question. Oh, very well. My parents, yes, I knew them. I was no orphan. And no, they didn't deserve a demon like me. But they got me, and that's the way the world works. You there!" he jutted his chin at a lanky boy named Ben who appeared stunned at the attention. "What the devil is that on your head? You suppose you're a duck, do you?"

Ben's eyes rounded and his fingers touched his baseball cap. The other boys laughed and one of them punched Ben on the shoulder.

This bit of levity warmed up the other students. They started calling out their own questions.

"Are you married?"

"How'd you avoid the cops?"

"Why does my dog eat rocks?"

"Will you come to my birthday party?"

"Have you ever tried a chocolate bar?"

As the barrage of questions rained on him, Jack scowled at the teenagers with growing irritation. They noticed his glare at last and fell silent.

Marian finally spoke, "What did you do to that poor girl in the vidscene?"

"That one? Why, nothing as didn't happen to the others, little mistress," said Jack. He allowed his anger to show through. It wasn't difficult—the anger was always there, simmering under the layer of calm that he wore, like a coating of white ash over burning embers. He glared, and curled his lips in a snarl. "Et 'er up, as I recall. Except the toenails. I keep them in a wee kettle to flavor my tea."

Several of the teenagers gasped, but Marian held her ground.

"Do you hate girls?" she asked.

Jack grinned. Now he knew he had her. He turned his full attention to this beautiful 16-year-old, drank in her youth, her innocence, her dreams. He looked through her eyes, deep, as if peering into her intimate soul, that dearest place where they already knew each other so well.

"Little mistress, you misconstrue. There's no finer thing in all creation than a girl, is there?"

Marian hesitated. "Well ..."

Jack gestured at her, hands reaching out with his palms up. "Look at yourself, love. You're a man's most personal ambition."

Marian shook her head, doubtful. "I don't—"

"Marian, I'll let you in on a little secret. I'll be drinking thoughts of you every hour for a month, on account of seeing you this moment. Are you blind to your power over men? My dear, you're a scarlet rose, awakening amidst the heather."

Jack inhaled deeply, savoring the sight of her. Marian blinked like an owl in daylight as air haltingly filled her lungs. After a moment they slowly exhaled together, in perfect sync.

Jack's face flushed. A powerful love swelled inside his chest.

"You're a teardrop, Marian, pure and clear, transforming daylight into all the colors of the world."

Her eyes grew wider, simultaneously spellbound and devastated.

"My dear, you shine like Easter morning! You—"

"Clarence!" Lucia's sharp rebuke cut through his rhapsody.

Jack suffered a flood of hot rage. He flung his body at Lucia, hands outstretched like talons, his face marred by murderous intent. But an invisible wall slammed him backward with equal force, and he sprawled onto his side. Stunned, he panted for a moment, and then he began to laugh.

"Never, never. Never would I believe it," Jack muttered.

He took a breath and sat up, searching for the wall that was not there.

Lucia spoke to the teenagers. "I think Clarence is done answering questions," she said. "Let's move along and let him get used to his new residence."

Residence? Jack thought. Not remotely. He would find a way out of this place, and to repay his captors he would unleash his numerous talents upon the unsuspecting world outside.

Marian cheeks glowed, still ringing with words. She cast several glances back at Jack. He did nothing to delay her departure. He remained on the floor, working at slowing down his breath and heartbeat.

Once calm, he examined his surroundings. The three visible walls were bare and dull. There was an upholstered chair and settee. Everything seemed perfectly lit with unyielding daylight, but he could not judge the source. He rose to his feet and touched a small blue symbol on a wall. A sink slid out. Amazed, Jack found that water flowed into it endlessly, and he could change its temperature by touching along the spigot. A few feet to its right, pressing a different symbol opened an invisible door into an empty closet, all white and polished. More symbols provided instructions for bathing and eliminating wastes, each in their own tidy alcove. Back in his main room, the blade rested in mid-air against the invisible barrier, tantalizingly close. He pounded on it, hung his entire weight on it, and slammed it with his chair, but nothing would release it.

On the other side of his invisible barrier, hundreds of people wandered past, gawking, blathering nonsense, and forcing that irritating incident in Whitechapel to replay again and again. He spoke to no one, glared at everyone, and turned his back when he could not endure it a moment more.

A few hours later Lucia reappeared, accompanied by a stout man of later years. A halo of white hair framed his balding head, and he wore expensive clothing in the form of a rich, dark jacket and red necktie.

Jack stood. "Couldn't resist my charms, Miss Lucia?"

"Have you been trying to charm me? I didn't think I was your type." Lucia allowed a smile to tug at her lips, and she met his gaze as if daring him to protest.

"Why would you suppose a rare prize such as yourself would not be my type?" He met her dare with an easy grin and unflinching eye contact.

"Clarence, I'd like to introduce you to Devin Cross. He's the authority here."

"Welcome, Clarence." Cross's voice resonated like a cello. "We are delighted to have you with us."

"Can't say as I share the sentiment, Mr. Cross."

"No doubt," Cross replied with a smile. "Yet you made quite an impression on Lucia's group."

"Did I?"

"Yes, they'll be talking about you for months. One girl, Marian, I believe, can speak of nothing else."

Jack grinned.

Cross nodded. "You put on a good performance. We want you to keep it up."

He stared blankly for a couple of heartbeats. "I'm not sure I follow. You *want* me to rave and froth and act an utter fool?"

"Yes. It will help our guests remember their visits, and that's important to us."

Jack shook his head, clasped his hands behind his back, and began to pace. "That's rubbish, 'ey? Are you saying I'm in some kind of theatre?"

"No, it's not a theatre. It's a zoo, Clarence."

Jack looked around his room. "I don't see any animals."

"This zoo is the first of its kind. It contains living characters from human history."

Jack's hands clenched into fists, fingernails digging into his palms. "You must be joking. You brought me two hundred years into the future to put me in a bloody zoo?"

Cross nodded vigorously. "Oh, yes! We started with an invention that allowed us to view the past. So much enthusiasm! So much support! But years went by and all we had to show for our work were reports of how the history books are inaccurate. The public lost interest. Then we discovered a way to open a gap in time and slip a person through it. I'll be blunt, Clarence: we need funding to keep doing this remarkable research, so we created this place, where people can interact with the past directly."

Jack clenched his head between his palms. He gritted his teeth. "I see. You threw me in here so you can swoggle a few pennies, 'ey?"

"Well ... frankly, yes."

Jack stared at Lucia. "This seems reasonable to you, does it?"

She stood silent, arms folded across her chest.

Jack turned away. "Why should I cooperate? What's in it for me?"

"Fame, of course," Cross replied. "Isn't that one of the reasons you killed *all* of those pretty girls? To have an impact? Those kids today may not remember Napoleon. He blathered incessantly about Russians and the science of military conflict. He nearly put them all to sleep. But they *will* remember you. Marian is telling everyone about you. Word will spread and they'll be lining up in droves, hoping to be seduced and attacked."

Jack's eyes drifted toward the infamous knife. He walked over to it, reached out, and rapped his knuckle on the barrier that kept it safe. "I love this knife," he said. "It's been a friend, more reliable than day turns to night. I'd like to introduce you to it, sir. I'm contemplating the manner of skewering you. I'm thinking I'll stick you like a hog and slice you into fat, pink ribbons."

Cross beamed. "Remarkable! And here I thought you preferred girls to old men like me."

"Fear not. I'd make an exception for the right bloke."

Cross smiled. "My boy, that's exactly the sort of thing we want from you. Keep it up!"

Jack stared at Cross, and then at Lucia. His eyes burned with hatred. "When I get out of here, we'll see if you're still so keen on it. Now it's time you left. No more chirping, little birdies. Go away."

Cross's smile grew into a grin, "Lovely to have you with us, my boy. I look forward to your antics."

"I'd like a quick word with him, Devin, if you don't mind." Lucia spoke to Cross as he turned.

Cross nodded and walked away. Jack focused his fury on her, the Red-Headed Treat. He imagined her lovely skin blistering in the heat of his anger.

She turned to Jack, hands clasped together. "He spoke the truth, Clarence. Please believe me, there's nothing you can do."

Jack's voice shook as he asked, "I'm a prisoner here?"

Her lips pursed and she looked down. "Yes. Mr. Cross has thought of everything. He expects you to try to escape, and he expects to enjoy watching you try."

"I daresay he may be quite disappointed," Jack muttered.

"Clarence, you can have a decent existence here if you accept it. Live up to your part and you'll be treated well. Maybe it won't be so bad."

"Maybe it'll be worse," he growled.

She set her lips and waited.

He raised his eyes and their gaze met. He searched for the familiar reflection of guilt, of quiet longing that women so often held for him. Her eyes were deep gray, dark, and unruly, like stormy skies in August. He found no reflection for him there.

"Will you help me, Lucia?"

She shook her head, frowning. "I can't help you escape. But perhaps there are other ways I can help."

He turned his back to her, and when he glanced a few minutes later she was gone.

Days passed. The miserable visitors continued to parade through. He talked to some, screamed at others, ignored most. He grew accustomed to the routine—all the visitors ogled the Whitechapel murder scene, and then bugged their eyes at the knife. They stared at him like they expected him to kill somebody for their entertainment. Many of the kids called out to him, or insulted him, or threw things at his barrier. Each day Jack dreaded the hours when visitors flooded the Hall, and felt his soul lighten when the Hall closed for the evening.

One day he heard a familiar voice.

"Hi, Clarence," Marian said.

She smiled as he turned to her. She wore a bright yellow summer dress with bare shoulders and white sandals.

"I can scarcely imagine how this could be the case, but you're lovelier than I remember," Jack said. "You're breathtaking."

She blinked rapidly and took a breath. "I thought maybe you could, you know, give me some advice about boys."

He tilted his head. "You want advice from me, 'ey?"

"Well, I mean, you're a boy, so maybe ..." she faltered, working the small white handbag she carried with both hands.

"I'll give it a toss, Marian. Go on then."

"Okay, so, have you ever, you know, have you had a crush on a boy—"

Jack arched an eyebrow, smiling.

"Well, no, that's not it. Not *you*. I mean, like, if you were a girl, and I know you're not, obviously, but if you *were*, and you couldn't think about *anything*, because there was this person in your mind, and you can't stop thinking about him? And you know you shouldn't think about him, like it's the stupidest idea in the world, I mean monumentally stupid, but then he's there with you in your dreams, and you don't want those dreams ever to end. And you long to go back to those dreams, but you know it's wrong to think about him, so you can't sleep at all and ... Clarence, do you know what I mean?"

She turned away, her face flushed a deep red.

"Maybe so," Jack said, his voice soft. "Go on, Marian, don't be coy."

She took a sharp breath. "When we first met, the way you looked at me. It was so ... Well, you looked at me as if ... as if I were in your dreams."

Jack nodded. "Amazing! How could you possibly know that? That's precisely how I felt."

Marian closed her eyes, sighed, and inhaled slowly, savoring his words. "Did you really mean those things you said to me?"

"Every word. Every single word, my dear. I feel it now, seeing you again before me."

She stared, eyes wide, pupils dilated with intense emotion.

He rubbed his forehead with his fingertips like he had a splitting headache. "But I should not have spoken to you like that," he murmured. "I've regretted it ever since."

"Don't say that!" she said. "Those things you said, they were the most beautiful things I've ever heard."

"Well that's just bloody great!" he said, smacking his palm sharply on his thigh. "I thought I had nothing to lose, I figured I may as well speak my mind. Never could do it before. Had to keep my thoughts to myself, even the beautiful ones. But here you are, unable to sleep for thinking about a *murderer*. And here I am in a bleedin' cage!"

Marion moved to the edge of his enclosure. She reached out a hand and pressed it to the invisible wall, fingers spread. At last he looked up, eyes damp with sorrow. He reached out his own hand and aligned it with hers. They held still like that for a moment, breathing in sync, trying to feel the warmth of the other through the barrier.

"Really, Marian, don't you have any sense?"

Lucia stood at the edge of Jack's enclosure.

"This is none of your business, Lucia," said Marian, dropping her hand. Her expression showed more shame than anger.

"Isn't it? Well, how about this, Marian? Shall I inform your parents that you're skipping school in order to play fluttering heart games with Jack the Ripper?"

She glared at the girl, stern as a magistrate.

Marian dropped her eyes.

"I thought as much. Go! Go on back to school and don't come here again."

"She's right, Marian," said Jack. He stood slowly and took several steps away from her.

Marian looked at him unbelieving. "But—"

"No, please, Marian. It grieves me to see you when we can't be together. Don't come back, it will only bring pain for both of us."

He hung his head and his shoulders drooped.

"Don't worry. I won't come back!" Marian shot this over her shoulder and stomped away.

They watched her go. Moments later, Devin Cross sauntered toward the display from the same direction. He smiled at Jack when he arrived, the smile accompanying a look that made Jack feel like the goose at Christmas dinner.

"You sly crocodile," Cross chuckled. "You made certain she would come back."

Jack sat in silence.

Cross chuckled again, "You're misreading the situation, Clarence."

"Am I?"

"Yes. We have no objection if you want to seduce the young girl. Well, Lucia does, but the rest of us have no problem with it. Marian's in for some heartbreak, but that would be true regardless of the object of her affections. No doubt other boys are waiting in line to disappoint her. The problem here is that you think you can somehow use her."

Jack's fury and hatred began building again. His fists clenched and unclenched and his jaw rippled as he ground his teeth.

Cross grinned. "There's no way for you to change the basic premise of your existence here, Clarence. Nonetheless, believe me, I do hope you'll keep trying."

Cross waited for a reaction, but got nothing. The round little man smiled at Jack's silence. He nodded in a jaunty way to Lucia, who returned the nod politely, and he walked away. Jack cast a scorching glare after him.

"Clarence," said Lucia. "You should listen to him. He's right."

He glared at her. "He supposes I'm manipulating that girl."

"Aren't you? Honestly, now."

"Maybe I am. Maybe, but that's not my intent. I don't plan to manipulate her or anyone, for that matter. It just happens."

She looked at him thoughtfully. "Are you saying you actually meant that poetic nonsense you dished up when you first met her?"

"Of course. I felt all those things just looking at her. It just came out! I don't lie. I don't intend to lie, at any rate."

"Hmm. I see. That explains something I've wondered about you."

"Does it?"

"You adapt your emotions to fit the moment. The most dangerous lies are the ones you believe when you speak them."

He processed the woman's words silently.

"But then the moment is gone, and the feelings that made your words true have vanished. What happens then, Clarence?"

He didn't answer. He didn't care. Her words just made his head spin. Was she right? Did his existence amount to nothing real, nothing tangible, nothing he could hold? His gaze turned to the knife hanging on the wall, shining and untouchable, mocking him. He rested his face in his hands to hide the tears that had formed, from rage or despair he could not tell.

When he looked up again she was gone.

Lucia returned a few days later, accompanied by Marian.

"Clarence," Lucia said. "Marian has volunteered to keep you company, in the hopes that it will help keep your spirits up. The notion delighted Devin, so despite my opinion, here we are. But no talking about your feelings, both of you. Believe me, I'll know it if you do."

She wagged a scolding finger at them. Then she motioned to her left and a security guard brought a small chair and set it beside the enclosure.

"I'm going to read to you, Clarence," said Marian, a smile accompanying her dancing eyes. She seated herself and rummaged in her pouch.

Jack watched as Lucia and the security guard departed. He fetched his own chair and seated it next to Marian.

Their smiles matched.

"What's this about?" he asked.

"Jane Austen," said Marian. "My favorite author. She's so wonderful, I know you're going to love her. This book is about how a man changes and grows so that he can be with the woman he loves."

Jack grinned and shook his head. "An odd choice. Couldn't you pick something more in line with our situation?"

She arched an eyebrow at him, still smiling. She produced a printed antique book from her pouch. Opening the book to its first page, she began to read.

Weeks passed with little to separate one day from the next. Jack paid no mind to the visitors. He ignored the children who were determined to goad him into responding. Women paraded by, looking him up and down and saying things to him more brazen than the prostitutes of his day. He found himself sinking into a dismal state, the only respite being the hour each day that Marian came to read to him. He longed for those moments, when her soft voice caressed his ears, her presence like cool raindrops on sunburned skin. Lucia always hovered nearby but did not interfere. Then Marian would leave him, and each time his depression rose to consume him, as if someone had snuffed out a candle, enveloping him in darkness.

His beard inched out a fraction each day. His hair grew scraggly and dangled in greasy clumps. His body withered. He found himself less and less inclined to speak, especially with Lucia always lingering on the fringes of sight. After some time he barely spoke at all.

One day, once Marian had completed reading *Pride and Prejudice* and started on another book, she stopped in mid-sentence.

"I can't ignore it anymore," she said. "You're in such a state! Clarence, you haven't been eating."

He shook his head, not wanting to discuss it.

"Clarence," she said, clear and direct enough that he met her eyes. "This is no way to live."

Jack abandoned his reticence and slammed his fist on the shield. "You suppose I don't know it? I'm living it, aren't I? All night and all day in an endless, dreary cycle. I do the same things, I think the same thoughts, I walk the same circles, I eat the same tripe. People pass, free as songbirds, and they're all so bloody unhappy. In my day I supposed I was unhappy too, but now ... now I'm just meat in a cage. In here there is no life, no hope, no future. I'm dying inside."

Jack realized he'd barely said a word in weeks. It surprised him how good it felt to speak. The sensation of reconnecting with life was tantalizing. Waiting for her reply, hands trembling, he noticed that she had a perfect face, truly a work of art, high cheekbones, heart-shaped, bright green eyes, lovely beyond words. He wanted to gaze at her face forever. The desire startled him, but not so much as realizing that the warmth of life he felt had less to do with speaking and more to do with speaking to Marian.

Marian had listened intently and now she gazed at him, her eyes shining with new tears. "Well, you do have a kind of choice," she said. "You can live what life you have in a haze of misery. Or you can engage with the people who care about you, and come here to see you all the time, and who hope to understand you, at least a little."

"There's one other choice, Marian." His voice was laced with challenge. "The only real choice."

"Clarence..."

"Death."

She put her hand to her lips. "You can't mean that."

"Can't I? I was done-for long ago. Cross stuck me in here, against my will. Healed me and caged me, he did, against my will. I'd rather be feeding worms than abide this anymore. I'd do the job myself but I've no way to do it. Cross 'as made certain of it."

"I want to help you, Clarence. But you can't ask that of me."

"You want to help me? Death will help me."

She blinked and shook her head, startled at the direction of their conversation. "I can't—"

"Don't stand out there and protest. You don't know what it's like in 'ere. Nothing's ever been so clear to me."

He sunk to his knees. Tears flowed freely. He dashed at his cheeks with his fingers.

"Kill me, Marian."

"Clarence," said Marian, her voice rising with alarm. "You're so dramatic! Can it truly be so bad?"

"I'm weeping like a swaddling babe. Never did cry before. Not as I can recollect."

She searched his eyes. He just looked back at her, his cheeks wet, eyes red and brimming. He willed the despair in his belly to spread outward and envelop his soul in darkness, for her to see and judge.

She furrowed her brow and studied him. "I can see it. You've given up."

He hung his head, silent.

She watched him a moment more, her breath shallow and her eyes still threatening tears. Finally she stood and tucked away her book.

"I'll speak to Lucia. She cares about me, and you too Clarence, believe it or not. Maybe an appeal to her kind heart will convince her."

She walked out of sight and Jack moved to the back of his cage. He touched the wall that turned into a cot and flopped into it. Laying prone, examining the perfect ceiling, he thought only of Marian until he fell asleep.

For three days she didn't return. Misery cloaked him in gloom and oppressed his every breath. He paced in his cage and paid no attention to any of the people in the Hall. His time in the enclosure seemed endless, and he longed for darkness, for nothing.

After the third day of her absence, the public areas emptied, and the slam of the heavy entry doors rang down the hall. The lights extinguished and Jack slumped onto his cot.

Hours later, with sleep still eluding him, Jack slitted his eyes as a panel magically appeared out of a solid wall. It slid open. Marian stepped through, entering the cage.

"Clarence!" She hissed in a whisper.

He sat up and rested on an elbow. "Thank the heavens. Have you come to kill me?"

"Yes."

"How does it work?"

"I've brought you something. A poison. You just swallow it. Quick and painless, just how you'd want it." She took a few steps into the room, set her small handbag on the little table and began to hunt in it. "Here it is," she said, producing a small blue pill.

She looked up, but Jack was no longer there. Her eyes grew wide. She glanced toward the knife hanging on the wall and her breath caught. It was gone.

"Clarence ... ?" she looked left and right.

Jack's voice came from directly behind her, "You've never been lovelier, my dear."

He stood at the gap in the wall, blocking her way. He had moved undetected and now positioned himself between Marian and her exit. He held the vicious blade in his right hand, as easy with it as if it were an appendage of his body.

"Clarence! No!" she scolded, hands trembling.

He took a step toward her, and she stumbled back, further into his cage.

He smiled. Here at last he permitted her to see the monster they all sought. But the monster had never hidden in his eyes. It lived in his smile. He showed her the smile of a predator, the leer of a jackal, the grin of a python gripping a kitten in its coils.

"I wasn't lying when I said I wanted to die. If I can't kill anymore, there's no point in carrying on living. But here you are within my grasp, aren't you, my darling? Pretty as a garden in June. Marian, you're the answer to my darkest desires. You're the savior I've been hoping for."

He lunged for her, quick and silent as a shadow. She leapt to the side, swifter than he expected. She edged around to keep his little table between them.

Jack drank her in: pupils dilated, pulse hammering in her neck. He knew that adrenaline coursed through her body. He imagined the icy chill tickling her spine each time she caught his smile.

She gave a breathless squeak, "If you kill me, they'll know it was you!"

"Ha! Know it was me? What of it?" He inched toward her as he spoke. "I've got the whole world to hide in, haven't I? But I'm not going to bolt quite yet, oh no. I've a mind for some fun and games. Let's have some fun, 'ey?"

He lunged at her, swinging the knife. His face glowed with joy, the pleasure of the hunt apparent in his grin. She managed to avoid his reach by a fraction, no more, and somehow kept the tiny table between them.

He showed her the knife. Her eyes widened.

His grin broadened.

"Why me?" she gasped, stalling for time and easing toward the gap. "Don't you care about me?"

He nodded. "I fell in love with you, Marian."

She scowled at him. "If you think you are in love with me, then why would you kill me?"

"You still don't understand, my dear. I only kill women I love."

She stared at him, dumbfounded.

"If it helps to know it, you are far above all others. I confess that I can't stop picturing your face. I would expect to be less enthralled when I haven't seen you in days, but it was quite the contrary, wasn't it? Your face haunts my waking eyes. A few weeks more and I'd be helpless to think for myself."

He knocked the table aside and leapt at her. She couldn't move quickly enough. He knew he had her at last. He slashed the knife in an arc, shifting his shoulders to gain the leverage necessary to tear through human flesh, even skin as tender as Marian's.

But his weapon passed right through her.

And she was gone.

He snapped his head, looking left, right, behind, above. "No!" he shouted. "It can't be—"

The lights came on. Applause soon followed.

Devin Cross stood right outside the cage, grinning and clapping. "Bravo! Bravo! Well done. You put on an extraordinary show, Clarence!"

"How ..." Jack stuttered. He looked back and forth between Cross and the place where Marian had stood.

"A projected vid-scene, my boy," said Cross, like an indulgent uncle. "Just like the one showing you in action in Whitechapel."

Jack hammered his hands on his forehead. "No! But she was looking right at me. I had her!"

Cross winked at him and chuckled. "Of course you did, my boy. You did and you didn't."

"No," Jack whispered.

Lucia walked up to stand beside Cross. It was almost more than Jack could take. His knees nearly buckled beneath him.

She smiled, and he saw a trace of the monster he knew so well.

"In case you're curious ..." Lucia nodded to Cross.

He pulled some sort of device from a coat pocket and poked at it with his fingers.

There stood Marian, right beside Cross, a Jane Austen book in her hand.

Cross twitched the device with a finger and Marian laughed, as if Jack had told an off-color joke. Then he manipulated the device again and Marian vanished.

Lucia's smile remained in place. "She is real, Clarence, don't doubt that. But she had no part in Devin's little prank. I had to stay nearby in case the real Marian wandered up."

"You said you wanted to help me!" Jack yelled at her, his voice breaking. His soul screamed at the betrayal exploding within.

She nodded, "And I meant it, Clarence. I meant it wholeheartedly"—her eyes, those stormy eyes with depths like an ocean, gazed deeply into his—"when I said it, that is."

"But ... but I can't live like this."

Cross replied. "It may not be forever, my boy. With our abilities to heal you, you might die in 150 years."

"No," Jack whispered.

"With any luck, by then we will have invented a way to live eternally. But you won't be entirely alone. Marian will visit and read to you every day, right here, just beyond your reach."

Cross waved his little device at Jack, took Lucia's elbow and began to guide her away.

"Wait!" Jack's voice shook.

They paused, looking back.

"I just ... I can't ... Lucia, tell me. Am I in hell?"

Lucia shook her head, eyes filled with pity. "Were you expecting anything else, Jack the Ripper?"

Playing Man
Scott Dyson

THE MONORAIL GLIDED through the depths of the Amazon rainforest, blending with the lush green and gold vegetation that lined the track and filled the views from all windows in the train. Animals paid the sleek vehicle no mind; the teeming plant life remained unaffected by its motion.

Jordem Lun stood at the panoramic window on one side of the train, transfixed by the breathtaking sights in every direction. The depth of color, the vibrancy of the life on the other side of the flexiglass was awe-inspiring. Brightly colored birds flew between the tops of the exotic trees under the canopy, and giant mouse-like creatures climbed among the branches.

Is there anyplace else in the universe quite like this planet? he wondered.

Jordem turned, raised a frothy red drink to his lips and drank.

Strawberry daiquiri, he mused. *Another thing that no place else seemed to have.* The alcohol in the beverage was already giving him a pleasant buzz behind the eyes. In space, these sorts of heady delights would be considered wasteful, sinful extravagances. Here on Earth, though, the strawberry plants still grew and the sugar for rum was available in abundance.

A vacation in this place is worth the expense, he thought as he wandered across the viewing deck of the train.

Too bad it's not all play-time...

His fellow tourists stared awestruck at the utterly alien scene surrounding them. It was a less-than-once-in-a-lifetime proposition for all of them - the stuff of comscreens or travelogues.

"Dr. Lun?" A pretty, young female monorail staffer tapped his shoulder. Jordem widened his eyes and nodded. "Comm link for you." His clenched teeth relaxed into a smile as he nodded and followed her to a private room at one end of the deck.

Jordem flicked the button to activate the comm unit. "Lun here."

"Dr Lun," the feminine voice on the other end was unfamiliar, "we have information we believe you would be interested in. It concerns your purpose here on Earth."

"Who is this?"

Jordem refused to break the awkward silence which followed ...

The caller continued. "We need to meet with you. Soon."

Jordem remained silent.

"Dr. Lun?"

"I'm listening."

"You're staying at the World Hyatt near the border tonight. If you would be so kind as to visit the hotel's lounge, one of our people will be in contact."

"What sort of information?" Jordem stalled. "Why should I interrupt my vacation to meet with you?"

"We both know you're not here on vacation," the caller said.

Jordem allowed the pregnant silence to linger once more. "Look. I don't know what you're talking about, but if you people are *so* interested to meet with me that you'll interrupt my days staring at this *amazing* scenery and sipping daiquiris, then—"

"If it's that important to you, our agent will happily cover your bar tab—for the entire evening, should you like."

Jordem considered the offer with an arched eyebrow. His expense account *was* nearly maxed out. Plus, maybe these people could shed some light on the true reason he was on Earth.

"How will I know your agent?"

"Our agent will know you." The caller let the pause sink in for a moment before continuing. "Someone will suggest that you drink to the cradle of life. I suggest you do so, for your own sake."

"What does that mean?" Jordem asked, but the caller had already hung up. *Cradle of life?*

Jordem lowered the comm link unit and stared into space as the beautiful scenery whizzed past. He barely heard the attendant ask him if he was finished with his call, nodding distractedly and handing over the unit.

He silently cursed his superiors' arrogance. *Secrets like this cannot be kept long or well*, he thought. *Obviously this one wasn't ...*

Still, he didn't plan on being the one who confirmed what might be the biggest story in recorded history. Besides, they couldn't be certain—tests needed to be run—the very tests that had brought him to this Garden of Eden.

They aren't paying me enough for this job, he thought, as the priceless view scrolled silently past, almost unnoticed.

∞

Jordem surveyed the expansive lounge at the World Hyatt, opulently furnished with plenty of wood and gleaming metallic surfaces. The huge semi-circular bar didn't even seem to put a dent in the size of the room. Jordem sauntered over to it, admiring the lighting effects behind the beautifully arranged bottles amid tasteful but obviously expensive ornamental glass and dark mahogany.

He sat on one of the comfortable stools, which automatically adjusted for his height and weight and placed him at an optimum level relative to the polished steel bar surface. He rotated around on the stool and gazed back toward the curved windows which overlooked another gorgeous rainforested landscape.

Just beautiful, Jordem thought. *It would be a true shame to waste this kind of an experience.*

He sincerely hoped it would not come to that.

A tap on his shoulder jerked him from his reverie; Jordem jumped and pivoted his head toward the source of the touch.

"Lovely view, isn't it?"

Jordem exchanged one beautiful view for another. She was tall, slim, with brown hair and the most perfect, striking smile he thought he had ever seen. A fitted blue dress accented all of her feminine assets. It *almost* matched the blue of her eyes.

She laughed. "Hello, Dr. Lun."

"Hello," he said, forcing his mouth to move as he focused on her face. She looked to be about his age, mid forties. It was the almost-imperceptible wrinkles around the eyes that gave her away. "Have we met?"

She shook her head. "Not until now. I thought I might join you for a drink."

"Certainly," he said. He swallowed the lump in his throat, and then recalled the mysterious comm link conversation from earlier. "What should we drink to?"

She turned toward the rainforest, the low back of her dress exposing a delicious curve of soft, creamy skin. "How about we drink to the cradle of life ... Earth?"

Jordem swallowed. *So this was their agent.* Somehow he'd been expecting someone a little less glamorous. *Pull yourself together,* he told himself.

"Yes, I'd like that."

He raised two fingers. The bartender nodded and shortly delivered up a pair of strawberry daiquiris. Jordem met the mysterious woman's eyes with his own as they clinked glasses and sipped.

After a few minutes of silence, Jordem decided to fish for more information.

"So, what *really* brings you here tonight?"

She smiled again. "Right to the point. I like that." She set her drink on the bar and shifted her gaze toward the window. "Incredible view, isn't it?" she repeated.

"It certainly is," he agreed as he eyed the curve of her hip.

She gently touched his arm. "How rude of me! I haven't even introduced myself, have I?" She purred out a laugh.

Jordem thought it sounded like bells.

"I'm Alnay Snow. I'm with the Department of Preservation."

Jordem frowned. "You're not an off-worlder?"

Alnay waved a hand vaguely. "My position requires me to travel off-world extensively, and I have a weakness for your products. But no, I am a native and a resident of Earth. Did you know that fewer than one hundred humans were born on Earth last year?"

"Really? And you were one of them? I mean, not last year, obviously," he ran the back of his hand across his forehead, "but you were born *here?*" He nodded toward the window.

She nodded. "I was. I love living on Earth. Who wouldn't, right?" She nodded at the window.

"I don't know," said Jordem. "I mean, it's a great place for a vacation, but I'm not sure I would want this experience to become commonplace or routine."

"I know what you mean," Alnay agreed. "But there's nothing routine about living on a planet like this. I think you have an idea of what I'm talking about."

Jordem raised his eyebrows again. *Now we find out how much she knows* ... "I'm not sure I do ..."

"Dr. Lun, we'd like to ask you to finish your vacation as planned. We would like you to return to your employers and we would like you to report that things are normal here ... *without* making your tests."

"Tests?" Jordem tried to play dumb. "It seems you know more about why I'm here than I do." He wasn't going to make it easy.

She put her hand lightly on his wrist. Jordem stiffened and went still. A small sting pricked his skin and he jerked his hand back.

"What did you—"

"Oh, I'm sorry. My ring must have jabbed you." She held up her right hand, showing off a ring with a large solitaire emerald mounted on it. *I don't see any sharp edges on that ring,* he thought.

"Should we adjourn to your room, perhaps, and continue our discussion on more private terms?" Her left eyelid shivered down in the hint of a wink.

A trap? Jordem wondered. *Or maybe I'm just the luckiest guy on Earth tonight...*

"Certainly." He stood and caught himself; the alcohol already was going to his head a bit. She offered her arm and he grasped it, steadying himself.

She led him through the maze of hallways and elevators.

"Floor number—"

"Eighty-five," she finished, smiling at him.

How does she know where I'm staying? Jordem thought. Something was off ... but he just couldn't think ... of anything, really. He swayed toward Alnay, and she caught his larger frame easily, almost elegantly.

"Too much to drink?" Her eyes sparkled.

The doors opened onto his hallway, but Jordem could barely stand. He wobbled toward one side of the hallway, then the other. It was all he could do to bring his hand to his face. An inch-long scratch was etched into the flesh, barely slick with blood—

That's one hell of a ring, he thought as he fell to the floor, and slipped out of consciousness.

—∞—

Jordem awoke in bed. But it wasn't his bed. And it wasn't in the hotel. It wasn't even comfortable. He tried to get up, but a wave of dizziness hit him.

"Ahh, Dr. Lun!" A male voice; not Alnay Snow. Jordem winced with disappointment. He couldn't decide if he wanted to get even with the woman who had drugged him or if he wanted to get her into bed.

Both, he decided.

"I'm glad you're awake. We have a lot to do." Jordem blinked against the lights. A tall thin man approached and handed him a glass of liquid. "Drink this. It's our 'hangover cure' of sorts."

Jordem eyed the glass. "I've had a *lot* of strawberry daiquiris since I've been here. Seems to me that this is quite a bit different from those rum-induced hangovers." He examined his wrist. "Don't remember any of those drinks having a sharp edge."

"Rapidly acting sedative. Administered through a small scratch on the wrist, I believe. Can't even see the scratch. Surely you guys are familiar with the technique."

Jordem drank the liquid. His headache started to fade almost immediately.

"Better living through chemistry." The thin man twisted one corner of his mouth up in a sardonic smile.

"What do you mean, 'you guys'?"

"You know. The corporation. The owners of this vacation racket, among other things. Your employers. They use it a lot. Maybe you've even used it a time or two yourself."

"I don't know what you're talking about, friend."

"Doctor."

"Yes?"

"No. I was referring to myself. I'm Dr. Damid Snow." Jordem's eyes widened. "Alnay's brother and her second-in-command at the Project."

Jordem stared at the scientist. "Brother? Like from the same parents? Both of them?"

"Yeah, she received the good genes, plus brains. I just have the brains." *That laugh*, Jordem thought. Maybe he *was* a Snow after all.

Jordem rubbed his temples. "So why kidnap me?"

"Kidnap you? Hardly. We want to take you on a little diversion from your itinerary before you continue your vacation. Then we will return you to your regularly scheduled programming." He laughed again.

Jordem rolled his eyes.

"I'm guessing it's too much to hope that you mean a diversion like a ski trip in Antarctica or something?" He looked around the room. Data screens were mounted above work areas in three different places, and two showed video feeds of the jungle. The third was dark.

"Feeling better?" Alnay's lithe form glided through the doorway.

Jordem rubbed the back of his head. "Thanks for picking up the tab last night ..." he muttered.

Alnay made her way over to him and tapped him playfully on the shoulder. "What can I say? You're a cheap date."

Jordem grinned. He nodded at Damid. "Maybe *you* can talk some sense into this guy."

"Actually, we're hoping that I can talk some sense into *you*." Alnay wrapped her arm around his shoulder, barely brushing the stubble of his neck.

She's definitely the more persuasive Snow ... Jordem thought.

"Go on," he swallowed.

"The answer is *yes*." She almost cooed the words at him, her lips rounding suggestively.

For a moment, Jordem considered telling Damid the two of them needed some privacy.

Then he remembered what had happened to his predecessor when he failed to accomplish his mission.

"'Yes' what? Okay, look, maybe I'm *not* just here on vacation. The truth is ..." he took a deep breath and steadied himself, "... somebody's been messing with the monorail. Tearing things off the supports, cutting wires, that sort of thing. My employer doesn't like it much, so we drew names out of the hat, and I'm the lucky guy who gets to sip daiquiris while figuring out who's damaging their *precious* train. So if you two know something helpful, I'd *love* to hear it. Otherwise, I'm only a few days away from figuring out exactly what they mean by 'permanent administrative leave.' Something tells me that it's not an all-expense-paid trip to the World Hyatt for the rest of my life."

Jordem willed his face blank, lest he expose his lie. *It's mostly true,* he thought. *At least half-true,* he reconsidered.

Damid shook his head. "You can play dumb all you want, but I think you'll be *very* interested in what our little Project here has found lurking in the shadows of the forest floor."

Jordem steeled his gaze. He looked at Damid, then at Alnay. Her eager face pulled him toward her. She bit her lip and nodded, eyes bright and dewy.

Jordem shrugged, "Okay then—a private tour of the forest floor with 'Oddball' and his sister it is."

"Oh, I love that old vidshow!" Damid said. Jordem looked at Alnay for clarification.

Alnay just smiled and motioned for Jordem to follow her. They passed through a series of corridors and finally into a sheltered vehicle port housing a Jeep.

"Go ahead and have a seat," Alnay opened the side door of the vehicle for him.

"Hop right in, sit right down!" Damid sang the words and laughed again.

Alnay gave him a sidelong glance. "He thinks he's funny," she said. "He's always been like that."

Jordem nodded. He resisted the urge to make a cutting joke. Under other circumstances, this brother-sister banter might be cute. At the moment, it just felt like his hangover had returned.

Jordem took a seat in the front, and Damid sat behind him. Alnay slipped behind what Jordem surmised were the controls. He'd never been in a land vehicle like this one. *This could be interesting,* he thought as he pulled his door shut.

"Buckle up. It's the law," said Damid from behind him, giggling again.

Jordem arched an eyebrow at Alnay. She merely shook her head. She pulled a strap across her body, pinning her to the chair she sat in. She was wearing a khaki green button-down shirt, and Jordem liked the way it cut across the soft curves of her...

He pulled himself out of his reverie and turned straight ahead. Damid handed him a similar strap. "Put it on," he suggested.

Buckled in, Alnay started the vehicle and pulled onto a dirt pathway into the heart of the jungle.

Jordem enjoyed the scenery, still rapt, as they drove through the forest. Up close, the size of the trees was far more impressive than it was from the monorail. Jordem marveled at the uniform irregularities of the lush green leaves and the smooth tan bark covering the trunks. Their vehicle passed several herds of smallish brown animals which skittered away from the Jeep as it approached.

"What are they?" Jordem asked.

"They're known as 'capybara,'" Alnay answered. "The river isn't far from here."

"What are the large gray-brown animals I saw from the monorail?"

"Tapirs, probably. The tour operators have their ways of making sure at least a few are visible at various points."

"Are they as big as they look?"

"Absolutely," she said. "There's one." She pointed in between the trees. Jordem squinted, amazed at how well the animal blended in with its surroundings.

"They're even more impressive up close," Jordem said. He couldn't take his eyes off the beast.

"So are the jaguars," Damid offered. "But they don't take too kindly to us invading their territory."

"So what *else* are we going to see?" he asked. Now that he knew what to look for, he scrutinized the shadows between the massive trees.

Almay smirked.

Damid touched Jordem on the shoulder, "What do you think of when you hear the word 'village'?"

"A collection of small-ish buildings, mostly residences. Perhaps a common area with a vid screen and an interactive communal terminal. Some basic necessities, maybe a grocer or a pharmacy. Shipping depot. People milling around, interacting with each other ..."

Damid smiled and shook his head.

"Think of why you're here, Dr. Lun," Alnay said.

"Look, I'm not sure what you want me to say, but I'm here to take in the scenery and sip some drinks with umbrellas in them while trying to solve the case of the missing monorail panels. Now if ..."

Before he could finish, they passed directly underneath the monorail track, and Jordem thought that maybe he *did* understand. The beam was so high up in the air; the passengers were only seeing a fraction of the truth lurking on the jungle floor.

Damid chimed in from the back seat, "They'll protect their investment in the easiest, most cost-effective way possible. Elimination of whatever is in their way. Won't matter what it is, or *who* it is. That's why you're here, isn't it?"

"Damid ..." Alnay warned.

Jordem shrugged. "I don't know. It's not my job to tell them what to do. It's my job to report my findings." He looked back at the monorail track. "And right now, they're concerned with the recent incidents of sabotage to their property. You wouldn't know anything about that, would you?"

"If you're accusing us of vandalizing the monorail tracks or the power centers, the answer is absolutely not."

"Not *us*," Damid echoed Alnay.

Jordem looked over his shoulder at Damid, "But you know who's doing it then?"

"You'll see," he grinned.

Jordem wanted to slap him. Again.

Instead he affected a smile. "Great. Anything to make my job easier."

Alnay pulled up alongside a tree near a platform built about twenty feet off the ground.

"This is where we go to observe." She unhooked her seat belt and got out of the vehicle. Jordem pulled on his belt, but it didn't give way. Damid laughed; he opened Jordem's door for him and reached across him to push a latch. The belt retracted, hitting Jordem across his face as it did so.

"Twentieth century technology—solid and reliable. We still use it here on Earth. It might not impress you off-worlders since you're centuries beyond it, but it does the trick."

"I'll say," Jordem smirked. "We don't have anything like this, a vehicle that you would drive yourself. Everything's automated."

"Loses something in the translation," Damid said.

Jordem stared at him blankly.

He looked for Alnay; she had already started climbing a ladder toward the platform. *Does this place ever run out of good views?* Jordem thought.

He felt the faintest hint of a backhand across his chest. "Stop checking out my sister," Damid said, though he punctuated the thought with a snicker.

Alnay looked over her shoulder and narrowed her eyes at the two men. "Come now. Hurry."

Jordem grabbed the first rung and hauled himself up. He had never climbed a manual ladder before, though he'd seen them at construction sites. The muscles in his legs rebelled against the effort of raising his weight upward. Alnay pulled herself onto the platform, with Jordem and Damid close behind.

"Sorry," Alnay said. She pointed in front of her. Jordem groaned. "Another ladder?"

She nodded and began climbing. "We need to hurry. We're on a strict schedule and you need to catch the next monorail."

Jordem hadn't even thought about the fact that he had undoubtedly missed his scheduled train.

"They think you're hung over in your room. At least, that's the message we left with the hotel desk."

"It was half-true ..." Damid said.

Something in his tone made Jordem think the doctor wasn't talking about his excuse for missing the train.

Jordem needed little help keeping his eyes upward as Alnay continued to ascend in front of him. It was far better than the alternative— looking down.

"How many more ladders?" he asked Damid.

"This is it. Then we just cross the rope bridges and from there we'll be able to observe."

"Rope bridges?" Jordem gulped. He didn't like the sound of that. He sighed and continued climbing. Reaching the upper platform, he grasped Alnay's proffered hand as he summited the final rungs.

He finally ventured a look downward.

A wave of dizziness hit him. His head swam as his legs turned to rubber. He tottered. Alnay grabbed his elbows, tugging him to a sitting position.

"Vertigo. First time this high up?"

Jordem shook his head. Damid climbed onto the platform. "I've never noticed it ..." He'd visited the top floors of tall buildings, traveled in glass-bottom atmospheric floaters on other planets, watched planets while his shuttle approached or departed. But he'd never felt anything like the crippling sense of helplessness produced by gazing down from this platform.

"How will he manage to cross that bridge?" Damid pointed ahead. Jordem turned in the direction of Damid's outstretched finger.

It was as bad as he feared; the 'bridge' was a single–albeit very thick–cable, with two slightly thicker ropes to hang onto, and many short lengths extending from the handhold ropes to the main cable.

"I don't know. We can't carry him." Alnay turned to Jordem, "Can you manage without looking down?"

"I'll have to," Jordem shrugged. He stood, looking upward.

"That's the ticket," Damid said. "The cable is quite thick, and even if you stumble, you won't fall. Just keep looking up and slide your feet along."

"We don't have much time," Alnay said. "Are you ready to try it?"

Jordem nodded.

Alnay walked out onto the bridge; she moved quickly and surely. He followed, looking at the tree tops and doing as Damid had suggested, sliding his feet along as far as one would go, then stepping with the other, feeling for the rope. It was as thick as a log, and it wasn't as difficult as he had feared.

One foot in front of the other ...

He pulled and shuffled his way along the 'walkway' for what seemed like miles. Eventually, his foot hit something hard, something sturdy. Jordem sighed with relief as he felt for the next platform and all but skipped onto it.

This platform was different, sheltered on three sides by a curtain resembling a wall of green leaves. Heavy metal rails outlined the periphery, and transparent flexiglass enclosed the area under the rail, giving it a sense of permanence the other platforms had lacked. Multiple telescopes were mounted on the far side, all pointed in the same direction.

Alnay lifted the hinged lid of a metal box mounted on the rail. She flipped a switch on the enclosed console.

The curtain of leaves parted slightly. Damid stretched out his hand to slowly inch the camouflaged wall of greenery open farther, enough for two people to look through the gap. He motioned for Jordem to join him. Jordem stepped to the rail and peered down into the clearing below.

"Look through the scope," Alnay said quietly, as she took her brother's place at the rail.

Jordem placed his eyes to the binocular lens. "You people *love* your twentieth century technology, don't you?" he muttered.

"Yes, well we don't want any more high tech stuff out here than there already is," said Damid.

The lens brought a smattering of buildings into view. All of the structures looked the same, with thatched roofs and walls of smooth poles—trunks of trees. Large green fan-like leaves covered the thatched roofs.

"It looks—primitive," Jordem observed. He felt his heart thundering in his chest. *It can't be ...* he thought. When he'd read the reports by the monorail techs, he'd thought they were just exaggerating.

He turned to Alnay, "Are these the vandals?"

She raised a skeptical eyebrow at him, "We're well beyond your little charade now, aren't we, Dr. Lun?"

Everything was quiet. Alnay's exposed shoulder brushed against his shirt-sleeve as she raised her own binoculars to her eyes.

"Nothing's happening," he commented.

"Watch," she pointed. "There!"

Jordem turned his lens. Something was coming out of one of the huts. He thumbed the zoom feature on the lens, and looked closer.

"A ... primate?" he said, incredulous. The ape walked across the compound and knocked on another door. It opened and another primate emerged. The pair stood on a crude porch, their mouths moving. Communicating?

No ... *talking!*

"Chimpanzees, to be more accurate," Alnay said. "There are several such tribes in the area. They seem to concentrate around the monorail line, though perhaps there are others out there, more hidden."

Jordem's jaw dropped. He hadn't really believed, until this moment, that it was true.

"You're here to evaluate the developing sentience of a species on Earth," Alnay stated, her voice steady and even.

Jordem's resigned nod and frown were all the confirmation the Snows needed.

"What will your employers do with that information? What happens if another species has evolved intelligence? What happens to the corporation's interests here on Earth?"

"Okay," he started. "Say you're right. We've got a *whole* village of these apes down here, and—"

"Chimpanzees," Damid interrupted.

Jordem nearly reared back and popped the scientist in the face. "And these *chimpanzees* are the ones causing trouble up above on the monorail. Do you know how *big* this thing is? It goes well beyond land ownership, beyond leases paid by World Hyatt and other corporations. It's just—"

Jordem stopped himself. He still couldn't open up to these two completely ...

... yet ...

"I believe my employers would act to safeguard their business interests."

"How?" Alnay asked.

"What do you mean, 'how'?" His lips pressed straight, then he opened his mouth to resume his tirade. Alnay interrupted, tapping him on the shoulder and pointing back at the now-very-active apes in their village.

The apes' actions were at the same time alien and familiar. Their posture and the way they moved their limbs seemed odd, but the whole scene—there was something very 'human' about the way it played out before Jordem's eyes. Still, did looking human make them intelligent?

"So you are saying that these apes *are* sentient?"

"Are *you* sentient?" Damid asked. "Because they seem to do everything humans do."

Jordem furrowed his brow. "Chimpanzees. They aren't native to the Amazon, are they?"

"No. We actually believe that it's part of why they've evolved sentience. The stress of an unnatural environment, the absence of human interference for a thousand years, and the presence of technology in limited quantities in this area may have given them the boost they needed to become cooperative and develop a language."

"Language?"

As if on cue, the platform speakers came to life, and the sounds of two chimpanzees conversing sprang from them.

"Sounds like gibberish."

"Not to our computers. Look." Words flashed across the screen.

–... *Banana, shell half milk, mix, cook ten taps*–

–*Eat good?*–

–*Kids like, good food healthy*–

Jordem smiled as he realized that even super-evolved chimps still could have mundane conversations about cooking dinner.

"Taps?" he asked.

"How they measure time," Damid tapped gently on the metal rail with metronome-like steadiness. "We think they developed it from the monorail supports. There is a regular ping that resonates from them constantly."

"We could have shown you this in the lab, but I didn't think it would have the impact of seeing it in person," said Alnay. "So now, the question is, do you need to perform your tests, and what will you report to your corporate masters?"

Jordem didn't have an answer. "So they really have evolved sentience," he said, more confused than ever. *The implications ...*

∞

All three monitors in the lab now showed different chimpanzee colonies. Jordem studied them, trying to discern any differences between the tribes. The animals were spreading out across the jungle.

Except it's wrong to think of them as 'animals' now, isn't it? I should think of them as 'people,' just different from 'human people.' Jordem's brain hurt worse than when he had woken up from the sedative.

"So I ask you again, Dr. Lun. What will you report to your employers?" Alnay watched Jordem, rapt in front of the monitors.

"There are two possibilities, as I see it. If I report that these chimpanzees have evolved sentience, they'll almost certainly hush it up. They may even decide to exterminate all of the colonies ..."

"Assuming they could even *find* all of them," Damid said.

Jordem ignored the doctor. "... and then there would be no threat to their interests from either the sentient beings ... or from those people seeking to protect them. If I report that they aren't sentient, there is a distinct possibility that they may proceed with the extermination anyway. After all, they *are* vandalizing their monorail. Who knows how much they make off that cash cow? And if they're not sentient, they're the property of whoever owns the land, right? They could say that the animals were on their property and were impeding their business interests—just another pest to be dealt with, and there would be no recourse."

"So the question is, how evil are they?" Damid tilted his head to one side.

Jordem shrugged. "Evil? I'd say they're ... uninterested in anything but the corporate purpose. Generating wealth." He turned to face Alnay and Damid. "If World Hyatt Corporation owned most of this planet instead, we'd probably be having the same discussion about them."

"So why send you here? Why find out the answers at all?" Alnay asked.

"If I report the truth, they can't simply exterminate the chimpanzees openly. That path requires great secrecy and stealth."

Understanding dawned on Alnay and Damid. "If they're not sentient, they can do whatever they want. Openly."

Jordem nodded. "But if they aren't sentient, then why do anything about them? My guess is that they already know the answers they sent me here to determine. I mean, how hard would it be for the corporation to get their hands on video of what you showed me today? Maybe even from someone in your Project ..."

Alnay and Damid exchanged glances. Jordem could almost see them mentally examining each of their colleagues, trying to identify which one might be a traitor to their purpose.

"So I think the corporation's hope is that I return with a verdict of non-sentience. That you mislead me, knowing who I work for. That you want to keep your secret longer. So the question is, how should I proceed?"

"Expose them," Damid said. It was neither a question nor a request. "Earth is not simply a zoo, to be used for the amusement of some wealthy off-worlders and the economic gain of your employers at the expense of its resources. And now it belongs to these sentient chimpanzees as much as to us."

"We had hoped that a report from you indicating that there was no sentient species other than mankind here on Earth would be enough," Alnay said. "But if it's not ... if there's still a threat, I think that the news must be disseminated as widely as possible. I also believe that the announcement should come from you and originate off-world. Our communications are monitored here. Everything goes through your employers. Privacy is nonexistent on Earth."

Jordem digested this. He knew there were sophisticated automated spy systems that would pass routine communications through, but block any and all that were in the least bit sensitive or suspicious. On any planet but Earth, he could broadcast the news, make it impossible for his corporation to eliminate an entire sentient race.

"Why don't you travel to one of the off-worlds and get the story out?"

Damid shook his head. "No travel permits for us. Not since this all started. Residents of Earth are not currently allowed to leave. Only the tourists come and go, even if some of those tourists *do* secretly work for the corporation, but cover it up."

Jordem grinned. It was the first one of Damid's jokes he had understood all day.

"It's up to you, Dr. Lun. What will you do?" Alnay moved closer to him and widened her eyes. *A man could get lost in those eyes,* Jordem thought. But right now it was just a distraction—one that he didn't need.

"I can't be the one to make a public announcement," Jordem said. "But I *can* be the one to provide the source material to ... to whom?"

She took his hand. "There are—colleagues—at universities and foundations on many planets. There are journalists and comscreen personalities who we believe will be sympathetic to this cause." She leaned into him. "We can provide a list ... help you make travel plans ... but we need *you* to do this ..."

Jordem looked at Alnay, then at Damid. And his course of action became obvious.

Jordem stared through the monorail's flexiglass windows, entranced by the mountainous scenery outside. The train was passing the ruins of an ancient human civilization, a people known as the Incas. They had been decimated when the Spaniards came to the Americas in search of gold and riches for their king. The ruins had been restored a number of times, so that they looked suitably old, yet could still be viewed by tourists.

Jordem had noticed the ruins on his previous monorail trip through the jungle, but he looked at them in a new way now. He saw, not Incan people, but a sentient primate race, standing in the way of great wealth that the powers-that-be in the world wanted for themselves. Vast wealth that was measured not only in terms of the tourism business run by the corporation, but also in terms of the renewed resources of a still-rich planet.

These new sapient primates, in turn, saw the evidence of a technology far greater than they had achieved—in the power stations and monorail tracks, in the floating trains in the sky—and they would bow before its power.

It was humanity's responsibility to stay out of the way of the development of intelligence for a second time on Earth. But would they?

Jordem Lun fingered the tiny chip drive he carried in his pocket. It contained everything he would need to make sure that the information was released in the optimum way, to the right people. He would delay his corporate masters' quest to "steal the Incan gold" until a vast audience knew what was at stake on the planet that had once served as their home. He could only hope that those with the power to influence even powerful corporations would act in the correct manner.

He would trust Alnay and Damid Snow—and their organization—to manage the public cataclysm likely to unfold after his revelation that humans were, for the first time in their history, not alone.

You'll Be So Happy, My Dear
John Hindmarsh

"GOOD EVENING.

"Yes, I am the proprietor of this humble little repair shop. You saw my advertisement, the one I so cunningly worded, on the internet? Good, good.

"A space/time/dimension transfer core? Hmmm. I'll have to search my inventory.

"The advertisement? Well, before I explain that, may I see your hands? No, it is not a trick. Certainly not. It's ... it's fortune telling, if you will. Now, come, your hand, don't be shy. Yes, that's a lot better. We can hold hands. See how it relaxes you, instills that necessary modicum of confidence?

"No? Well, be patient, my dear, it will. There. That didn't hurt a scrap, did it?

"Where were we? Oh, yes, the advertisement. You are looking a little pale, are you—? Very well, I will tell you.

"For years now I have been marooned here, on this tiny, scruffy planet. Years? It feels like centuries.

"Yes, marooned. Although perhaps marooned is not as precise as I need to be. I was fleeing, you see, from a fast patrol ship. They almost had me, back at Alpha C, but I managed to skip a bit further and then they lost track of me. I think that colorful planet, the one with all those rings—very pretty, don't you think?—deflected their tracking system. And my little ship managed to limp to a landing on this planet.

"Good fortune, you might think.

"You are looking pale—do come and sit for a while. Don't protest, it will be no trouble at all. My repair shop will close the front door automatically and, really, you do look pale. My, but you have a tiny hand. So soft, so delicate.

"Now, where was I?

"Oh, yes, my good fortune. Not really. My little ship was completely written off. Completely. I exaggerate, I know. I was able to recover some bits and pieces, including the gold core of the drive unit. Unfortunately the ship as a ship was a total wreck. There I was, shipwrecked, almost destitute, and a fugitive as well.

"A hopeless position? I can see by your eyes, the way they flicker from side to side, that you have some idea of what I mean. But no, not hopeless. I mean to say, us Xerggianths are a very resourceful species.

"Oh, my dear, I am so glad you were sitting down, you must have had rather a shock.

"Your hand feels so soft, did I mention? Very nice, such a pretty little hand. Well, it did not take me long to set up my repair shop. It even pays its way with work from the locals. Well, what else could I do?

"Strange thinking, you might say. Look, here I was, a fugitive, cut off from my home planet, isolated from my fellows. Oh, I know, the GalFed have banned intersystem travel by Xerggianths. I think it is so unfair, don't you?

"I had to recoup, you see. I had to build up my reserves. Even if I was lucky, very lucky indeed—yes—to capture a ship capable of getting me away from this tiring little backwater.

"Now, don't struggle. You are such a pretty little thing, and you don't want to bruise that lovely skin, do you?

"Of course my plan worked. I do not know what it is about this system. It seems to have an adverse effect on every spaceship entering its region of influence. There have been one or two rather nasty crashes, don't you know? I was unable to find any survivors at all. Most unfortunate. Sad, really. Most of the time the problems are minor, electronic glitches, mechanical failures—all candidates for self-repair, if the shipcomp is intelligent enough. Oh, I am so glad, let me tell you, that most shipcomps are such little idiots.

"My, you are trembling, aren't you? A fever, do you think? So pale, and now a fever. Dear, oh dear.

"Perhaps if you lie down?

"Here, I'll release your hand.

"Oh, I'm still here, don't look so anxious. There, I'll put my arm around you. Comfortable? Good. Now let me see—what was I saying?

"Oh, yes. Most shipcomps are completely unable to handle these minor repairs. The pilot—you, in this instance—comes exploring, seeking assistance for some insignificant fault that most vidset technicians could repair with their eyes shut tight. Why, it's so simple. You discover the internet here, and which advertisement do you see? Mine, of course.

"Mine, mine ... oh, forgive me, please?

"I'm sorry; it's just that the humor of it appeals to me, so you will forgive me? Normally I am not carried away so. And your fever has worsened. See, you are perspiring. Your forehead is all damp.

"Perhaps—and I am so reluctant to suggest this, because you may get the wrong impression about me, and first impressions are so important in a relationship, don't you think?—but, well, perhaps you will feel better if you take off those heavy clothes. They are ideal for the cold weather outside.

"But it is very warm in here.

"Warm and very private. No one will see you, I can assure you. It's easy to do. I'll keep my hand here, on your neck, to comfort you. Such a pretty neck. Oh, you are so beautiful. I daresay you have been told that thousands of times, hmmm?

"Yes, go ahead; take off those heavy clothes while I continue my little story. I am certain you are finding it exciting?

"Relax, my dear, no one is going to hurt you. Why, it would be the last thing I would wish to happen to you. Now I have lost the thread of my story ... where was I? Oh, yes, all those responses to my advertisement—you would be surprised. Even a Xlogh, but what would I want with one of those ugly creatures? All that silicone—ugh! Let's not talk about him. The mess took days to clean up. But you—you are absolutely perfect. Why, the humanoid shape is so convenient. And female. Well, that was an unexpected bonus, I can tell you. There now, relax.

"Feeling better?

"Good. I knew if you would relax ... Remember, I'm your friend.

"Happy?

"No, perhaps not yet. You will be. We just need a little more time together. See, my hand is still on your neck. So very reassuring, isn't it?

"I know we Xerggianths are not very popular. Don't you know, it's all that malicious gossip spread by those GalFed troopers? There's a nasty lot, I can tell you. They will not listen to reason, I don't know why. Those primitive types give me shivers down my spine. Oh, don't disturb yourself, my dear, you are safe with me, so safe. They haven't established themselves on this nasty little backwater planet. Oh, I'll be so pleased to see the last of this place. And you will be so pleased to help me, won't you?

"You are the prettiest little thing, your bare skin so soft and white.

"Yes, I know, it is the drug. We—I can tell you, can't I?—we secrete tiny amounts through our hands, through the fingers and palms, just enough for you to absorb. It takes only a little while and there you are—so relaxed, so happy—and you just lie there and listen. Be patient, my dear. We will get down to business soon. I have one or two matters to attend to first.

"What I need to know is—pardon me, this is so uncouth I know, but I also must remove my clothing. Just look the other way if you find it too embarrassing. Everything will be all right soon, you'll see. First, I need to know where you left your ship.

"Now, now, don't get so agitated. It will be safe, yes, very safe in my care. I promise I'll look after it for you. And yes, I am positive I can repair it; you should have every confidence in me, my dear. Do tell. Do tell me ...

"Ah, yes, that's right, tell me exactly where.

"Good, good.

"Relax, relax. You have never seen a naked Xerggianth before? No, I daresay not. Well, we are a strange species from your perspective. Particularly from your current perspective, yes? Oh, I do want your body. Don't you think it is nice to be needed? Yes, I do want you so much. There is no need to be apprehensive, my dear.

"You see, we don't have a male and female differentiation. What? That? I think you would call it a proboscis. Yes, that is the correct term. I know, I know. Just think of the experience. Besides, I must have a pretty little body like yours ... it's so enticing. I'm sure you'll be an ideal mistress for me. Those curves, lovely and smooth. Yes, you'll make an excellent hostess.

"Very well, we'll wait a little longer. The drug is working and it won't be long before it takes full effect. Relax, my dear, relax. I promise you will be so happy. See, I now have both hands on your body and that little extra dose will soon take effect. There, there.

"I told you it would not take long. Please don't look so anxious. I'm so confident you will be able to cope. There, that is the full effect of the drug. No, it won't send you to sleep. You will remain wide-awake all the time. That is the best, don't you think?

"Of course, if the inhabitants of this filthy planet—have you had a good look at them? Humanoid, I grant you, but totally incompatible. And so brutal, so primitive. I tried, I can tell you, I tried a number of times and with a variety of specimens, some male, some female. A complete disaster, my dear, let me tell you. Not like you at all.

"It won't take long now, you'll see.

"I forgot to mention the drug also paralyzes your vocal chords—gradually, mind you, and without harm. Very ingenious, I think. It is always so amazing to me. Every time I think the process is marvelous. Well, just consider—once we touch our potential breeding, um, recipient, a single touch starts the entire process. Oh, yes, we need to maintain contact, but the first touch starts it all, you see. And of course, the drug has an effect on me as well. Haven't you noticed?

"Now this is what we have both been waiting for. Don't struggle; the pain will not last for long.

"Perhaps you would not have screamed, but it is prudent to be certain, don't you think?

"Ahhh. You are relaxing. Good. It won't be for much longer.

"There. I am sorry that took a little longer than I anticipated. You are still conscious? You have excellent stamina. And such a beautiful body. It should be able to nurture—what, about fifty, I would guess—Xerggianth eggs. Yes, they are all in there. Oh, don't worry, the effects of the drug will continue. It is quite permanent, my dear. Why, you won't feel a thing as they grow and then hatch. It will be only four weeks and then success—you'll be a mother. Oh, I know, you won't be able to care for the young ones—well, not in an active sense, anyway. They will be so appreciative of your lovely body, so soft, so soft.

"Oh, there is one more thing.

"I had the basement expanded for just this purpose. Nice and cozy it is, too. You will enjoy it. And nurturing my offspring—you will enjoy that too, hmmm?

"Ah, here we are.

"See, you have company. It will be so nice for you. Oh, no, you won't be able to talk to each other, but you will be able to watch. And I will come and check every day. You will be so cared for, so wanted.

"So ... *mine.*"

Skipdrive
Morgan Johnson

―∞―

WHEN WE FOUND THE THINGS floating in the darkness between stars, we should have been more afraid. Instead, a giddy joyous wonder gripped the world like a fever. Every news feed shared the pictures of the two massive creatures spinning slowly somewhere past the Oort cloud and speculated wildly.

"Proof of alien life at last?" asked the Gawker News Network.

"17 Amazing Facts Scientists Have Learned About The Spinners," offered Huff-Feed.

"Russia Sent A Probe To Chase Comets. You Won't Believe What They Found Next!" was Google's attempt to capture eyeballs.

We couldn't read enough, know enough about those dark shapes.

Here is what we thought we knew: at the extreme edge of our system, just past the distant ring of ice and dust that marks the blast radius of our own sun's kindling—the accretion disc—life was waiting for us. Alien life forms the size of humpback whales floated in the black. Encrusted with rock and ice, they looked like nothing so much as a mad child's drawing of a cuttlefish. The first two we found sported tentacled limbs floating motionless in space and eyes larger than a man placed in a ring around a cavernous mouth.

The very best radio telescopes and laser rangers were trained on the lurking things. Each day the news was full of speculation. Did they have hearts or brains? Were they alive? Were they explorers from an alien world? Could they be dormant, awaiting an intelligent culture to wake them up?

Seriously, we should have known better.

The narrative the media settled on was predictably optimistic: the things were organic, living ships sent by a benevolent alien race to explore the galaxy. They were probes of a sort, like our Voyager, taking a message to the stars.

Of course we had to have them.

And of course, once we found two it took little effort to find more. While our ship—my ship—was being outfitted to race out ahead of the Chinese and the Pan-African ships to get our hands on the beasts we found more. Lots more.

Some days it seemed that wherever the astrophysicists looked they saw another Lurker. Once the eggheads knew what to search for it was easy; they found dozens. Some of the Lurkers were as small as a car while the largest would have given the largest dinosaurs a run for their money.

There were contests to name them on board the U.S.S. *Melissa*. The smallest one—the thing that looked like a turtle with eight limbs and no head—ended up with the name Raphael. Private Corrigan won the lottery and came up with that one.

Our Chaplain, a bubbly Unitarian from Hawaii, she named the largest Leviathan. Everyone groaned at that. Too obvious. No art.

Sardines being sardines, the rest of the Lurkers ended up with names spanning a breathtaking range of vulgarity. It's the Navy, after all. We may have been professionals. We may have been seasoned combat veterans of the Pluto Conflict. But if you show us a life form fifty yards long shaped exactly like an erect penis, well, we're going to name it the Cock Rocket. Can't be helped.

No, I didn't take part in the name lottery. Whoever won had to stand up and shout the name for everyone in the mess to hear and I just haven't been comfortable with attention since the accident.

But I dreamt up some good ones.

∞

The U.S.S. *Melissa* was the last of the hive ships. The only survivor of the Pluto Conflict, and even then just barely. Trust me, I have the livid purple and silver scars to prove it. When she was built the idea was novel: a modular ship, constructed in space, that could be whatever you needed it to be. She looked from the outside like a squished shiny orange. Looking close you'd see that her surface was covered in hundreds of hexagonal doors in all sizes like winking eyes. Airlocks, of course, leading to maintenance bays and cargo pods and fueling hubs and every sort of service a growing space fleet needs. On the inside it was a different story.

My grandfather served in the Navy, back when that meant boats in the water and not hurtling through the void. He had photos of his time on a submarine, which was basically a long skinny spaceship that moved under water. Weird, right? He used to complain endlessly about his time serving—not that it stopped mom from following in his footsteps. The food was terrible. His shipmates were dullards. The boredom scraped away civilization, leaving behind a yearning raw ache where your heart should be. But mostly he complained about the space. Grandpapa was a tall man, over two meters, and he spent his entire service ducking and running back and forth through narrow corridors, the air slick with condensation.

His stories sound like luxury now. I pull up the vidcaps of his chats with us sometimes—I don't know why, just sometimes being miserable and feeling sorry for yourself is better than feeling nothing at all—and there's a part where he gets off on a tangent about a particularly awful ship he crewed and he says, at the end, at least you'll have it better.

It always makes me laugh.

The *Melissa* is the third ship I've served on. As maintenance chief, I know her every bolt and plate. Her bundles of wires are more familiar to me than the mangled reflection I see in the mirror. I love the bitch. So when I say that she is the most uncomfortable ship in the Navy you should know I'm not exaggerating. The eggheads that put her together forgot to include space for a crew at first. Fills you with faith, doesn't it? One hundred and sixty-three atmo-locked reconfigurable independent bays mounted around a central spinning hub, outfitted with conventional drives. The outer bays are each separate and flow around each other so that the docking hubs on the inner ring can get cargo or personnel to the correct bay as quickly as possible. She was designed to outfit and supply and repair an entire fleet at once.

From the inner ring it's quite beautiful, like a giant beehive spinning before you, every hexagonal cell full of boxes and tanks and grease-covered half-naked grunts taking machines apart. When Nicolai and I were still together we'd go stand at the edge of the ring, thirty feet of empty space stretching between us and the spinning rooms full of busy little workers.

A marvel of human ingenuity, to be sure. But they forgot living quarters. They forgot lavatories. They forgot a mess hall. So at the eleventh hour, when colonist aggression grew out of hand, they carved out living space on the edge of the inner ring. Rooms little bigger than coffins. Showers so tight you couldn't sit, let alone shave your legs. They put the mess hall in one of the smaller rotating bays. You ever try to eat while every thirty seconds your entire room jumped in a new direction? I swear every sardine aboard the *Melissa* lost weight on that tour.

I personally lost about forty pounds of bone and muscle and skull when the bay I was in was imploded by a crazed colonist ship on a suicide run.

She was an extremely useful ship, the *Melissa*, and that's why we were picked to go out to the edge of known space and to stuff our little beehive full of those lurking things.

We were all set to go, too, and then China and the Pan-African Alliance announced they were sending their ships—their closer, faster ships—to fetch the first real alien life humanity had ever encountered. So the plan had to be changed. We needed the Russians. Our old allies from the Conflict were the only ones with a ship fast enough to get there in time.

The Russians could get there but they had no place to put any specimens they caught. We could hold all of them, but would take weeks to get there. The solution was obvious, like chocolate and peanut butter.

Through the center of the Melissa they drove the Russian Kerensky-class corvette, the *Chernobog*. From a distance the two ships together looked like a pencil stabbed through an orange. We were in a hurry so we worked double shifts. Triple shifts for those who could take it. Grafting the two vessels together in an unholy amalgamation. The engineers were pretty sure—really—that the Hoffman-Streibling Drive wouldn't just tear the two ships to pieces. But there was that chance. The skipdrive had only been used a handful of times before.

Mostly I was worried about Nicolai. He was mustered to the *Chernobog*—the "Chorny"—and it'd be the first time I'd see him since the accident, since half my face and skull were ripped off when the walls around me crumpled inward, since I lost an arm and a leg and a few ribs to boot. No one knew that I'd been tied down in that empty cargo bay, that I was wearing my one set of stockings and nothing else, waiting for Nicolai to show up and take me again on the warm steel floor, our sweat making us slide and bump and clutch each other tight to keep from drifting apart.

He was late. Or I was early. I'd handcuffed myself to one of the safety rungs in the starboard wall. It wasn't our first time. Hell, at that point it wasn't our fiftieth time. The crew quarters could fit two people snugly, but unless those people were contortionists they'd have no luck getting busy in those cramped berths. It was an open joke. A handful of the smallest repair bays—too small for even the vipers the Navy prefers for ship-to-ship conflict resolution—were reserved permanently for R&R.

When the crew first began using the R&R cabins people snickered and made jokes, but as the Conflict dragged on and the colonists dug in, it lost any humor. At best you'd see the cold glare of jealousy in someone's eyes across the mess as you reserved your room.

It was our turn then, in the R&R cabin. The fighting had died down. The Collies had been quiet for days. Either planning something or hashing out terms of surrender, everyone agreed. Suicide mission hadn't been on the list. Kamikaze strikes weren't a thing you did. Ships were too precious, too few, to waste them. No one knew why they did it. One minute we were at a semblance of peace, stretched out better than naked in a dimly lit brushed-steel cargo dock waiting for our too-handsome-for-us Russian/Californian lover to engage in some conventional thrusting and the next minute a ship piloted by a starving madman tears open your world and pins you to a wall.

In the end, no one mentioned the stockings or the handcuffs. They patched me up with the cheapest cybernetics the Navy could get away with, gave me the minimum mandatory leave, and sent me right back up into the black.

Only now no one looked at me the same and my lovely Russian paramour had been assigned away as a liaison to some Red Navy boat.

—∞—

The captain gave a big speech before we made the skip. Everyone was nervous about the new drive—the Hoffman-Streibling Device. It collapsed space or pushed holes around space or did things that didn't make sense, no matter how many times someone sketched them on napkins. The short version was, the captain explained, that the drive would throw us across space-time like skipping a stone across a pond. The journey would take hours, not weeks. Then he rattled off a lot of optimistic nonsense about duty and science and frontiers of knowledge but I lost track of the narrative because at that point, in the largest bay, with all the crew and personnel huddled together, I caught sight of Nicolai.

I swear I could feel the seams of my flesh burn. The purple scars that marked where my skin ended and the flexsteel began ached and throbbed in his presence. He'd grown even more beautiful, something in his face was meatier. He'd put on muscle and changed his hair. He no longer looked like the prettiest sardine in the can but rather like a movie star pretending to be in the Navy for a scene.

He studiously ignored me. Not a glance in my direction. Not a single one. He must've seen me before I noticed him. Seen the scars and the perpetual bruising that mottled my face. He probably had a new lover on the Chorny anyway. A guy like him? How could he be single?

And then everyone was applauding and cheering and I guess the captain had finished his speech in a particularly rousing way.

"Elizabeth, what a lovely speech, don't you agree?" The Chaplain's bubbly voice snared me as I was about to try and catch Nicolai's eye.

"You're the only one who calls me that, y'know?"

"I've never been one to embrace formalities, Chief. You might think that makes me a poor fit for some organizations but I've always considered it a strength." The woman's eyes sparkled with mirth. Was she intentionally distracting me from Nicolai?

"Just call me Eliza, okay?" I turned to leave and she hooked my arm, pulled me aside.

"The captain asked me to speak to you."

My face burned. They know. They all know. We'd thought our trysts were a secret all those times but every boat has its spies. I was prepared to be ordered to stay away from Nic, to keep our relationship professional.

"He's concerned about the effect the drives might have on your," her eyes roved across my scarred left side, tracing the silvered circuitry that glowed so faintly beneath my bruises. "Well, other crew have reported night terrors after traveling with a skipdrive and you are the first with an enhanced, ahh, brain to undergo it."

"Tell Captain Harch I'll be fine." I knocked on my skull and pulled a smile. "I don't sleep. No sleep, no night terrors."

Her face told me it was exactly the wrong thing to say. "Just let us know if you feel anything out of the ordinary. Skipping across the universe has driven others mad, they say." She flashed a bright smile, squeezed my hand and left to talk to someone else.

Nicolai was gone.

Hours after our rousing pep talk we were ordered to our bunks. Strap in with the safety webbing, the officers said, the skipdrive can be a little bumpy. One of the senior engineers from the Chorny, a woman with the blackest skin I'd ever seen and the bluest eyes, too, described the feeling of skipping as like having your eyes rammed down your throat while simultaneously getting a message that your parents were dead.

It was worse than that.

The added weight of the *Melissa* did something to the calculations. Prolonged the experience. They swore the math was correct, blamed the problems on the size and shape of the *Melissa*. The Chorny was a slim dart of a thing, cutting through the other-space like a scalpel. The *Melissa*, well, she was a big beautiful woman. When she walked by you noticed.

The skip should have tossed us one AU out from Earth and it should have taken three seconds. Instead we ended up four AUs out and it took five minutes.

Five minutes of wails and moans cannonballing through our little brushed steel coffins.

"Oh god. Oh god. Oh god." A voice cried out.

"I see things in the darkness!" Another voice.

"Kill me! Just make it stop!" And another.

And then, as the skip dragged on, the wails of pain and anguish lengthened and deepened. They took on a rhythmic hum.

"Oh god. Oh god. Oh oh oh god yes!" A voice cried out.

"There's hands in here with me. In my berth, I can feel so many hands. They're, oh fuck." A second voice whimpered.

"Don't let it stop. Don't ever let it stop!" The third voice screamed.

Mostly it gave me a nasty headache. I don't dream. I don't even really sleep. Most of my left hemisphere is silicon now. Silicon and titanium and a billion billion tiny circuits. All I need to do is activate the *end of day* subroutine and I spend fifteen minutes reviewing old memories, locked away from the world, while my systems do their thing. Fifteen minutes and I'm perfectly refreshed and ready to go.

I miss dreams. I miss the surprise of it all.

As it is I choose what old memories to watch, what to relive. And sure, maybe I spend a little too much time replaying the greatest hits of Eliza and Nicolai. Maybe when I'm maudlin and the rest of the crew is drunk and I'm doomed to sobriety by my cybernetics, maybe then I replay the moments before that ship slipped through the docking bay doors and stole my life away. Maybe I savor the feeling of erotic anticipation, when I'm restrained and hot and wet and just so ready for Specialist Nicolai Trutencz to come aboard the U.S.S. *Eliza*. Maybe I hope when I replay the memory—when I relive it all again in perfect detail—that a madman, howling about hungry stars, won't die on top of me, thrown from his ship.

Maybe my lack of sleep hasn't led to the most healthy post-trauma habits. But in that moment, with the rest of the crew caught up in ecstatic terror, I was pretty okay with it.

∞

No one would talk about it afterwards. It was like the whole crew were cousins who'd been caught kissing by their stern parents. The shame and excitement induced a hushed conspiracy of silence amongst us all. When talk about retooling the drive, about fixing the skip problems came down from on high, the response was unmistakable: why bother fixing the skipdrive? We made better time than we expected and would easily reach the Lurkers ahead of the other nations' fleets. Wouldn't it be better to just push on through two more jumps and let the crew suffer the effects like the hardened professionals they were?

And that was that.

We had enough time to run maintenance checks on the *Melissa*, to scarf down some lukewarm rehydrated potato soup, and to change out of any clothes that had been messed or ripped open during the skip. And then we did it all over again.

∞

The second skip was much worse.

When the skip engines punched a hole in space time and chucked our craft through it felt like the bottom dropped away from the universe. Gravity stopped working, inertia was a distant memory, light didn't behave properly. The flat planes of the Melissa's interior warped and curved. Nothing was sacred, not even the laws of physics. Everything was permitted. The seams of my body ached, especially in my skull. It began as a cold pressure, like an ice cream headache, but then it pushed and pushed like fingers trying to pry my head apart.

I tried not to scream.

In the berths around me my shipmates squirmed and moaned. The inter-planar ecstasy arrived in a crashing wave, rolling from one side of the craft to the other. Hushed whimpers quickly grew into full-throated cries of joy. The crew knew what to expect this time; there was no resistance. What did Nicolai see when the rush hit him? Who did he cry out for? Near me, Private Absalom screamed the name of his wife back on Earth. Engineer Lee spoke in a husky voice I'd never heard before to some man named Abdul. And this whole time I thought she was queer.

Post-skip interviews confirmed that the second skip brought visitations from loved ones both real and imagined. Crew affirmed seeing their wives and husbands and girlfriends and boyfriends—sometimes all four at once for the service members from the Free States of New Jefferson. Lieutenant Krall claimed with utter sincerity that she had made love to Simon Belfort. She swore affidavits with full knowledge of how it sounded. Belfort is the protagonist of Lt. Krall's favorite romance series, a whip-cracking hunter of vampires who falls into doomed romance after doomed romance. He was fictional, imaginary. But Krall wouldn't back down from her claims.

I've read a few of the Simon Belfort books from Krall's personal stash. They weren't my thing.

The head shrinkers wanted to put the lieutenant in lockup, said she cracked from the skip. The Russians who used the skipdrives back in the Conflict kept pretty mum about the whole ordeal—they were Russians after all—but the crews had privately claimed a sort of psychosis emerged amongst the more eccentric onboard. Skip madness, they called it. Well, it sounded better in Russian.

Krall insisted she wasn't crazy and demanded a full medical scan. The doctors tried to keep the results quiet but secrets are impossible on the *Melissa*. Too many doors. Too many ducts. Too many nurses like Dory Canta.

Nurse Canta kept me supplied with the inhibitors that kept my body from rejecting my cybernetics. I shouldn't have needed them—I was months past the rejection stage—but I did. Dory couldn't wait to tell someone about Krall's write-up. The big woman was bursting at the seams with the knowledge.

"The gyno scan found recent evidence of sexual activity." Dory tried to parcel out secrets, to drag out their enjoyment like a good supper.

"So she diddled herself in her bunk. I hear Michaelson damn near painted his berth white during the skip."

Dory shook her head, her eyes sparkling with wonder. "No, Eliza. They found the other kind of evidence." Her grin would have embarrassed the cheshire cat. "The sticky kind."

"But the Lt. isn't seeing anyone. She's got a fella back home."

"And the security logs show no one entering or leaving her berth."

This was way above my pay grade. I fixed ships. I repaired coolant leaks. I managed a small team of grease monkeys.

Dory's face shone with excitement.

"What aren't you saying, Nurse Canta?"

"They analyzed the sample. It's not human."

∞

Before anyone could really process the information we were there. The second skip had tossed us further than we expected, as if something out at the edge of space was pulling us. We arrived at our destination, near those terrible floating Lurkers, and years of training kicked in. You don't get through a war without being able to compartmentalize. Collectively we took the knowledge about Lieutenant Krall's visitation and decided to freak out about it later, when the job was done. We dealt with it just like we did any other too-big-to-think-about phenomena: we made jokes.

"Next time I'm going to think real hard-like about Arden Jackson. I've had a thing for her since that one movie, with the Vikings." My engineer second grade, Dooley, was a giant blond hunk of muscle who never knew when to stop talking. "She'll be my next skip-fuck."

"You gonna give her some *samples* for souvenirs?" Engineer Lumno never left his side. She was as tall as Dooley but half as wide and twice as smart. "Pull a reverse Krall?"

"All I'm saying is, if the Skippers want some more specimens I've got plenty right here for 'em to taste." He grabbed his crotch and pantomimed humping Lumno's leg. He couldn't see the blush enflame her cheeks, but I sure could. There was no doubt who Lumno saw when she skipped.

"What about you, chief? Who you gonna dream about?" Dooley left off the humping, and returned to his maintenance check.

I tapped the side of my head. "I don't dream, grunt. Not ever."

That shut him up.

"Dooley, you ass," whispered Lumno.

His silence didn't last. While we checked and rechecked every tow hook and short range shuttle in our launch bay Dooley methodically described every woman he hoped would visit him on the return trip. Lumno's name never came up.

∞

The *Melissa*, still wed to the *Chernobog*, had skipped in nearly on top of the Lurkers. In shuttle range of three, when the sensors painted the blackness they found dozens more. Too small to see from Earth they hung in space like bait. No two were alike. The smallest was the size of a car and looked like a crude drawing of a seahorse. The largest barely fit into our corvette bay. Most were not much larger than our two-man Scorpion ships.

We should have been careful. We should have taken one on board and studied it, analyzed it. This was the first real complex alien life we'd ever seen. Who knew how dangerous it could be? But then it came out that Ukrainian separatists had retrofitted the Indian *Kali*, that infamous destroyer, with a stolen skipdrive. It could arrive at any minute. If the conflict got hot we stood no chance. We'd be hopelessly outgunned.

The Scorpions and the larger ten-man Buzzards worked nonstop lassoing and pushing and dragging the Lurkers into every empty bay we had. Command wanted nothing left for the *Kali* to find. If there were Lurkers the size of meatballs out here past the Oort cloud, we had orders to stuff them in our pockets and leave no crumbs behind.

My crew kept busy refueling and repairing the Scorpions. They weren't designed for towing large masses in space and the rear cable assembly put undue strain on the chassis. One ship, piloted by a rookie from Michigan with the call sign Dirtbelly, tore itself in two trying to tug a Lurker shaped like a fanged donut into bay ninety-seven. Dirtbelly and his engineer, Dushayne Wiltz, were our first casualties.

They weren't the last.

After the Dirtbelly incident Command ordered twice the safety checks, twice the routine fittings. Dooley and Lumno didn't sleep that first day. They just chewed down their rip fuel and dug into the job. Dooley never shut up though.

I saw Nicolai frequently that first day. He was assigned to one of the Buzzards—the big nasty warships designed for maneuverability and killing. Technically they were N-77 Firehawks but with the crazy cant of their wings and the ugly knobbled cockpit stuck to the front they were too ungainly for that name. So they were Buzzards or, if you were assigned to one of the claustrophobic vessels, Shitbirds.

Nicolai's Buzzard was on a defensive patrol, circling the *Melissa* and the Lurkers, looking for threats. In the Sol system we had every rock mapped, knew every loose screw hurtling around Uranus. The computers took care of everything. Out here we didn't have so good a picture of the landscape. At any moment a dark asteroid could hurtle out of nowhere and rip everything to pieces. One wrong hit on the Chorny's reactors and we'd all be glittering stardust. The Buzzards protected us. They blared noise on every frequency, listening back for even the tiniest ping. Focused plasmatics could heat the surface of the toughest rock if you had enough time, give it just enough push to stay away.

It was thankless work requiring unflagging attention. If they did their job well the *Melissa* was peacefully buzzing with normal activity. If they failed, we were all dead.

Unspoken was the dreadful thought that the Lurkers would awaken and reveal themselves to be enemy craft. Unspoken also was the fear that the *Kali* would appear on top of us and it would be down to a single Buzzard's gunners to decide whether we went to war with India or if they dusted us first.

Nicolai still wouldn't look at me. He'd jump off the Buzzard like everyone else and stride over to the head, to the makeshift mess tables, to the showers. The rest of the crew might nod or chat, eager to talk about the crazy shaped Lurkers they saw, the rocks they deflected. But not him. My beautiful Nicolai, the last man who touched me, kept his eyes from my scarred and alien face and hurried out of sight.

∞

After three days of nonstop loading we were ordered to take a rest break. This was not a popular order. It wasn't just that we finally had something to do after months of post-Conflict busy work. It wasn't just that the *Kali* might pop in at any second and smash us up like a kid's piñata. It was that they wanted to get back into skip-space as soon as possible.

Those six hours of rest may as well have been a prison sentence.

We needed it though. Accidents and near-miss rates crept up the longer we worked. Dooley accidentally pumped a Scorpion's cockpit full of coolant. If Lumno hadn't been at his heels, sweating for him, he would have killed the two flyboys catnapping in the ship. And it wasn't just my team. From all around the ring of the *Melissa* came reports of near-death experiences. A cook pouring lye into the miso broth. A sanitation engineer mixing chlorine and ammonia and leaving it next to an air intake. A Buzzard pilot nodding off at the stick and launching his whole crew off into deep space. No one died, but it was a miracle. Three days on the job, on rip fuel and coffee, and anyone gets sloppy. Brains need rest. Well, normal brains do.

At Command's behest, the medical staff broke out the post-combat sedatives—the ones usually reserved for calming down front line teams whose nerves were screaming with adrenaline. Paired up with borrowed Marines from the *Chernobog*, the medical teams made sure every single active duty personnel got shut-eye. When they found me I was elbow deep in a rebuild of one of the smaller skiffs. We hadn't needed them yet, but we'd rounded up all the biggest Lurkers and smaller ones kept appearing wherever we looked. Too small for the Scorpions' grapples to be effective, for sure. Command hadn't demanded the one-man skiffs yet—they knew how terrifying riding one of those glorified surfboards away from a ship could be. But I knew it was coming. We'd filled nearly all the bays with those meaty Lurkers, but a few of the smallest rooms were still vacant.

It was Nurse Canta who came to give me the downers, accompanied by two of the ugliest men I've ever seen. That's the thing about these Russians: the pretty ones have cheekbones honed by evolution to decorate the most gorgeous faces you've ever seen. They look like fairy-tale princes and princesses forced to work alongside us mortal instruments. But when those Slavic genes go wrong—hoo boy—it's like staring at a giant thumb that also hates you.

"Eliza," Nurse Canta's voice was exhausted. I wondered if she'd be the last to get the sleepy pills.

"Dory," I nodded. Didn't look up.

"We have orders to get you some R&R, girl. How about you crawl out of that lawnmower engine and go lie quietly in your bunk for a spell?"

"Pheno-barbitolene?"

The Russians glanced at each other, worried I'd be trouble. My tone was off. Three days of nonstop labor made even me a bit raw. The brutes had fresh scrapes on their knuckles. The left one, Krazny, walked with a limp. The right one, Kurpetskin, had a fresh shiner that made his thumb-face look like he'd been fingerprinted with the largest ink roller ever.

"Dory, that shit won't work on me." I tapped my head. "Just make me crankier than I already am. So why don't you and these two moose hit the next name on your list."

"You're the last name, cybergirl."

"Don't call me that," I snapped.

Dory raised her hands in apology. "Just go to your bunk a bit, 'kay? Power down, run your program or don't. I honestly don't care. No one wanted to go to sleep and it's been a huge pain in my ass and they didn't even give me the sexy *Russkis* for my shift and I need to get some shuteye too and the only thing preventing me from doing that is your grease-stained ass. So up you go, Chief. Toddle off to bed or these humorless apes will taser you and drag you off. Understood?"

Krazny frowned. It made his whole face look like a wad of rumpled tissue paper. "You know we speak English. Why do you say such hurtful things?"

Dory patted him on the arm. "I'm just tired, you big bear. Don't get your borscht all hot and bothered."

I wasn't sure the taser would even work on me but I had no urge to test the theory. It'd probably blow out half my brain and leave me paralyzed, which almost sounded like a relief right then, but I had so much more work to do.

They escorted me across the access gangway all the way to my bunk. Our path left the outer ring of bays and circled around the inner ring. The interior catwalk was free of the usual bustle. To one side stood the brushed steel walls that held our endless berths, stuffed full of the sleeping crew. On the other side, across the ten-meter gulf separating us from them, spinning slowly, squeezed into our modular containers, were the Lurkers. We all stopped and stared. How could you not?

I hadn't seen them up close yet, just heard descriptions and seen the pictures. What struck me most was the infinite complexity of the beasts. The outer ring rotated slower than usual—the biologists were worried about motion on the great rough beasts—giving us plenty of time to study them and wherever I looked I saw more to goggle at. One of the largest

Lurkers in sight looked like a sleeping eyeless dog the size of a sperm whale. But instead of one mouth it had a row of them all down its neck and belly. Its skin looked like fresh chocolate pudding at first glance, wobbling gently with the motion of the craft, but closer inspection revealed it was a second Lurker shaped like a jellyfish wrapped around the first.

"Is like zoo, yes?" Kurpetskin volunteered, unsure of his words. "Animals in cages for children to see?"

Dory shivered. "But who's in the cage here? The size of these things—if they wanted to they could rip right through this hull and eat the lot of us."

"Is good thing they sleep then."

They led me to my bunk. "Yeah," I said, "it's a regular slumber party in here."

If sightless eyes watched me as I circumnavigated the sleeping berths, I didn't tell anyone.

∞

"Here we are, at your bunk." Dory yawned.

"Do I get a good night kiss at least?"

"Maybe next time."

"Just so you know, as soon as my subroutine is done I'm going to be back in my shop, elbow deep in something."

Dory shrugged. "Just because your mind doesn't sleep doesn't mean your body doesn't get tired. You're still human. The muscles need rest. But seriously, Eliza. I don't care. My orders are to get you into your bunk. What happens after that is somebody else's problem."

I blew a kiss at the big Russian thugs and squeezed myself into that coffin-sized container. Dory winked and closed the door. And then I heard the unmistakable sound of a bolt sliding into place.

"What the hell, Dory?" I yelled, banging on the door with my metal fist.

"You're locked in, sweetie. Just like everyone else. Might as well get some rest. The doors will open in six hours exactly so if you have to relieve yourself, use the emergency tubes."

I screamed myself hoarse, but no one came. Eventually I gave in and ran my dreams program and meditated, mentally reviewing the engines I needed to fix and keeping my mind as far away from the Lurkers as possible.

∞

Klaxons blared three hours later. Screaming madness filled the *Melissa*. It was a law of military strategy that no plan survived contact with the enemy. Also that if you want the enemy to attack, take a nap.

The *Kali* had appeared.

She was an ugly ship, thin and angled like an attacking wasp with reticulated weapons platforms curving up and away from her body like the arms of her namesake. The *Kali* was nearly impossible to hit, faster than greased shit, and loaded down with enough firepower to slag an entire moon. She held a crew of fifty-plus trained combat veterans. The *Kali* had more confirmed kills than any three other ships in the black put together. She didn't have an ounce of fat on her nor any room to bring aboard a Lurker. She was out here for one reason only: to stop anyone else from getting their hands on them. She was the absolute pinnacle of weaponized human engineering. She was terrifying and beautiful and I wished that one day I'd get a chance to work on her.

The skipdrive tears a pucker in the universe, Lumno had explained to me once during a particularly tedious teardown job. Skipping out of the universe is undetectable—no radiation, no burst of noise. You're there one second, gone the next. Not so with the re-entry. Skipping in is a messy process, like cannonballing into a pool, only you're a thousand-ton starship and the water is all of space-time. The resulting gamma burst is fireworks and fanfare for any sensor listening. The arrival is a giant neon sign, hundreds of miles wide, saying "We Are Here." During the Conflict the Russians always skipped in behind enemy lines, in the thick of it, firing on all sides. If you're going to be noticed, the theory went, *be noticed*.

The *Kali* popped in and the ship's sensors went apeshit. Emergency personnel were awakened with automated injections of amphetamines and nausea-blockers. I caught the micro arm as it swiveled out of the ceiling and directed the injection into my pillow. I didn't need to be blasted with a gallon of military-grade speed to be awake. Pink fluids seeped into my cushion, some sensor in the wall beeped, proud at having accomplished its one little task, and my door sprung open.

Orders from Command came piping in. Lieutenant Wabash, his words crashing on top of each other, "Chief, we need you to secure all the bays. Lock them down for emergency maneuvers. Make sure our little zoo doesn't get thrashed about." Wabash was on loan from the Chorny but spoke with a posh British accent. No one liked Wabash.

"We getting ready to skip out, LT.?" I spoke as slowly as possible, just because I knew it would grate on Wabash's meth-fueled pace of the world.

"Negative, Chief," he barked. "The brains say we have too much mass to use the skipdrive safely. We damn near broke the thing hauling the *Melissa* out here and this menagerie we've filled our pockets with has more than doubled our weight."

"That can't be right. How can these half-dead meatballs weigh more than our two welded-together starships?"

"Above your pay grade, Chief. Now I suggest you get moving. The *Kali* is outside of firing range and Command plans to keep it that way. As soon as you get those cages strapped down the *Chernobog* is going to burn stardust."

He didn't need to tell me twice. I had to sprint around the entire inner ring to all the access points, locking down cells sector by sector. Normally they floated somewhat freely, sliding around each other in an intricate dance like hundreds of gears meshing in harmony. The smaller bays shot around the larger ones like a river parting around a stone. Halting the dance was difficult. It took time. Time we didn't have. Without our cargo holds frozen our top speed was a fraction of what the bird was capable of. They should have woken up more engineers. There were a dozen, maybe twenty, people on board who had the access and knowledge to get this done. They only woke up one.

As I was finishing the final sector, sweat dripping from my skin like life rafts fleeing a sinking ship, the communicator chirped again. Wabash.

"Blast it, Chief. Why aren't those compartments secure yet?"

I didn't answer. It was a complicated process, one that I planned to rewrite if I got out of this alive.

"The *Kali* is nearly on top of us, Eliza. She's weapons hot and bearing down. Get those bays locked down or we'll have to jettison the entire *Melissa* and run."

With a sound like a tomb closing, the last of the spinning cargo bays lost their independence and fused together. Getting in to any of them would be harder now. You'd need an acetylene torch and a skiff, or hope that your bay was one of the six that met up with the gangways.

"Done," I barked. And then the Chorny roared to life, jerking the *Melissa* like sled dogs pulling a sleigh and hurling me across the catwalk with the momentum. They'd pushed the stick all the way in instead of the textbook slow acceleration. Crazy fucking Russians. From my vantage point I could hear beams bend, beams shatter, beams snap under the sudden force. I also heard my ribs snap—a sound like stepping on popcorn—as my good side impacted the catwalk railing and I began a slow, almost comical tumble over the side. My brain split into two competing consciousnesses: one worried about the rest of the crew, stuffed into their bunks, when the G-forces hit. The bunks weren't aligned properly with the Chorny's impact vectors; they pointed every which way. Some people would be pressed into their toes or back and be fine. Those who slept with their heads aligned on the trajectory would get smashed hard into the steel walls. Not everyone would survive this maneuver, but more would survive than if the *Kali's* torpedoes put a thousand holes in the hull.

The other part of my brain, the machine, was already pulling up schematics of what was under the inner ring's catwalk. The answer was not reassuring: precious little. A straight fall of a fifty meters then. A ghastly splatter onto the thin skin that divided pressurized inner space from the lethal vacuum outside. Maybe with my metallics I'd have enough weight to penetrate that barrier. The computer wasn't sure. It depended on angle of impact. Aimed just right my left arm would sheer through the steel like a syringe through skin. Then atmosphere would be compromised and with nearly all of the crew still in a drug-induced sleep there'd be no one to fix it. The thought of Dooley and Lumno and, yes, Nicolai all suffocating in their sleep shot a cold terror through my belly.

Guess I'd better try and live.

The calculations and resultant fear took a fraction of a second. Not enough time to grab onto the railing, but enough time to find the slick steel wall below it and push off with every bit of my cybernetically-enhanced body. My synthetic arm and shoulder and hip and leg punched the wall like a car accident, casting me with a nerve-deadening thump out across the gulf between the rings, sailing over that empty space like a bullet made of meat and regret, my parabola carrying me out and away from the catwalk and down straight into the glassteel face of a docking bay. I landed fist first, shattering the door, spinning like a cartwheeling drunk, marble-sized chunks of safety glass raining about me, before hitting something wet and soft with an audible *splat*.

I wasn't dead.

The ship wasn't bleeding atmo.

The *Kali* hadn't ventilated us yet.

I'd call it a win except I was half-submerged in a Lurker shaped like a pile of meatballs ringed by snakes.

The astrobiologists and xenobiologists and theoretical biologists hadn't wasted any time studying the creatures. As soon as the first Lurker was aboard they'd quarantined the cargo bay and set up shop in full hazmat suits, planned for absolute zero tolerance for contamination even at the micro level. Whatever the eggheads discovered they didn't share with the rest of the class. The scientists ate in a special mess, slept in special rooms. Command said it was a precaution against contamination. Had to keep those who had contact with actual alien lifeforms away from the rest of us. The rest of us thought it was to prevent knowledge from being leaked, not germs. It chafed a bit. Made them seem better than us. We'd gotten used to the officers having their own grub room. They needed a space to bitch about their charges, we understood that. But the nerds getting another separate room while the rest of us crammed into one mobile bay? No one liked it. Space was at a premium after all. But the mention of possible alien parasites or infections or toxic discharges was enough to quell even the angriest sardine.

Which is all a round about way of saying that I thought I was the first living human to have actual physical skin-to-skin contact with those awful stinking presences. Waist-deep in a pile of fleshy meatballs the size of a van, I didn't feel too excited about the honor. It was probably the reek of ammonia the beast gave off, or the concern that at any second it could awaken, or maybe that if I slipped any deeper into its poorly differentiated mass no one would ever find me.

The Meatball's skin was dry and rank like a desiccated corpse. The mass underneath was slippery. Even with my forceful impact I hadn't managed to puncture its skin. Maybe I bruised it. Squirming on its surface felt like being trapped on a water bed full of suet—a water bed four meters tall. I reached up, grasping for purchase, and felt my cracked ribs grate against each other. My cybernetics weren't responding at all. The arm hadn't liked punching the glass very much. With my one good arm and leg I tried to swim across the mass of the Meatball but every motion sunk me just a bit deeper.

One arm and a leg wasn't enough. Even on dry land I could barely move when my cybernetics were off.

I called for help.

But who would hear me? There were maybe a dozen essential personnel awake and near as I could tell all of them but me were on the *Chernobog*, in the C&C. On the whole of the *Melissa*, throughout her one hundred and sixty-three cargo bays and crew berths and aching, claustrophobic tunnels, I was the only one awake. And I was going to be the first human in the history of everything to be killed by an alien.

Because I fell on it and asphyxiated in its folds. So I shouted. Again and again I shouted. It'd be almost three hours until the ship came awake. Could I last that long? The computer in my head wasn't broken yet—thankfully, or I'd be dead—and the calculations were simple. At my rate of descent I'd have forty minutes at most until I asphyxiated in this stinky flesh-bag's embrace. But—more calculations—only fifteen minutes until my voice would be so muffled that no one could hear me.

My comm unit was nowhere to be found. Probably it was lost in the folds of the creature or smashed at the bottom of the divide. I had no way to call for help.

And then, a voice. An impossibly cheerful voice perpetually half-laughing at some private joke. "I'm awake," it said softly. "What seems to be the problem?"

I couldn't see past the flesh of the beast, had no idea what this rescuer looked like. Was he handsome or scarred? Was he a voice in my imagination, some last-minute creation to make me hold on just a bit longer? Or maybe it was the beast itself, this Lurker at the edge of space, finally roused from its slumber and speaking with a voice like a kid from Boston.

"A little help?" The voice was so calm I felt embarrassed by my panic. Struggled to make my voice normal as if being sunk deep into an alien creature was a perfectly common problem to have in a day.

"Oh yeah, hey. You're stuck up in there pretty good." He laughed at some private joke. "I don't have a ladder in here. Or any rope to toss up to you. You don't realize the enormity of these creatures until you get up close to them and let their presence wash over you." He shifted some boxes. This bay must have been one of the last utilized. All the others were entirely stripped of their contents, as if a fifteen-ton alien hippopotamus-eel would need to use a hydrospanner set to open these doors.

"When I was a kid," he continued, rooting through clanking containers, "skyscrapers were my thing. Not just the engineering that kept them from collapsing like lesser structures, but their size. I loved it. My mom would yell at me 'cause every day I'd sneak out and lie on the ground at the base of the Prescott Tower—the two-hundred-story one?—and cry uncontrollably. My head would be against the wall and the edifice would be my entire world. It felt like it was going to fall on me or like I was going to fall into it. She always thought I was crying from terror or guilt but it wasn't like that at all." He paused. "So I think I have a solution to your problem, but it's going to be kind of gross."

My face was slipping down into the folds of the thing like loose change between sofa cushions. I couldn't even respond.

He grunted and I knew instantly that he wasn't military. It was the exhalation of a man unused to labor that didn't involve a computer screen. A wet tubular structure slapped into my hand. Sticky and spongy, I held on to it with every shred of muscle in my one working arm. The civilian grunted and wheezed and whimpered, but he *pulled*. May his ancestors forgive all he did later, right then he pulled.

Inch by painful inch he hauled me up and out of that alien crevasse. The folds clung to me, hugged me with a damp insistence. If I didn't know the beast was dormant I would have been terrified. More than terrified. And then with a sudden heave I crested the peak of the thing and somersaulted out, landing on my back next to my savior, my head resting against the pooled tentacles covering the ground around the Lurker.

The civilian stood over me, holding one of the sticky-slimy tentacles in his hands. Purple goo stained his hands, his shirt, his pants. That same goo I knew stained my good hand and clothes as well. My rescuer was a bony young man, bent and bearded. He had shining beady eyes that flitted around the room, taking everything in. He wore a button-down shirt and khakis. If Military was a fixed point in space, this guy was at the opposite end of the universe from it.

"See, what I felt at the base of that tower wasn't fear, it was relief. The idea of being swallowed up by the monolith of the building, of falling into the sky, merging with the black stone, was a great freedom. It was a dream come true for me. The sublimation of self into a greater being. You're military, you must know about that. The relaxation of not having to make choices anymore." He smiled a shy, inward smile. "I'm Jeremy by the way."

"Eliza," I snapped a sarcastic salute.

"Oh I know," he laughed his private laugh again, "you're *famous*."

I laughed too, trying to join in on his game. "Because I'm the poor broken cybergirl. I get it." Now that I could move I popped up the service plate in my arm and started the diagnostic procedures.

"Oh no," he said. "Because you're the girl who doesn't dream."

I didn't like the way he smiled when he said that.

Or the way he fingered that yard-long slip wrench in his hand.

"Jeremy, I see a lot of boxes in here. A lot of odd boxes. I thought maybe this one just one of the last Lurkers to be packed in storage but it's not, is it?" My arm was coming back online. Hopefully the rest of my body would soon follow.

"This is the fifth we brought on board." He ran a hand along the bumpy meatball surface of the thing. "She's not as attractive as the others so I thought my fellow researchers would overlook her. They're such lookists, these guys. They want an alien that *looks* like an alien. Something majestic and terrifying with visible characteristics. I knew they'd ignore my girl here. As if this was her true form in the first place." He giggled, wiped his nose on his shirt sleeve. "The others have been physically dormant. But this one—I always had a knack for choosing the best subjects—no one was even looking when she extruded these tentacles." His eyes flashed with delight.

"How long have you been in here, Jeremy? How'd you skip the lockdown? Everyone should have been accounted for, tucked away in their beds for mandatory rest. That included civilian personnel too." Purple smudges seeped in at the edge of his corneas.

"It really is a shame you don't dream. They were so angry that they'd missed one. All those fresh minds popping into their world but one of them was still hiding. Hey, did you ever feed carp in a pond? You toss in those little food pellets and suddenly the calm surface of the water is broken by all of these hungry, gasping mouths. They poke out of their world just the tiniest bit in a ravenous clump, desperate for nourishment." Jeremy rubbed the Lurker again. He was nearly hugging it. "Those first skipdrives, back during the Pluto Conflict, those were our first handful of crumbs we tossed into their water. Just a tiny signal telling all the biggest predators that *something delicious* was on its way. They live out there, in the skip-space. This form here before us is just an extrusion into our reality. It's just lips, a mouth."

He spun at me again, eyes unfocused. He had that mean wrench resting across his shoulders like a broadsword. "Do you know why we never saw them lurking out in the black before? It's not because our telescopes weren't powerful enough or because we didn't look in the right place. It's because they *weren't there*. Not until those amazing Russians started taking shortcuts through their home."

My arm rebooted, was working now, but the leg was too damaged. The diagnostic completed and beeped loudly. Even if my leg was operational and I could walk, where was I going to go? At worst I'd be murdered by a delusional nihilistic madman and at best I'd spend the next month in quarantine after having unplanned contact with an alien specimen. Unless the *Kali* shot us out of the sky first, that is.

"I've studied your schematics, you know. The design is really quite ingenious. The doctors did some ersatz rewiring in your head that's extremely impressive, solves some of the shortcomings of the earlier generation implants. But the lack of sleep *is* a problem. Without sleep they can't talk to you. That worries them. *You* worry them. You're the fly in the ointment. The monkey in the wrench. But I had an idea." He held the massive spanner in two hands. "You might not sleep voluntarily. But what happens to your mind when it's unconscious?"

Before I could answer he swung the wrench into my skull and knocked me into oblivion.

―∞―

A smell like a knife driving through my eye woke me from the eternal dark of my mind. Military-grade smelling salts don't pull any punches. And they're just about the most unpleasant way possible to wake up.

My eyes popped open like torpedo hatches prepped for live fire. Standing to my side was the twitchy squint, Jeremy. And kneeling over me, a comical look of concern making him even more handsome than usual, was my Nicolai.

Smelling salts aren't the worst possible way to wake. There are more painful options.

Deep purple stained Nicolai's big hands, fading to a peaceful lavender at his forearms. Tracings of pigment highlighted his veins, crept up the side of his neck toward his eyes. It was like he'd passed out at some crewmen party and people had played Draw On The Drunk with him. But it wasn't people who'd done this. They were the farthest thing from people.

"She's awake," Jeremy said in alarm. Like I was a bomb ready to explode.

Maybe I was.

"Eliza," Nicolai's voice was the low murmur of a concerned father. "My *Lizabeta*. We were worried about you. Doctor Arraf was ... overzealous with his methods. It was not supposed to be like this." Nicolai was different. Even beyond the purple alien juice in his veins, he was different. When we were together doing whatever it is we did in those dimly lit cargo bays there'd always been a distance in his eyes, a hesitation. And it wasn't just with me. Nic could have gone so far in the Navy if he only gave a damn. He was bright and loyal and brave to a fault. But half the time he couldn't be bothered to care. There was something of the teenage boy in him at all times, the mindless, pointless rebellion. He said no just for the sake of saying it.

His lazy defiance was always there, between us like a wall. I knew we could never really be together—back then—until he got over whatever it was that held him back.

And now he had.

All trace of rebellion, of resistance, had fled his eyes. He didn't have the crazed zeal that afflicted Jeremy Wrench-Hands, just a clarity of purpose that I found maddeningly attractive—tied there on the floor in the tentacles of some ravenous star beast as I was. Here, at long last, was that Nicolai I'd been searching for all those sweaty, sticky afternoons.

"You look good, Nic. Purple suits you." It didn't. It was an ugly shade on him, making his olive-toned skin look ghastly.

A sad smile creased his face. "Why did I wait so long to talk to you, Eliza?"

"I'd love to give you a hug and make up but as you can see, I'm a bit tied up at the moment." I wriggled my good hand. It felt like half my body was wrapped in those viscid tentacles. Bound at the wrists, elbows, knees and ankles, lying on the wet floor as beautiful Nicolai dominated my vision—it reminded me too forcefully of the times we'd spent together.

"They think it is best, little bee." Another sad smile.

Jeremy interrupted, his body alternating between perfect stillness and spasmodic gesticulation. "Why are you pussy-footing around, man? We are *running out of time*. Make the pitch and let's go!"

Nicolai sighed. His eyes met mine and he shrugged as if to say, *can you believe this guy?* "Very well. Doctor Arraf is on a timetable. The *Kali* is a tricky pursuer and is, despite all our best efforts, gaining on us. We do not have much time at all." He reached out and stroked my face right where the cybernetics joined flesh. His fingers traced the livid scars. "I am so sorry for what happened to you. It is my fault, you know, that this happened. If we hadn't been arranging one last rendezvous that day. If I hadn't asked you to tie yourself down. If I hadn't been running late, then you never would have endured such pain, my little Eliza bee."

It was too much. I'd played out this conversation in my head so many times. It always ended with him kissing me, telling me that the scars were all in my imagination. In my fantasies Nicolai would strip me naked, walk me over to a mirror and force me to look at myself and I'd see finally that the scars were all in my head. I'd look for real and the ugly red-purple pathways that marked my injuries would be just the faintest traces of silver, like I was a rich man's car all filigreed in silver whorls. And then Nicolai would lead me to the bed, apologizing all the way, mur-

muring his love to me, swearing he'd never be late or leave me again, and then he'd take me for a spin and test out my new handling and maybe my cybernetics would make me even more amazing in bed.

But here, steeped in the alien muck with Doctor Paranoia watching—it was a perversion of my fantasy. A deep rage roared to life in my belly. Had the things peered into my mind after all? Had they pulled out my fantasy and then, oblivious to the finer points of the human mind, dangled it here covered in excrement? Or was this honestly in Nicolai's heart? Did it even matter?

"You can make it up to me, Nic. Untie me. Give me a head start and we'll call it even."

In the corner, at the edge of the shattered bay window, lay one of the emergency skiffs. That was how Nic got in here.

He grinned and shook his head. "Always such fire in you. That is what I loved." A stab in my heart, that one. "But, no. Freeing you would anger these angels from the deepness. You are like a demon to them, an invisible presence of mischief that threatens all their plans. They demand your problem be solved. We have but two options in our hands. Doctor Arraf, he wishes to take the coward's path. This little man would smother you with a pillow while you were unconscious." Nicolai shook his head. "But there is a better way. A way that honors life." He stood and walked to the rough-skinned beast, ran his hands along its flanks.

"I don't think I can be like you, Nic. I don't dream. These monsters can't get into my head like they did to yours. Even if I wanted to let them, that part of me is gone. Sheared away in a different bay somewhere."

"No," Nicolai said. "It is this same room. Funny coincidence, yes? The repairs were extensive so you can be forgiven for not recognizing it. But the address number—No—I shall never forget that. I ran towards it, heard your wailing and that madman's ranting. This number is burned on the back of my eyes, little bee."

"It's really a shame you have so much brain damage," Jeremy interrupted. "You wouldn't believe how good slip-space feels. Most of the crew, one taste was enough to make them long for more. Two skips, pulled and prolonged and directed by these wonderful beings, convinced more than half the crew that this was our destiny. Think about it: a life of unending pleasure. What does that sound like to you?"

Jeremy and Nicolai watched me excitedly, waiting for my answer. "It sounds like a lie."

"No," Nicolai *tsked*. "It is heaven." He knelt at my head and ran his strong fingers along my scars again. "You have been in so much pain, Eliza. So much. It clouds your vision, makes you see enemies where there are friends and angels. These wonderful entities, they have assured me they can heal your scars. They can rebuild your flesh and your mind. They have evolved past our understanding of matter, my love. There is nothing they cannot do. They can take away these machines in your tissues. They can regrow your brain just as it was. They can rebuild you."

Could it be true? Once you accept that there are higher beings, creatures that can live for strange eons in the darkness between worlds, anything seems possible. My mind raced at the possibilities. The computer in my head was busy on its own projects, estimating the *Kali*'s approach, guessing at how fast we could arrive back at Earth with our twisted zoo.

"You will be beautiful again." Nicolai grinned like a lover offering a spoonful of ice cream to his date. "But you must choose it freely. The miracles they work, they need the mind's acceptance."

"But the *Kali* is gaining," I stalled. "What will it matter if I get reborn? We'll be perforated and then nuked into dust."

Jeremy slithered in next to Nicolai, gazed down at me with his manic beady eyes. "Maybe. Maybe," he hissed. "Or maybe the *Kali* spent too long in the slipstream, too. Maybe all the people on board are rushing over here to join us. To protect us. To guide us back to Earth where we can share our knowledge with everyone."

"Is that what they told you?"

"You must choose, my dear busy bee. We have much to do still, the doctor and I. Nearly everyone is still asleep, you see. There are but a handful of us to serve as harbingers of this message." His fingers stroked my scars again, tracing a path of pain and shame on my skin. "Think of how it could be between us again. We could live forever with their blessing. Eternal youth, eternal health. Nothing is outside their grasp."

He was so close to me. I could smell him and he smelled like my Nicolai. The sweat on his brow. The spice of his aftershave. It was him. If he'd kissed me then, bound on the floor, I knew I would have given in. Would have said yes and been remade. I was a mess. My leg was a useless hunk of steel now, fluids drip-drabbled from a crack near my knee. My ribs ached where they'd cracked in the impact. The seam of my shoulder burned with the earlier exertion, threatening to become a lasting agony. I probably ripped some muscles deep down. My body was one giant ache, a temple of pain.

"Yes, Nicolai." I said yes. Why did I say yes?

He beamed at me. I'd never seen him so proud.

"Help her sit up. She can't receive the sacrament like this."

Jeremy wiggled his fingers under the metal of my cybernetics and grunted with the strain of trying to lift me. He slipped and skidded in the pooling purple muck, smashing his face into the floor and coming up covered in goo. I would have laughed if I wasn't so terrified.

Nicolai frowned. "Can you sit up, Eliza? I had forgotten how much you weigh."

"Sorry, Nic. All my systems are down. I can't even flex my fingers." His beautiful face always made me want to lie, to say what he wanted to hear.

"Da. Da." He nodded. "I will untie you. Please do not try any monkey business."

Jeremy stepped back, hefted that mean wrench in his beast-slick hands.

Every night when other people dreamt I'd been reviewing my memories of this man. For him we'd been apart over a year. We had distance. For me the wound had never healed. It should have but I couldn't resist picking at it. I'd spent the last months replaying that footage with my silicon brain over and over, feeling his hands on me, feeling him enter me and his hot breath in my ear as he whispered filthy delights and promises of things to come. And then, always, the memory of that accident and the look of disgust at seeing me ripped open on the floor. Not concern. Disgust.

As Nicolai untied me, I searched his eyes for any trace of the old him. Was that man who abandoned me as soon as I was broken still in there? Was the man who made me laugh with naughty suggestions as he fucked me still alive? I didn't see those Nicolais anywhere.

"We need the blessing," Jeremy muttered.

The surface of the Lurker rippled beside Nicolai. It'd been so still, so inanimate, I'd forgotten it was a living being. For a while it was as if someone had dropped a dump truck of half-rotten meat in our personal cargo bay and we'd just decided to have a nice conversation next to it. But not now. Something wordless passed between Nicolai and the Lurker. They were in communication. Was he acting of his own will as he said, or was he merely a puppet to these monsters?

The flesh of the thing parted and a pseudopod pushed forth, extruded by some internal force. It resembled nothing so much as a thick beefy mushroom half as big as a man, the stalk covered in lumpy purple fruits. Nicolai bowed his head as if in prayer. Then he plucked one of the purple globules and handed it to me.

"Eat this," he said. "And we can live forever."

The fruit resembled a bruised, dripping pomegranate. The heft of it shocked me, as if it was carved from stone and not made of flesh. Purple juice stained my fingers. I expected some sweet, cloying scent but it had no odor at all. I was still lying on my back, playing possum. "Can you help me up, Nic? It's hard to eat lying down."

He propped me against the Lurker itself, the liquid meat of the thing rolling under my weight. Sitting, I held the fruit. Nicolai smiled at me, crouched close and smeared with that alien goo. Behind him, Jeremy tapped on a tablet computer he'd produced from somewhere, wholly absorbed in its contents.

"Go, Eliza. Join us. Eat the offering." Nicolai nodded excitedly. He looked like a parent on Christmas morning watching a kid open presents.

"I need to thank you, Nic." I said, raising the fruit to my mouth.

"No, you don't."

"Yes, I really do. You've given me what I've been craving ever since the accident."

He grinned again, showing his perfect white teeth stained purple at the roots. "Healing. *Da.* And closure as well."

"No, Nicolai. You've given me something to hit."

The expression on his face as my words sank in was one I'd cherish for the rest of my life, however long that'd be. If I got out of this intact I knew I'd be replaying that look every night in bed. The next look, too, was pretty choice, as my cybernetic arm flared to life and smashed his pretty face with an uppercut. The force of it lifted Nicolai several feet off the ground. He soared up and back, blood spraying from a bit lip, jaw broken, only to collapse unconscious in a ragdoll heap on the floor.

Doctor Jeremy, the snake, hardly had time to react before I took that deceptively heavy fruit in my enhanced hand and hurled it perfectly into his face. The rocky fruit caught him in the temple and bounced his head off the shuttle bay wall with a crunch.

Behind me, the Lurker rippled.

I threw myself forward onto my hands just as a mouth gaped open in the side of the beast. It began as a seam where my back had been, but then it deepened and split and yawned open. Within were more tentacles and the glint of bone-white teeth. I scrabbled across the floor, over the mass of serpentine limbs that slowly came to life as I passed, writhing and coiling and feeling about for me.

It couldn't see me. My mind was too different. I was a blank spot in its vision. But it could definitely feel me. Shit. Hand over hand I hauled myself across those grasping limbs. They groped at me as I passed, looping around my metal leg and then slipping off when they failed to find meat. More and more of the questing limbs spilled forth from the chasmic orifice. It was only a matter of time before it caught me.

Inch by painful inch, my ribs cracking and splintering, I hauled myself across the floor like a deranged inchworm. Pushing myself upright, into cobra pose, preparing for another forward lunge, my fingers slipped in the purple muck and I crashed down hard onto my face. Blood gushed from my nose and sizzled on the alien goo. And then the tentacles knew exactly where I was. They smelled the blood. They sprang into the air, a whirling storm of limbs, and then they crashed down upon me, seizing my neck and ankles and wrists. Squeezing tightly, they hauled me back towards that hungry chasm, that gulf in reality. I looked, just for a moment, into the mouth of the beast and saw a never-ending plateau of stars. Nebulae, pink and gold in the sidereal light, stretched out forever inside the monster like an obscene tongue. A peace fell over me, an awful imposed peace like a narcotic and my struggles weakened, my grip slackened. The tentacles yanked me across the floor like some fisherman reeling in his catch and lost in those hypnotic stars I could do nothing but weep.

My mind wanted to be inside the creature, to become another star burning with certainty in the void, to be released from caring or needs or pain—to never feel cruel judgment's scorn like a sunburn on my skin—the promise in that gulf was of sweet release from all that mattered. I closed my eyes and stopped resisting and let myself be pulled inside that sticky mouth.

And then: I was a little girl again, staring at a monitor in class as the first colony ship set down on Mars. I sobbed with joy at the wonder of it all. "Human ingenuity," my teacher said, "knows no bounds. As long as we keep fighting and keep our eyes clear we shall always succeed."

And then: I was a teenager and my father took me to the Air and Space Museum. He pointed up at the first warship, an American Direwolf, bristling with guns. "It's a shame, kiddo, that we ever needed such weapons." His voice was sandpaper and honey. The cancer hadn't taken him yet. "But us humans, we're descended from a million years of war.

It's in our blood. The trick isn't to keep it locked up. The trick is to channel it." The memory ended just before he told me about the disease eating away at his lungs.

And then: I was back in that doomed cargo bay, handcuffed to the wall as the enemy's viper plowed through steel and skin and bone, shearing me in two. Only this time the memory refocused, the camera of my mind's eye moved from my broken bleeding body to the madman colonist, bearded and starving, dressed in rags stained purple, as he toppled out of the craft babbling. "You need to tell everyone," he grabbed my head, leaned in close, pressing our foreheads together. This isn't how I remembered it. Why is this not how I remembered it? "Tell everyone that it isn't safe out here. The darkness is alive and it is hungry. It's ravenous and insane." His voice was torn though his eyes—filling my vision—were absolutely calm. "We brought one of them down to the colony. They wanted to weaponize it. But you can't use the devil like a sword. It devoured us from the insides out, turned us on each other. It promised peace and brought only war." He glanced up, a noise at the door. "Tell everyone to go back. Go back." The door exploded inwards. The colonist's body jerked as taser rounds lit him up from the inside and then Nicolai was there, looking at me like I was broken.

The computer—that sneaky little bastard in my brain—it wasn't going to let me give up.

I opened my eyes and saw that terrible mouth before me, still reeling me in. It was old. Older than anything had any right being. Whatever muscles or mechanisms it used for physical activity were badly atrophied. I'd assumed it all-powerful but it stood newly revealed as a half-dead thing, luring prey close to gobble them down. Bracing my feet on either side of the monster's slavering orifice, I wrapped my cybernetic hand around a tentacle close to the root and *pulled*. The limb strained and stretched, slipping in my fingers, but I held on tight. My grip could powder stone. The thing never had a chance. With a sound like cloth tearing the tentacle ripped free, spraying purple and black gunk everywhere.

The smell was appalling.

The beast recoiled, tremors wobbling the surface, and I grabbed another appendage at the root and did it again. And again. And again. Tentacle after tentacle I braced and tore from that deathless mouth. Soon it stopped struggling, withdrew its remaining limbs and folded in on itself. I fell to the floor, drenched in alien fluids, and watched as the giant meatball wrapped impossibly inward and vanished like a drain clearing. The process took seconds. Whatever mouth it had forced into our world had been pulled back to the skip-space where the beast lived.

Part of me wanted to savor the victory, to lay back and smile and congratulate myself. But the machine told me to keep going.

There'd be others like Jeremy and Nicolai. Others sabotaging the ship. Jeremy's tablet computer chimed on the floor. It still worked, half-submerged in the beast's bloody effluent. Military hardware, built to take a spill. I half-swam and half-crawled over to it, my leg still entirely nonfunctional. He was tapped in to the ship's communication network, was watching everything on a dozen tiny windows. One flashed red, warning about the *Kali's* proximity. She was nearly in weapons range and she was flying hot, all her launch tubes open and her warheads armed. So much for joining the Lurkers in endless joy. Jeremy had seemed to think there was a way to outrun the pursuing ship. But what was it? I could have woken him, demanded answers. The smelling salts were somewhere nearby.

But there, I found it. The navigational officers and Command were arguing over open comms. Command wanted to jettison the entire *Melissa*, escape on the *Chernobog*. They'd built in mechanisms for quick release. Explosive bolts for the just-in-case. But navigation had locked them out of the system. The navigators were spooling up the skipdrive. They were going to hurl themselves back into the blissful emptiness of skip-space along with all the Lurkers.

"Damn the extra weight," they said. "We need to get these specimens back to Earth."

"Launching the drive while moving at this velocity is suicide," Command argued back.

"We need to bring them home, we have been chosen as their harbingers."

The diagnostics showed mere minutes until the skipdrive was active and usable. The separation sequence was nowhere near as far along. I tried to disable the skip, but navigation had everyone else shut out, even me.

There was no way I was going back into skip space. That hungry thing would be there waiting for me. And maybe this time the ship got stuck forever and never returned. Maybe it popped back into space with the entire crew mysteriously gone, like the first skip test so many years ago. Or maybe it arrived at Earth with its terrible payload, this zoo full of starving gods.

I hurled myself onto the skiff. I might not be able to walk on one leg, but I could surely fly the oversized scooter. Launching out over the divide between the rings, I resisted looking back. I knew that the things stuffed into every cargo bay would be watching me with baleful eyes. Their hateful appetite was a fire at my back. I maneuvered the skiff to one of the emergency terminals. Number three, my favorite. The skiff had an emergency package tucked into the seat. Standard issue bug-out bag stocked with rations, water and the thinnest, ugliest EVA suit you could ever hope for. I pulled the suit on in record time, struggling with my bad leg, and activated the terminal.

Being one of the chief maintenance officers gave you special privileges. Sure the job had crappy hours and low pay, but if there was ever a fire, a contagion, or an armed boarding party breaching the outer ring of hexagonal cargo bays you had the ability to purge the contents of all the bays at once. It wasn't even difficult. Open the right app and the system presented you with a giant flashing red button reading JETTISON?

So I pressed it.

One second the ship was hurtling along at breakneck speeds and the next there was a roar like every star in the sky crying your name at once with absolute rage. The bays spit forth their cargo into the darkness of space and where the cargo held on or was too heavy to jettison the container itself released and ejected itself from the outer ring.

Navigation paused the skipdrive. Their comms were silent. What was it like for them to hear their new masters drift away?

The *Kali* entered live fire range. The tablet terminal shrieked in alarm.

I piloted the skiff out across the expanse, aiming it through one of the absences in the outer ring where a particularly hefty Lurker had been expunged. Clearing the ship, slipping into open space with only the thinnest of emergency suits around me, I saw the terminal flash to life again as the *Chernobog* blew its explosive bolts, throwing the ring of the *Melissa* off like a spinning coin. Then the skipdrive fired and the Chorny vanished from sight.

Torpedoes the size of bears whizzed past me, heading for the *Melissa*, breaking up into a million razor-sharp flechettes as they neared their target.

Hurtling toward the *Kali*, toward my only hope of salvation, I piloted between the Lurkers who now unfolded like flowers, reaching for me with their tentacle-like roots. In the cold of space, absent any gravity to speak of, they moved slowly. There was no way they could grab me—the skiff was too fast. But they knew that. They knew everything. The lurkers extended all their tendrils and tentacles and thin whip-like limbs, grasping for each other like lovers. It could have almost been sweet if they weren't weaving a massive net meant to catch me, to catch the *Kali*, to catch their ticket to humanity.

My tablet went dark. I was either out of range of the *Melissa*—unlikely—or the flechette rounds from the *Kali* had done their job and ripped a million tiny holes in my home. There was no explosion, of course, no booming sound. The vacuum took away everything, gave nothing in return. It ate all sound, all feeling, all hope.

The machine in my head saw how fast the Lurkers wove themselves together, ran the calculations. I wasn't going to make it. Those nasty limbs were going to seize my ankles as I cleared the net and hold me tight. Would they devour me? Torture me? Take me back to their skip space home? If only I could make the skiff faster, jettison some weight.

I had a terrible idea.

The EVA suit was military grade, thin but functional. The best thing about military engineering, in my opinion, is the utility of it. The basic design of the EVA suit was old, some said it went back to the nineteenth century, adapted for space of course, but following classic military principles. All the navy uniforms had built in tourniquets. My *suit* had built in tourniquets.

Locking the skiff's autopilot onto the *Kali*, I snapped my belt onto a safety ring. Like a mountain climber hanging from a cliff face I dangled in space. My gloved fingers fumbled at the straps. The machine in my head calculated and recalculated the odds I'd slip through the net. They weren't good. Pulling the tourniquet tight on my upper thigh, I ripped open my EVA suit just above my knee. I dug my fingers into the mangled, bent housing until I found my emergency release. If my suit wasn't sealed tightly this would kill me quickly, probably before the Lurkers got me. I tugged the emergency release hard and warning lights flashed in my skull. The computer was alarmed. I jettisoned my leg.

It was artificial. It was metal and plastic and a pain in my ass but it was still me. Watching that leg hurl off into the waiting grasp of those things was like watching a friend close their eyes and never open them again. I wanted to mourn it, to mourn everything, but there was no time. I'd shed mass—a lot of mass—but it was still too close to call. I needed to ditch something more. I could have chucked the tablet, the tool bag, the emergency rations but they weighed almost nothing in the grand scheme of things. Four kilos wouldn't get me anywhere. So I pulled the tourniquet tight above my arm, at the shoulder and ripped open my suit above the elbow. The tourniquets held. They were designed for this—well not exactly for this, the Navy men didn't plan on a brave cybergirl throwing her limbs to a pack of pursuing hungry gods in space, but it was close enough. My arm was in better shape and easier to remove. I dug in, found the release and then took my arm off. For a moment I was shaking my own hand and I didn't want to let go. The cybernetics had been a part of my grieving and my coping. They were old friends. We'd had good times together, like when I punched Nicolai. That was fun. But the computer chimed again with the odds and I let go of myself.

My arm spun off into the void, impacting fist first into the eye of one of the great beasts. *Thatta girl. Make momma proud.* If you have to go out, go out swinging, my grandfather used to say.

If I could have removed the rest of my cybernetics to flee even faster I would have, but the suits didn't have tourniquets in the proper places for that. Instead I watched as the stars vanished one by one, as the tentacles of those hungry gods wove around me into a wall of night. When they caught me, would I tear open my suit and face the void first?

The odds were not in my favor. Even with the mass I shed, it would only take the lightest touch from a Lurker to spin me off course, to snare me forever and ever. I aimed for the largest hole in the contracting net—the only stars I could see—and waited. I flew through a cylinder of spinning tentacles, each reaching out to grab me, to be the first, like children impatient for dessert. Closing my eyes, I braced myself. Gripped the skiff with my one good hand, feeling off balance without my heavy metal limbs.

And just as the net closed about me, just as the last stars vanished from my view, a blinding light sizzled by me, painted a circle around the skiff. Grasping tentacles turned to ash, to vapor, under the laser's assault. It was the *Kali*. With incredible precision she burnt away every lurking limb within five meters of me and in seconds I was past them, through their claustrophobic net and hurtling towards the *Kali's* bridge. I tried to steer, to redirect the skiff. But it turns out you need two hands to fly one. Powerless to change course, I watched helplessly as the *Kali* loomed before me, her black insectile form now the only hope anyone had for what was coming.

I needed to tell them.

I needed to warn them.

Who knows how many on board had been contacted during their skip, how many had already turned against humanity in favor of these deathless monsters.

My skiff torpedoed through their bridge in a shower of sparks and shattering glass. I slammed into the far side of their command deck and was thrown free of my craft, my safety webbing strained past capacity. Hitting the ground hard, I pushed myself up on one arm and looked around for someone to tell, someone to warn. Blood welled up from the edge of my cybernetics. Something important had given way deep inside of me. The machine in my head was quiet.

A man lay trapped, half-pinned under my skiff. He had beautiful brown hair spilling down his shoulders and perfectly amber eyes. His right leg was crushed between the wall and my ship. I'd apologize later. I'd explain later. I'd warn them now.

Pulling myself to him I whispered, "You have to kill them all. Every last one of them." My voice was gone. He stared at me with horrified eyes, as if I was a monster. I brought my face close to his—close enough to kiss—and made sure he heard me. "The darkness," I said. "It hungers. They will devour all of us. You can't let them get to Earth." I was a raving madwoman, screaming my hoarse shouts into this poor man's face. I could see in his eyes that I terrified him. He'd been happy and at peace with himself until I came along, smashing into his world with my awful truths.

He had his own ship, his own crew, his own Nicolai.

And his Nicolai was there, rushing to the bridge with a weapon in his hands.

He saw me and took his shot.

Demon Rising
R.S. McCoy

SHE'S COMING. I could always tell when she neared. A strange thumping noise would erupt from my chest, starting low and quiet until it had moved up into my neck. An automatic smile would sprout across the blistery skin that graced my jaw.

The soft thuds of her feet grew steadily louder as she made her way up the stairs. The absence of the second, heavier set revealed she was alone. *Finally.*

I had waited all day, just as I did every day, for the sun to go down and the girl to make her way up. Her footsteps stalled just outside the door a moment before the brass knob creaked as the small hand turned it. A dim light broke into the room for the brief moment before she shut the door behind her.

"Pan?" she whispered, inaudible but for the vibration of muscles in her mouth. She asked as if she wondered if I was still there, although I didn't know why. I would never, ever leave her.

"Is it safe?" I asked in return. *Exposure must be avoided.*

"Of course."

I reached out one disgusting clawed hand to pull my body closer to the edge until I could just make out her shape in the darkness above me.

"Come on." She reached out her own petite hand to pull me up. The metal frame scraped the skin along my spine as I rose but I was careful to keep the pain from my face.

A small flame appeared and landed on the wick of a candle. "I'm sorry you had to wait so long. I know you hate it under there." Her face was especially sweet in the dim candlelight, a dark tendril of hair fell across her face.

"I don't mind," I replied honestly. There are worse places to be than under her bed. I had only flashes of memory from the before, but they were enough; I would never go back as long as I could help it.

"Here, I brought you something." She held out a small object, but I knew what it was before I even caught sight of it. She brought me one every time.

"You went again today?" I asked, attempting to hide my envy. There was nothing I wanted more than to go with her.

"Father says I can go as much as I like."

What father said about the zoo was no secret. She said the words every time she went. The carved wood animal was placed into my palm.

"Don't worry. You'll go with us someday."

I could only hope she was right as I marveled at the tiny creature in my hand. It appeared to be some kind of cat, but the teeth were long and sharp and it wore a thick patch of fur around its neck. And it had a tail just like mine.

"What do you call this one?" I asked as I clumsily turned the carving over in my hand as well as my thick, clawed fingers would allow. Yet again I wished I had ten small, capable fingers instead of the four useless ones I possessed.

"A lion. It's from Africa."

"Lion." I repeated, rolling the word around my jaw and savoring the taste of it. *If only I could see it for myself.*

"And look. It has a tail like yours."

I leaned down a bit so we could both look at the carving together. A strange feeling welled up inside me when I realized she had picked it out especially for me. She recognized the same tail and didn't think it disgusting. Maybe I would really get to go with her someday.

"Thank you, Katherine." Her delicate hand reached up to pull on my arm until I lowered to kneel next to her. I closed my eyes as her soft, warm lips met the cold, tough skin of my cheek. A *kiss*. She didn't always give me a kiss, but I cherished every time she did. I felt my wings jump open for a moment with the excitement before I could call them back.

I forced my eyes open to see if she was angry; I wasn't supposed to show my wings. But she only smiled and said, "Go on. Put it with the others."

Along the window sill sat the treasured collection of animal carvings. Aside from Katherine herself, they meant everything to me. I carefully placed the lion on the end next to the one called a 'gorilla.'

"Will you tell me about the lion?" I asked her, a bit forlorn without the warmth of the wood in my hand.

"Not tonight. Tomorrow's Sunday. You know that." On Sundays, Katherine's father took her to church to worship someone named 'God.' They started going only a few months ago, but already it was cutting into my time with her. Slowly I began to feed the hatred of whoever 'God' was.

"Tomorrow night?"

"Sure. Tuck me in?" She didn't need to ask. It was my favorite part of the night. I watched her climb onto the wide mattress and lay her handsome curls onto the pillow. My ungainly fingers pulled at the bunched up sheets at the foot of the bed and carefully drew them up until they rested just below her chin. For the thousandth time I wished I had lips to kiss her goodnight, rather than the scarred remains of flesh around my grim, exposed and yellowed teeth. I so badly wanted to give her a kiss.

"Goodnight Pan," she said as she smiled sleepily.

I blew out the single candle and made my way back under the bed, back into the darkness to wait for tomorrow, to wait for the story of the lion.

Within minutes, the comforting sound of Katherine's slow breathing filled the room. I didn't mind the dark the way she did, but then again, I could still see. I crept to the edge of the bed until I could just make out the shapes in front of the window. More than anything, they gave me hope.

There was one called a goat that had curved horns on its head just like mine, along with a patch of hairs that hung from its chin. I reached up a rough finger to touch the hairs that trailed from my own chin. As a force of habit, my finger moved up just enough to graze the lipless teeth and absent nose. *If only I could have the face of a goat.*

Instead, I had the feet of a goat with narrow hooves and a deep slit down the middle. How I hated them. They were loud against the light wood floors and more than once they threatened to alert Father to my presence in the house. They would be the key to my exposure, I was sure.

Next to the wooden goat was another, the one Katherine called a bat. It had thin wings of skin stretched across narrow bones and a pointed face with large ears. It was one of her favorites. There was no denying that my wings were the same, thin with dark skin and interwoven with veins, though mine were nearly ten feet across fully spread. And Katherine hated them.

I so desperately loved her and wanted her to love me in return. For the most part I thought she did love me, all except for those wings. Maybe someday I would ask her, if I ever found the courage.

Amongst the other animals carved of wood were a giraffe, a zebra, a snake and the gorilla. Each had their own shape, and their coverings, too, according to Katherine. A giraffe had spots while a zebra had stripes. A snake had scales and the gorilla had fur.

Every shape and sized animal was welcomed at the zoo. I could only hope they would welcome me as well. *If only I could see it for myself.*

One of them called a peacock was said to have the most beautiful colors. Its wings were large, so large that it can't fly, and filled with blues and greens and golds. The brown of the wood carving hardly did justice to its beauty, or so Katherine would say.

There were animals from all around the world, places called Asia and Africa. Would they welcome me? I didn't know where exactly the before was, only that it was dark and I didn't want to go back.

I listened to Katherine's slow breathing as I dreamt about what it would be like to be an animal at the zoo. Sleep never came to me, not in all the time I had been with Katherine, but still I could dream. I wanted to be with the animals, almost as much as I wanted to be with Katherine. I wanted to go outside and see the world, more than just the one room.

The pink of the morning streamed in through the window as the heavy boots came up the stairs. "Katherine?" Father's deep voice boomed just before he opened the door. All I had ever seen of him were those shiny brown boots.

"Come Katherine. It's Sunday and we don't want to be late." She sucked in a deep breath to wake as the bed sunk from Father's weight.

"Can I wear the new yellow dress?"

Yes, the yellow dress. I had wanted to see her in the bright colored fabric since Father had bought it for her earlier in the week.

"Of course. Don't forget your hair." The familiar sound of a kiss came just before the weight lifted and Father moved back down the stairs.

"Did you hear that, Pan? I get to wear the yellow dress!" Katherine squealed as her small feet touched the wooden floor and took off to get dressed. For a moment, I considered pulling myself out from under the bed to see it myself, but I knew it was too dangerous. Father might see me.

Faster than I was ready for, she slipped on the dress and ran down the stairs in eagerness to go to church. Part of me was upset just that she had left, but another part burned with jealousy. I didn't want her to be excited to see anyone else. I wanted her to be satisfied with me.

Once I was sure they were gone for the day, I crept out into the room and unfurled my wings. They hated to be pressed so close and the stretch liberated, even though they barely missed hitting the two sides of the room.

Desperately I wanted to stand at the window and gaze down at the city. People would be walking past on their way to church or somewhere else. Some would ride on horses, and I itched to see one. So long I had heard the sounds of their hooves sinking and sucking in the mud.

There had to be a way to leave the room. As sure as I wanted to avoid the before, I wanted to get out and go with Katherine, wherever she went. Even to church to see God. I would go, if that's where she wanted.

I spent the day admiring the wooden carvings and thinking of how I could get out. I had to leave without being seen; she was always clear about not being seen. There seemed to be only one answer. *Night.*

Later in the evening when her small feet climbed up the steps, I summoned the courage to ask her. "Pan?" came her familiar call into the dark.

"Is it safe?"

"You know it is. Come on." I pulled myself carefully from beneath the bed as she laid a small flame onto the candle.

"Pan?" Her voice quivered in a way I hadn't heard before. Immediately I knew something was wrong.

"Yes?"

"Are you a helper of Satan?" She spoke in a low voice despite the hush, seeming nervous for how I would answer. Her trepidation infected me as well, and I struggled with how to answer her confusing question.

"I–I don't know. I don't think I help with anything called a Satan." A moment later I added, "What is a Satan?"

A wide smile lit up her face, brighter than the meager candle light had any right to, and immediately I began to relax. "He's pure evil."

"Satan is a person?" It hardly sounded like a name, but then again, I had only known of Katherine and Father.

"Well, not a person exactly. Father Rickard says he is God's enemy." Instantly it became clear how she would be worried about this Satan. For whatever reason, Katherine loved God. An enemy of God was an enemy to her.

"Why would I help him?" While I was certainly no fan of God, Katherine was, and there was little I would do to displease her.

Again her features fell and her eyes rested on the rough grain of the floorboards. "Today in church, Father Rickard said that Satan has helpers. He said they are evil, and they look- He said they look like you."

My breath caught in my chest in fear of what it could mean. Would she send me away? Did God mean more to her than I did?

A moment later I caught sight of the girl, frightened and nervous. "Katherine?" I knelt in front of her to let her arms fly around my neck and her chest fall onto mine. Warm tears splashed against my shoulder amidst her shaking sobs.

"It's not true is it? You're not really Satan's helper are you?" she managed between gasping breaths.

"Of course not. I've never even met him." That seemed to calm her and I wasn't long before her head lifted to reveal two puffy pink eyes.

"He said Satan has helpers, they go around and do his evil work. All the helpers have horns, and wings and a tail. He said they kill children."

I struggled to gently wipe the tears from under her eyes as I contemplated that someone would really kill a child, that someone would kill Katherine. A person had to be truly evil to do such a thing.

While we worked to compose ourselves, I remembered my decision from the afternoon but questioned if the timing was right. Then again, maybe it would help to cheer her up.

"Katherine, would you take me to the zoo?" I asked hesitantly. I had waited for this moment for a long time. In the answering silence, I quickly questioned asking her so soon.

"What do you mean? I told you I would take you someday."

"Let's go now. It's so dark, no one will see me. I can get you to the zoo and back and Father will never know."

An instant later, she jumped from my arms and ran across the room. My heart sank.

"I'm ready." She emerged a moment later with a loose shirt tucked into her pants and her boots already on. On her face she wore an excited smile that warmed me to the core. *It's really happening.*

As quietly as I could manage, I leapt forward to scoop her into my arms. She was nearly weightless for the strength in them, but I enjoyed her closeness all the same. I carefully moved toward the window and pushed aside the carvings.

My hand glanced along the animals I had dreamed about, and now I was finally going to see them. Silently I pushed open the frame of the window and felt the cool night air against my face for the first time. The moon shone brightly above us and the streets were quiet below. *This is going to work.*

One hooved foot stepped up onto the ledge followed by the other, and a moment later I stepped down. In a flash, my giddy wings flew open and pulled us back up and away from the ground. I held Katherine tight, so she wouldn't be afraid and cry out. Her heart beat loudly against my chest, but only in the exhilaration that matched my own. We had done it.

"Katherine, which way?" I asked when I realized I had no idea where to go. Given enough time I could have found my way to the animals just by smell, but she had to be back before Father woke.

"Over there, about twelve blocks or so." My wings effortlessly pulled us along, strong and free like they had never been before. Within a few minutes, the sign for the zoo could be seen in the bright light of the moon.

"That's it down there," Katherine said as she pointed towards an open area. My hooves made a small sound as they made contact with the stones and my wings folded along my back again, satisfied.

"Over here!" Her hand pulled me eagerly along towards a row of metal bars surrounding an enclosure, and my heart raced with the possibilities.

Within seconds, I heard hooves against the sand as a tall animal emerged from a thin wooden house. Its legs were as long as my body and its neck extended up twice that high. Brown blotches covered all over, though I didn't need to see its colors to know its name. *Giraffe.*

Far more elegantly than I would have expected from a creature with such height, the giraffe walked to the fence and hung its long neck over until our faces were only inches apart. A long black tongue trailed out of its mouth to bend and flick across my neck and shoulder. Despite the strangeness of the touch, there was no doubt that the giraffe was as happy and eager to meet me as I was to meet her.

"Wow! I've never seen him do that!" Katherine jumped up and down excitedly to see the giraffe so close.

"It's a she," I laughed in return. Katherine pulled me along a few feet until we reached the next enclosure. A great grey beast with a large horn sauntered over until it stood with its body pressed against the metal bars.

"Do you know this one?" Katherine asked. I shook my head in response, but of course she already knew. She hadn't told me about it, and she hadn't brought home a carving of it. I had never seen such an animal before, but I recognized the tough skin that draped over its body.

Without intention, my hand reached out to touch the skin that matched my own, prompting a playful headshake that rattled the horn against the metal. Katherine laughed out heartily.

"It's called a rhinoceros, but everyone just calls it a rhino."

Rhino. I moved my hand along his back and shoulder for another minute or so before moving on. My hooves graced each cobblestone without fear of being heard, and for the first time in memory I stood tall in my own skin.

Katherine's hand pulled me along for a few minutes before she would break away and skip ahead, then circle back to pull me along again. I had never seen her so excited, and my own feelings agreed. The animals even seemed drawn into our energy. Each and every one had come as close as the metal bars would allow.

The lion paced along the fence and let out a throaty growl when I rubbed her chin. Three gorillas approached with speed and pounded the metal with enthusiasm. A she-bear stood tall and let me stroke the thick fur of her belly.

Birds of more colors than I could have ever imagined called a hundred different sounds and songs. Bats flew quick and low in a special house made for flyers. A strange jumping animal called a kangaroo hopped towards us and licked the thick fingers of my hand.

Animals of every shape and size, sound and color emerged from their sleep to greet us across the metal fence, as eager to see us as I was to see them. A deep resounding feeling began to set in. *I belong here.*

Without really meaning to, I allowed my wings to unfurl, to experience the open freedom, the exhilaration of being open.

"Katherine!" Father's deep voiced boomed out from the darkness behind me. I spun on a hooved heel, scanning the night for the source of the sound, terrified for what it meant. *How did he know?*

The early morning colors wouldn't show for a few more hours. She would have been back in bed long before he woke. *This shouldn't be happening.*

At the sound of her name, Katherine ran over and appeared behind me, her small hand sliding quickly into mine.

"Katherine! Get away from that thing!" shouted Father as he emerged from a shadow near the section of birds. *Thing?*

Father approached slowly, holding some sort of metal device aimed our way, followed by at least eight other men. He was a good bit taller than most of them, his shoulders broader. A thick beard covered most of his jaw but there was no denying the resemblance to his daughter. It was the first time I had seen more than just his boots.

A noise sounded suddenly, so loud it brought back images of the before to distract me from the searing heat in my wing. The metal tube Father held released a plume of smoke, and there was no doubt that we were in danger.

Easily I lifted Katherine by the hand until she curled against my chest for the second time that night. I pulled my wings up to arc over my shoulders and provide a thin barrier between her and the smoking tube.

"Christ, it's got her! Don't shoot! He'll kill her!" I could see Father lower the tube and raise his arm up in front of the others. He thought I was one of those things that kill children, when he was the one holding the dangerous metal device.

"Pan?" Her small voice crept up from under my chin, a tremble revealing her fear.

"I won't let anything happen to you." I tried to sound confident, though I felt the opposite. My wing still burned from the pain of the metal tube, and there were a half dozen more. I thought of maybe spreading my wings to fly, but the exposed moment might be just enough to let her come to harm.

Another booming sound erupted just as burning pain and heat shot into my lower leg. In an instant I dropped to a knee and held on to Katherine tightly, struggling to make sense of it.

Father began shouting, but this time directed at one of the other men, though I couldn't be sure. The fire in my leg distracted me from all but Katherine. I would do everything to keep her safe, but I began to doubt how much could be done against the strange weapon. I clutched her tighter to my chest.

A moment later, the individual sounds were replaced with a chorus of booms and pops as a fire erupted throughout my legs. It was all I could do to sink down to both knees and keep from falling forward, falling onto Katherine.

My wings wrapped tighter around us and my arms squeezed her in close. An eerie silence settled over the zoo, a stark contrast to the volume just a moment before. Amidst the pain and confusion, I started to question how we would get out of it. With my legs so injured I couldn't even run. I was helpless to keep her safe and it was only a matter of time.

"Pan, let me down." If anyone else had asked, I wouldn't have even considered. As much as I knew it would haunt me, I hesitantly obeyed.

My wings pulled back slightly as her feet touched the ground, offering a glimpse of Father. Though I didn't know the features of his face well, his relief was transparent. He crouched on the stones and awaited Katherine's arrival in his arms. The smoldering heat in my legs paled to the ache of watching her run at full speed to get to him, to get away from me.

"Katherine! Are you alright? Are you hurt?" Father peppered her with questions without offering a chance to answer. If she did answer, I never heard. All I could see was her nod against his shoulder.

Standing, Father addressed the others, "Father Rickard told us all about this evil. It is God's enemy. Kill it." Katherine turned to face me but kept her back pressed against him. Her eyes captured mine just as the loudness erupted again.

My wings flew across me to offer what little protection they could, but still my chest began to burn. When one of them hit my neck, it was all I could do to leap into the air and ask my injured wings to pull me away. *Katherine.*

Slowly the sounds drifted behind me, but not before a final few hits reached my skin. The holes that graced my wings let through so much air, I questioned if I would get away. More than once my body sank towards the ground despite their effort.

When I finally did touch the ground, pink light skipped between the trees. Trails of smoke and steam rose up from what little skin remained of my tattered wings. Even through the odor of char, I could still make out the presence of animals around me. *But no men.*

I had made it outside of the city somehow. Birds sang sweetly to welcome the sun. Leaves rustled as creatures began to stir. A small brown rabbit hopped lightly just a few feet away. Yet all I heard was the harsh sound of the metal tube, the ringing in my ears and the crashing of my knees onto the stone. All I could see was a girl's face as she watched her Father try to kill me.

They had fired their weapons at me for being the enemy of God, a person I had never met.

And she didn't stop them. She didn't even try.

I knew there would likely have been nothing she could have done to change the events of that night. She was a child, after all. I had been the one to ask her to leave, and being my friend she agreed. *Why did I ask her to leave? What have I done?*

Before I fully registered the motion, one thickly fingered hand reached behind me to grasp the upper edge of a wing. A surprising strength remained to begin to pull at the torn skin and fragile bones, offering a renewed but tolerable pain. The muscles slowly separated in a large strip down my back until a final scream revealed my ragged wing in my hand before me.

The other hand soon reached back to find the other, and pulled at it with no less pain or release than the first. Somehow it comforted to hold my bloodied wings in my arms, rather than suffer their attachment any longer. Without those willful, disobedient wings I never would have left her room. I wouldn't be alone in the forest. I wouldn't have lost her.

I cast them aside and stood, examining my surroundings. The rabbit jumped at the sudden movement, but soon hopped close enough that I could have stepped on it. Truly, for a moment I thought about it.

Instead I lowered back down and extended a hand. Despite the thick skin and bulbous shape of my fingers, the rabbit came closer. She let me stroke the soft brown fur across her back and never shied. A small brown bird with an orange chest and narrow clawed feet appeared atop my shoulder.

A slow look around revealed the forest to be full of animals, all quietly approaching. A young deer moved gracefully. Some sort of insect with brightly colored wings flitted all about before landing on my knee and opening to reveal yellows and reds in a stunning pattern.

At once I understood. I will keep these animals. I would keep them safe, away from man, away from Father, away from God. I would share with them the devotion I once showed to Katherine.

I am Pan. And I will never forget.

Your Day at the Zoo
Frances Stewart

THEY TELL YOU when it's *your* day, of course—not something to miss. They took your samples quite a while ago—scrapings and blood–but until you got the notice you'd almost forgotten. They tell you to come half an hour before opening.

The staff, all smiles, escort you through the gate—there's no need to stamp your hand.

A wall of fish tanks lines the entry halls—full of tiny tetras, glass catfish, and glowing cichlids all ontologically recapitulating. You look into minuscule eyes, hunting for recognition or acknowledgement, but that will not come until later. Still, the glowing colors flicker pleasantly. Brilliant scales clothe each tiny body in endless possibilities.

Inside the monkey house, crouched figures scamper. As you approach, a dozen tiny mirrors gaze back at you from among leaves and vines. The diminutive marmosets glance furtively and dash away. A capuchin grins and bounces on a swing. His enthralled eyes follow your own, an unattended finger fumbling deep in his nose. You spend five minutes watching the colobus monkeys, which follow you everywhere as you walk around their enclosure. You see an infant, curled up between the paws of its mother in a pose so similar to a photo from your childhood that your heart flutters in your chest.

The Great Cats exhibit is a surprising letdown. The hall's attendant shepherds you to the best viewing spots, and even the reclusive jaguar slinks out briefly to stare up at you. A few early visitors come up to shake your hand. The staffer documenting your day takes pictures, but you move on politely as soon as you can. The exhibit feels ... *empty*. They're still majestic creatures, but you feel no connection. It seems you're not a cat person.

It's different in the Savannah House. Rhinos, giraffes, and elands each connect with you. Something indefinable in gait or posture—the wildebeest playing with its foal—is familiar, familial. You laugh out loud with a hyena that sounds just like your favorite uncle, the one who never drops a punch line. When a tiny gemsbok tiptoes stealthily out of the sun-speckled shadows, you watch each other unblinkingly for several minutes, until some noisy children startle it. As it breaks for the acacia thicket, it swivels its fine-boned head back over its shoulder for one last glance. For an instant, you nearly hurdle the rail and follow it to safety.

You're reluctant to enter the reptile house, but the staff gently encourages you. Many animals are sleeping, but the geckos and chameleons are fascinating. You strain to name the kinship here, but it floats like a faint scent on the breeze. Then you meet the anaconda.

It is draped on a branch, head resting on its coils as you approach. You wait, and its tongue flicks out. Then it flicks again, and the head rises as if drawn on a string, tracking invisible pheromones. Deep brown eyes open and follow the tongue as it points the way to you. The serpent shifts its massive coils, spilling down onto the leaf litter at the bottom of its enclosure, rustling towards the glass. Children squeal and adults gasp as it rises before you to stare directly into your eyes on seven feet of neck. A tear rolls down your nose—you have hypnotized a serpent.

As the day goes on, the bars and fences often frustrate you—it breaks your heart that you can't wrestle with the family of foxes who pounce and whine, playfully begging your company. But you find ways to interact, even through glass and steel. You howl with wolves across the park, play hide-and-seek with otters between the windows of their exhibit. You throw prickly pears to the peccaries and scratch the trunk of an elephant that will not stop playing with your hair and fingers. At the petting zoo, the goats, lambs, and even the pony smell like you.

They always save the best for last. The exhibit is closed to the public, just for you. In a small locker room, you strip down. It's for everyone's safety, they say. The animals know their kin, but they're still animals. It's *really* easy, they stress, for things to get out of hand. The way they talk about it, you're not sure it's the animals they mean. Just be yourself, they tell you. You're all part of one another, now. Then they guide you to the heavy gates.

When they open, you step naked onto the grass in the House of Great Apes. They're waiting for you—bonobos, chimpanzees and gorillas, in clusters that form a half-circle. For an uncomfortable moment, you all fidget nervously, unsure how to greet each other.

Then a baby chimp, craning over Mother's shoulders, leans too far and somersaults dizzily into the grass. Whoops of laughter melt the silence. You scoop the child up, kissing and tickling it as you return it to its mother.

You tussle and play with the youngsters. A gorilla toddler wrestles you to the ground in triumph, and you laugh as he howls in victory. Then he goes down in a pile of young bonobos and chimps, and the tussle continues.

When you are exhausted, you pull away. An over-eager young chimp grabs your hand and drags you back toward the fray. You gasp in pain, and a grownup intervenes—gently, gently! He pries the youngster loose and shoos him off to play. Then he strokes your hand, easing the hurt, and guides you to where the grownups are resting.

The bonobos and chimps are grooming one another, as if it was always this way—one big family. Some of the gorillas join the circle, and you join in the cooing and cheerful sighs. It feels like a quiet holiday afternoon, a circle of conversation—wordless, sweet intimacy that you've rarely felt outside the privacy of bed or cradle.

The elderly silverback stays away. As you watch how the others treat him, you realize he has lost a mate. With great deference you approach him. He huffs halfheartedly at you, but when you take his great paw in your hands he sighs. He settles himself more comfortably on the grass as you comb his thick hair with your fingers, teasing out the knots and burrs.

Time blurs here among this gathering of cousins. Nap, play, sit with children, groom, climb, chase down unruly youngsters, groom some more. You hardly notice the twilight creeping up. The cousins drift away in ones and twos, chimps and bonobos back to their own enclosures, gorillas off to their sleeping cave.

Then people come to take you back. You try to hide. You yell at them when they grasp you, cling to a branch and fight them. The silverback takes your hands in his and plucks them from the branch. He holds your hand and ambles along beside you as you stumble back to the exit. Before you step through, he cups your face with his great paw and strokes your cheek with a rough thumb. A chimpanzee calls a goodbye from her own enclosure, and you choke on tears.

Back in the locker room, they wash you in the shower, scrubbing off the grime. They disinfect your scrapes and inspect a pair of nips from overexcited chimps. They treat and bind two dislocated fingers and give you pills for later, for the pain. They thank you for helping to expand the reach of the zoo, and hand you a drive full of photos and videos.

Then they dress you and walk you to your car.

Serpent's Foe
J.M. Ney-Grimm

When the sun-disk descends below the western horizon, then does the sun god Ra enter the duat, *for his perilous passage through the Realm of the Dead. There he must battle many monsters—the chief of them Apophis—before he achieves the eastern gate, to emerge and rise with the sun-disk at dawn.*

—Egyptian funerary text

She-lion
Born helpless with eyes shut
Her mother moves her cub to a new den
Often, lest scent build up

She-lion
Hunts for her pride while he-lion watches their young
Working with her sisters so cleverly
Stalking, that all may eat

She-lion
Rampant on the shield of might
Couchant in the sigil of cunning
Royal, hear her roar

—hieroglyphic inscription on the fragment
from a forgotten tomb

ABRUPTLY SHE RETURNED to herself.

Where had she been?

The desert spaces of a dream, hunting as a lioness should? She didn't know. But this dim-lit vault looked different through waking eyes than dreaming ones.

Why didn't they sweep the floors?

Sand lay on the flat stone expanse in patches of dusty sparkles. The whole complex cried out for a scouring. Rust coated the iron bars of the cages, from their tops, anchored in the sandstone ceiling, to their bases, sunk into rock. Dung decorated the corners.

And the carcass of her last meal rotted against the bars separating her from the jackal next door. That black-coated beast gnawed at the bloody remains, his snout poked through a gap.

Fah! She lifted her forepaw fastidiously to lick it clean.

Movement diagonally across the broad corridor caught her eye. Another feline—a cheetah, not a lion—paced.

Back and forth.

Back and forth.

Prowling restlessly.

This is no place for me and mine. I, who carry the sun in my eyes by night.

She was caged, she who was meant to be free.

Who had perpetrated this outrage?

She shifted the bulk of her feline body, feeling the press of the cool stone floor against her flank. She lay in the exact center of her square enclosure, avoiding the bars—cold and radiating evil.

She'd been hunting, surely. Before she woke to this zoo. Or was she dreaming now of her imprisonment?

In her earlier dream, the grey shades of moonless night had enfolded her.

Tall strands of sun-dried grasses rustled in the almost-not-there breeze, brushing against her pelt. The bass rumble of bullfrogs mingled with splashing sounds. A rank smell of river mud crept close to the ground, closer than she.

Fah!

Her limbs were made for crouching, for stalking, for lunging from cover.

The faint scent of her prey traced through the cool air rising off the Nile.

Not ibis. Not hippo. Not croc.

Something ... tastier.

She lunged, hindquarters powering her forward, fore claws outstretched, ready to rend as she batted her meal to the ground.

Its nest lay empty—a trammeled area of matted reeds where the red deer had slept.

But not now.

Now it fled, zigzagging, its tail a flag in the night.

She gave chase. *I will feast!*

Nearer and nearer.

Her muscles bunched, then extended, driving her close.

The smell of the creature's submission lent her strength, transforming the draining pain of her hunger into her pounce.

And then the very air lay empty.

Where ... ?

No spoor on the mud. No scent on the breeze. No thud of panicked hooves in the ear.

Utterly gone.

From where would her feast come now?

Yet not all scent had vanished.

Behind her, a fresh aroma threaded the night: musty, dry, a whisper of fear.

She, the hunter, was hunted. The knowledge shivered through her empty belly.

All impulse to slacken her pace vanished as utterly as the deer. She raced onward, fleeing the riverbank, fleeing her pursuer.

What would hunt a lioness?

And toward what end?

Her breath came hot in her mouth and heaved her flanks. She was no horse, meant to race from river mouth to first falls. A sprint, not the marathon, was hers.

The mud grew dry and cracked under her paws, grew sandy.

She slackened her speed. Had she outrun that which chased her?

A rattle of the reeds behind galvanized her anew. Amon Ra! That she should come to this!

The desert sand provided easier running as she spurted for the Valley of the Kings.

I will escape my hunter and then defeat him. I, who protect the gods themselves, will do this.

The next moment she awoke. Or did she dream again? Which was it?

Gah! This confusion of sleeping and waking plagued her still. And another hunt failed! Her belly stabbed her.

She snarled.

The jackal, her neighbor, barked back and retreated to the far corner of his cage.

This is the dream, this underground place. I'll close my eyes and wake where I belong!

Snarling again, she lowered her lids. The smells of the menagerie—her lioness nostrils could distinguish each one—would vanish like the red deer.

The dank, dirty water of the crocodile's lagoon in the cage immediately opposite hers.

Begone!

The musk of the fox, asleep within a hollow log on the stone floor of its enclosure, next to the croc's.

Begone!

The tainted rot of her own abandoned meal, the carcass pushed aside for the jackal to gnaw its bones through the bars.

Get them hence!

Where was the incense, pungent and resinous, wafted from the censors of her priests? Where the perfumes, dabbed on the pulse points of her priestesses? This was no fit abode for her!

My wrath will vanquish you, my captor. Oh, be afraid.

The friendlier, clean warmth of the cheetah pacing the cage on the other diagonal drew her eyes open again.

She flowed to her feet and approached the front of her own cage. The bars were cold, so cold. What would happen, if she touched them? Would she grow equally cold and dead? Turn to stone? Pass into sleep?

You! She demanded of the cheetah. *How did you come here?*

But only a third hissing snarl emerged from her mouth.

Sssr!

Who had done this to her? Taken her speech? Taken so much?

The cheetah ignored her hiss, turning abruptly at a cage corner to pace back the other way. Iron clanged on iron, and the cheetah gave the dry cough of her kind. Reaction, no doubt, to brushing the burning chill metal.

Fah! I am the sun carrier! These beasts will heed me! Say I so!

She glared at the cheetah. At the snorting bull beyond the jackal. At the mantling falcon in the cage at her other side. Its wings batted the still air—foomph, foomph—and then folded close. The scents of the menagerie swirled.

You must be my allies, my servants. Mine! To find the door from this place into the night, dark and clean.

Somehow she would compel them.

Without words, without power, without freedom.

My will shall suffice.

She retreated from her bars, lounged down to the sandy floor, and defiantly closed her eyes.

I shall awaken now.

And she did.

Blinking, she stared down at womanly arms. Hers. Stared further at the sheer linen shift rounded by breasts. Hers. Followed the fabric folded across her curving lap to the vivid green matting on the alabaster floor.

I am woman. Not feline.

She sat in a backless chair, its cushion firm under her thighs. A slave knelt before her holding a hand mirror just so, its polished bronze surface reflecting—

My face!

No, *not* her face. Sekira's.

I inhabit the body of the temple's high priestess.

Which was meet. So she had done throughout Sekira's long tenure, feeling the woman's limbs as her own in religious dance, religious ecstasy. But now—

This time it seemed unwholesome.

"High One." Her handmaiden, Henutt, drew near. "The noontide comes. Your part rushes upon us."

Henutt lifted a palette of kohl from the tray on the tripod next to the mirror slave. Sekira's face must be painted.

"I would sup." Her cat's belly hungered, even now, awakened from its dream of hunger.

I have words. Yes! I have power.

But they were not *her* words. They were Sekira's. She *was* Sekira—for now.

The handmaiden lowered her eyes, not soon enough to hide the shock in their depths. Ah, yes. A priestess fasted before major rituals.

But I hunger and must eat.

Obediently, Henutt crossed to the table at the other side of the robing chamber. She passed through a bright rectangle of sun, cast from high above onto the brown-veined paleness of the floor. She poured from a golden ewer into a gold cup. The amber liquid drew a singing from the metal as it hit. Henutt brought the cup and a plate of almond paste patties to her high priestess.

"High One."

Sekira's belly stirred again, painfully.

Cinnamon and lemon spiked the almond patties. A hint of peach rose from the wine. She reached abruptly for the cup, knocking it in her haste. Wine sloshed over her fingers, cool, and sticky with the honey sweetening it. She lapped it from her palm, tongue warm on her skin, wine vivid and welcome on her tongue. Mmm.

"Highest!" Henutt was quick with a cloth, catching the drips before they stained Sekira's shift.

Sekira bit an almond pattie. Sweet with honey and cinnamon, sour with the citrus. Saliva flooded her mouth. Mmm.

Placing the plate on Sekira's lap, Henutt took up the kohl once more, stirring a small brush over the surface of the black ointment. She drew the bristles across Sekira's eyelid. The greasy feel of the stuff comforted her. She ate and drank while Henutt painted her. Black kohl around the eyes. Powdered malachite on their lids. Red ochre on cheeks and lips—dodging morsels of almond paste and sips of wine.

Then, attar of roses for the pulse points: ankles, wrists and elbow crook, neck.

And, finally, the wig. Heavy braid upon braid of dark glossy hair lifted onto Sekira's head, there to press her shaven scalp.

Henutt poured a last generous measure of rose oil on the wig's crown. Its slickness oozed down through the braids—just a drop or two—and slid across Sekira's skin. The perfume of it, floral and cloying, pressed against her nostrils.

A last swallow of wine to cleanse the mouth. Then she arose. The linen of her shift unfolded, falling straight to her ankles.

The slave placed her mirror on the tray and pulled thonged sandals from beneath the backless chair. Gilt and emeralds ornamented their straps. Sekira slid her feet into them. The slave tied the leather strings.

It was time.

She glided under the tall transom of the robing chamber's doorway into the temple's innermost court.

And stopped.

An aisle of priests flanked her way to the open air altar. Their oiled scalps—wigless—shone in the sun. Their robes, linen garnished with electrum thread, flashed. The emeralds of their massive pectoral chains glittered.

Enveloped in the clean scent of balsam, they waited for her.

Only for her.

She moved not, confronted by the vast sculpture beyond the altar.

Carved from sandstone, the woman sat enthroned, looming over the temple complex. One mighty foot emerged from the draperies at her ankle, graceful and perfect. Her hands lay open in her lap, beautiful as lotus blossoms. The curve of her waist, skillfully hinted by the sculptor, molded the folds of her shift.

She was womanhood perfected.

Deity.

With the noble head of a lioness.

She was Bastet, goddess against disease, protector of the pharaoh, the burnished Eye of Ra.

I am she!

Bastet stood still.

Enrobed in Sekira's human form, she stared at her divine form, come home to her memories of her life before dreaming, come home to a true knowledge of herself.

Then Sekira's limbs moved her forward through the ranks of the priests toward the altar and the smaller statue beside it. Another portrayal of the goddess, rendered in alabaster, carried from her inmost sanctuary—her home—for this outdoor ceremony.

This was the *sed* of the goddess. The ritual renewal of Bastet's divinity and strength.

My strength.

As the handmaidens had bathed Sekira, so the priests had bathed Bastet's stone form. When Sekira donned her shift, Bastet received hers. While Sekira refused to break her fast, so Bastet received these passed-over meats for her own.

She remembered. She remembered it all.

Venerated, worshipped, adored. And in return ...

I hold illness at bay.

I bear the shield of Amon-Ra before the pharaoh.

I carry the sun in my eyes through the night.
I maintain the maat *of life!*

She arrived before the altar. And drew back.

All lay in readiness: the unguents for her feet, the salves for her hands, and the perfumes for her face. Then the besom, the flail, and the rod to whip evil spirits from the daylight into their prison underground. And finally the urn of water, drawn from the Nile above the last falls, to be poured over her brow in purification.

All these, but there were more.

The palm wine, with which to wash the dead.

The spices to perfume them.

The natron for the drying.

Linen bandages and sealing resin, to be blessed before their use forty days hence.

All these, the tools of mummification, and one more thing: a jeweled knife, the length of Sekira's palm.

She knew then this was a dream. A dream—or a memory—of her last day before she dreamt in earnest.

The chief priest bent to raise a basket from the foot of the altar. Within lay a cat, short haired and elegant, and asleep.

Sekira's hands lifted the feline, oh so gently, onto the altar. She was old. Sekira's hands stroked her taupe pelt in reverence. She was sacred. Sekira's hands took up the knife, readying to drive the blade home, just behind the ears, in the nape.

I won't, Bastet vowed. *She will live out her old age.*

Sekira's shield hand cupped the cat's head.

She will enjoy the sun's warmth.

Sekira's weapon hand tightened.

Her weakness is not mine.

Sekira's shield hand elongated the cat's neck.

Her death and mummification will not be now.

Sekira's hands moved.

Amon-Ra! No!

Gasping, Bastet bolted awake.

Her eyes opened on the dim glow of the underground space with its cages side by side.

A lioness once more, she stood with her limbs stiff and outraged, matching her angry hiss.

How dare an alien power compel her to slay one of the innocent creatures under her protection! Let alone a sacred feline of the temple!

A weighty body smacked water behind the bars across from her. Sobek the crocodile had entered his lagoon to seek the rotted victuals he secreted there.

Fah! These carrion eaters!

She—fastidious and feline—ate only the freshest of meats, leaving any remains to her jackal neighbor. She could hear him now, his narrow snout poked through the bars, gnawing bones.

And yet these were her potential allies: wily Sobek, fiery Maftet, careful Anubis, and all the other prisoners in this zoo of twelve.

The rank odor of rotting flesh—sour and sharp and sickeningly sweet co-mingled—crawled into her nostrils and turned her stomach.

Her memory flashed back to the moment before she awoke: the cat limp in Sekira's hands—her hands—like the linen cloths that would wrap its mummified form, a single drop of blood leaking from the knife piercing its neck just behind the left ear.

Were she woman now, not great cat, she would weep. Who had persuaded Sekira to such horror? Who had compelled her—Bastet—to relive that deed, that interval of time?

The faint drift of reptilian musk breathed on the sighing of the air, creeping from the bare tunnel beyond the last pair of cages. Dry, menacing, with the hint of a rustle beneath it.

My enemy! The same from her desert dream. There, he exhaled. There, he waited. There ... *I will seek him.*

The cheetah's cough recalled Bastet from her reverie of vengeance. She flicked her tail in annoyance.

Pacing would do Maftet no good. Solving the puzzle of their incarceration required thought, not restless movement.

And I ... I am the thinker here.

She curled around herself, and then lowered her belly to the floor, tucking her paws beneath. The cool of the stone calmed her hot desire to wound ... someone.

One day they would slip, these servants of her enemy, servants she'd not yet seen, and then ... she would pounce.

I will take my freedom sauced with their deaths.

But now, now was the season for thinking, for understanding, for kneading the future into a shape of her own devising.

She felt ever more certain that this was no dream. These cages, these beasts, this menagerie collected by some power of malevolence—all were more than the stuff of slumbering imagination.

My desert hunt—that was dream. *My last ritual at the temple*—dream as well. This prison, strangely familiar, yet utterly strange: real.

This realm? I have stalked it.

These walls? The fires in my eyes once lapped their stones in golden radiance.

This below ground passage? I have traversed it.

Yet always I bided within my temple. Sometimes encased within the great statue of the inner court. Often within the smaller sacred statue of the sanctuary. More rarely within the flesh of her high priestess. And always—*always*—a pervading spirit on the breeze, within the perfumed smoke of the incense, one with the wisdom of the holy cats.

I was the ka *of that place.*

Worshipped.

Empowered.

Adored.

A purr rumbled in her throat.

These memories of her days eluded some deeper truth. The key to her presence here. The key to her freedom.

What of her nights?

This was night. An unnatural night, dimly lit, yet night all the same. And she had been ... not here. Never here. But somewhere like this when the sun's great disc sank below the land.

I, who carry the sun in my eyes by night.

No metaphor. It was truth!

And yet how?

Where had she spent her nights that followed those innocent days?

And how did those nights compare to this strange one?

Eyes still closed, she tracked the darkness, down and down through the blankness that should be memory.

And she awoke.

Within Sekira again.

The eyes of the high priestess were shut in slumber, and Bastet could see nothing. But she felt her womanly arms clasped across her lower ribs, her hips sunk deep within the cushions of her sleeping platform, her neck secure against a wooden head rest.

I belong here, not there behind bars. Here is my home. Here is my peace. Here is real. Not there.

A step sounded in the room.

Mios?

Now she remembered. Her son would visit her in the night. Not Sekira's son. Bastet's.

In the earliest of days, the Egyptians embraced him. Deliverer of Truth and Champion of Order, they called him. Never mind that he arrived on the winds, from nowhere, adopted son of their goddess, bearing her leonine head.

They built temples in his honor and claimed him as Ra's own.

In that era, he visited his mother openly by day.

Then came the Hyksos from the east, invading, burning, raping. And Egyptians noted his resemblance to the eastern gods. Not his leonine form, nor his lion-headed man form, but the third form: red-skinned and bearing horns on his brow. Like Shamesh, like Marduk, like Nabu—the cloven-footed ones.

Then they reviled him and gave him darker names.

Lord of Slaughter.

Knife-wielder.

Devourer.

And he visited her in secret only.

Did he come to her now? To help her in her time of trial?

He is my son, the child of my heart, my beloved. Never mind that before the war the Hyksos deities birthed him. They rejected him. *I found him on the sands, mewling, abandoned. And taught him all I know.*

She struggled to open her eyes, Sekira's eyes. The paralysis of sleep held them closed against her will.

Another step, softer.

Another step, heavier.

The murmur of voices.

The scrape of a chisel on stone.

And then she knew. This was her last night in her home. The night of the invasion. The night of the desecration. *Now* her memories returned.

Tall shadows with horned brows, moving in the dark.

The dead left in their wake—acolytes, players, priests, and priestesses—without wounds, yet limp like the cat, blood dripping from their mouths.

The blasted temple walls, scraped clean of their sacred writings, the hieroglyphs razed.

And one memory so fraught, so potent, so fateful—

Her cartouche and its doom.

Three sacred symbols, enclosed by an oval, expressed her name. So long as the writing or carving endured—on a temple wall, within a coffin panel, anywhere—her recorded name ensured Bastet would live forever.

The first glyph, the oil jar, signified her role as protector of the gods themselves, protector of the pharaoh, protector of the people. *I hold evil at bay even as medicinal balms defy sickness.*

A chisel had scored the temple's stone, removing her leading hieroglyph, the emblem of ease.

Her second glyph, two loaves of bread, symbol of the feminine perfected: love and nurture and acceptance.

The chisel moved a second time, gouging the name for her receptive essence.

Her third glyph, a goddess with the lioness head. Bastet herself. The chisel's swift edge debrided it completely.

Throughout the temple complex, the desecrators moved, killing, defacing, erasing.

And when the last cartouche disappeared ...

She woke up!

To the zoo. This dreaming of her cartouche an echo of that first time, the time it was real. Muzzy and distraught then. Furious and disempowered now.

Grr! Her growl ripened into a full-blooded roar, pouring through the cages with the force of a cataract, mingling with the animal smells.

Beside torpid Sobek, the fox yipped and pattered to a far corner. The cow beyond him lowed in pain.

So timid, her compatriots.

They disgusted her.

The falcon next door mantled its wings, achieving lift. It fell back when a silver chain jerked it short, the links clinking.

Bastet roared again.

She was protector of all Egypt and defender of its gods, but these pathetic creatures were unworthy of her. Let them molder here in exile. She would free herself and escape alone to race under the stars.

By starlight, she would be reborn, her skin painted red, her brow sporting horns.

By starlight she would become one with her enemy.

By starlight she would forsake her heritage and embrace a new one.

The jackal barked, a deeper, more commanding resonance than the high yip of the fox.

Amon-Ra! Who had generated those racing thoughts?

Not I. Never I. I deny them.

She swung her massive head around to stare Anubis down.

I am lioness! Hear me roar!

The jackal stood his ground, then seated himself deliberately, holding her gaze all the while.

Great cat and great canine sat and glared; she, hot and furious; he, adamant and cold.

Bastet faltered first, looking down.

Fah! The rotting carcass of her despised meal lay at her feet, white ribs rising from the bloody welter of skin and hooves and broken antelope legs. Turning away in revulsion, Bastet paused. What if ... ?

This was no food of hers, no. Nor anything she wished to touch. But *she* would be unworthy of her title were she to disdain a resource.

Fighting herself, she dipped her right paw in the stinking muck. It was slimy. Clotting. Foul.

Holding the forepaw up, fighting the urge to lick it clean, she backed on three legs just far enough to find dry stone.

With fetid blood, she drew the oil jar, fragrant and wholesome. The leading hieroglyph in her name.

Then another trip to the well of death for her ink—tainted ink—and she scribed two loaves of bread: the power behind nurture, the power of her womanhood. Her second symbol.

One last visit to the congealing pool of blood for the final glyph, most potent of all: herself as the goddess with the leonine head.

And the encircling oval that signified her divine royalty.

I am Bast!

But she was not.

Where were her powers? Where, her alternate forms? Erasing her cartouche had erased the better part of her. Yet drawing it anew recalled nothing of her greater self to her.

Her burst of will and rage transformed her not into a woman with a leonine head who possessed the strength to remake her world.

She remained lioness. Wordless. Powerless. Imprisoned.

Gah!

Pride would not suffice for this. Nor thought. Nor ferocity.

Vowing to withhold her roar, *it* roared *her*, deep and guttural, the visceral sound of a creature that kills to eat.

I am lioness! Hear my challenge!

But this was no challenge. Were she woman, she would blush. This was weakness, futility, impotent complaint.

Gah!

Her fury should make her strong. It always had in the past. From wrath came courage. From courage came action. From action came deeds. *I am strong!*

She crouched and pounced, descending on her prison door as a thunderbolt to an obelisk, her forepaw all muscle and might, batting her enemy to the ground, ready for her death bite.

The bars burned her paw, seared her jaws, and buffeted her body to the floor.

Dizzy and tingling, as though lightning-struck indeed, she struggled for breath. Blackness claimed her.

And she awoke to dream again.

Not in the temple this time. Nor in the desert night. But a stone tunnel all too similar to the one that held her cage: sandstone glowing gold with not one window piercing its tall upper walls.

Ah … now she knew this place. This one *and* the caged one from which she came.

As a lioness-headed woman, regal and strong, she stood now in the *duat*, the underworld ruled by Osiris. Here, Ra traveled from his setting at eventide to his rising afresh in the morning. Here, the souls of the dead came for judgment. Here, Bastet herself carried Ra's light while he walked darkened.

Yes. This was the *duat*, but she was not new-come to it. So too was the zoo that imprisoned her of the *duat*. The scent of the beasts—amphibious Sobek, avian Set, canine Anubis—lingered before the great gateway where she paused, sifting forward from some unknown distance behind her.

Ah! My cartouche is power!

Her name-glyph—drawn in blood—had brought her here, to another hall of the underworld. Freed from the menagerie by its magic, she would seek a further freedom now.

If I must battle Apophis himself, I will be free.

She studied the two pillars before her. On the right, Ra—carved in bas relief and painted gold—brandished a leaf-shaped sword. Across from him, on the left pillar, the image of the serpent loomed, pale hooded and rearing, dripping venom from its fangs.

She knew this gate.

"O, you who keep the gates because of Osiris."

And now she had voice. Coming from her woman's lungs through her feline larynx, the words emerged, unreasonably melodious and beautiful.

"O, you who guard these portals. O, you who report the affairs of the Two Lands every day to the Lord of the Dead."

She straightened her back and lifted her chin.

"I know you."

And she did.

He who dances in blood.

Hippopotamus-faced.

He who lives on snakes.

"And I know your names!"

Every night she had named them. Every night she had mastered them. Every night she had passed by each monstrous guardian unharmed, accompanying Ra to his rebirth.

Every night she passed into this hall, this very one awaiting her.

She knew what she would see when she stepped forward: a great vault upheld by a forest of columns, a platform at its center. Osiris would preside, seated on his throne in majesty, the double crown gracing his ram's head. Thoth would record, tablet and stylus in hand, his keen falcon's eyes making no mistake. And Anubis, black-headed and ominous, would conduct her to her judgment.

Never before had she been judged. That was for others. But this time—this time, she knew—her heart would be weighed against Maat's feather and found lacking or found guiltless.

She stepped forward, her bare womanly foot soundless on the cool, gritty sandstone floor.

There were the columns, carved and adorned, topped with sheaves of papyrus.

There was the platform, approached by three steps at the center of each side.

And there was the golden scale with the beast coiled beneath it, serpentine and hungry, longing for her heart.

Apophis' representative.

She stepped forward.

But the white-skirted figure who awaited her in the shadow of the first column was not Anubis.

Red-skinned and low-browed with horns curling above his pale eyes, Marduk took her arm and drew her forward, his hooves clattering on the stone.

She stiffened only a moment before she yielded.

The aroma of fire enveloped him. His fingers burned hot and repellant, slightly moist. He sneered, triumphant: "May Apophis eat your heart."

Bastet slowed, not in fear, but for dignity. She would walk at *her* pace, not his. And she would speak, asserting the melody of her voice against his deep syllables. *You will not intimidate me, Marduk.*

"My heart is pure."

"I think not!" He conducted her to the platform and up its steps. "Child-stealer!"

Another figure emerged from the column forest. Not Thoth, falcon-headed, but Nabu, the scribe of the Hyksos gods. His white skirt dipped below his knees, longer than that of Marduk, and a shawl covered his chest, but his red skin, pale eyes, and horned brow were the same. He carried a clay tablet in his left hand, a reed stylus in his right.

He said nothing. He didn't have to. Bastet could read his insolence in his stance as he climbed the stairs to the platform and came to rest beside the scale.

The serpent at the scale's pedestal uncoiled, casting rustling echoes through the hall, and reared up, hood unfurled. That was right, the only thing right. Always the beast waited on its meal.

But she shivered. This time it waited for her. She'd sensed it even within her cage: Apophis, her enemy, more so than the Hyksos gods who hated her.

A third figure approached from the far end of the vault. Not Osiris, as should be, but Bastet no longer expected the proper Lord of the Dead, now that Marduk usurped Anubis' place.

Shamesh—king of the Hyksos deities—paced forward, the folds of his ornately pleated white robes alternately revealing and concealing his noisy hooves, a heavy scepter gripped in his right hand, a scowl narrowing his pale eyes. She would get no fair judgment there.

Shamesh climbed the stairs to the platform and seated himself in Osiris' throne. "Begin," he instructed, his voice lighter than Marduk's.

Bastet straightened her already straight spine and raised her arms.

"I have not committed sin.

"I have not slain.

"I have not stolen."

Marduk growled.

Shamesh admonished him: "Peace, o judge."

Bastet continued through all forty-two of the denials.

"I have not purloined offerings."

How could she? She was the goddess to whom the offerings were made. They were hers to consume.

"I have not uttered lies.

"I have not uttered curses."

"I have done no evil."

Marduk lifted his arm.

She'd always wondered if this part hurt. Her son, Mios, said not. And yet they flinched, the dead.

Marduk's red fist passed through her breast bone to grasp her beating heart.

And she flinched.

It did not hurt. And yet ... she felt something. A vulnerability, a violation, a sense of trespass. Would she have felt thusly if Anubis, dedicated judge of all Egypt, were pursuing this rite?

Marduk drew her heart from her body, blood dripping from it, and placed it on the left dish of the scale.

Bastet felt hollow, empty.

Shamesh drew an ostrich feather from a fold of his robes and placed it on the right dish of the scale. "Let her be judged, who has never been so assessed before. Does she speak true?"

Nabu tucked his stylus behind his ear and released the clamp that held the scale in balance. The right dish dipped down, far down. Could a feather weigh so much?

Then it rose, and Bastet's heart dipped down, so far down. Had she sinned so much in all those ages of time?

The feather dipped again, but when it rose a second time, it did not descend again. Her heart was heavy, burdened with wrongs.

What wrongs were these? She had committed none!

And then she knew.

Not the mothering of Mios as the Hyksos gods believed. They had well and truly abandoned him, and her mercy counted for much in this weighing of her virtue. No, she had never stolen another mother's child. And never would.

Her sins were other: pride, arrogance, lack of ruth for the pitiful.

But I am strong and must be so, cried her silent and measured heart. *Would you have me weak? All Egypt is my care!*

She had not spoken aloud, but Marduk answered her. "Compassion for weakness is not weakness itself. Nor does weakness erase all other virtues, *Protectress* of the Innocent."

How had he, who judged her unfairly, also judged her aright? She who disdained her fellow menagerie inmates so recently, and disdained them as well in their power before the Hyksos came.

I have not blasphemed the gods. Thusly she had spoken, and it was not true. Every day had she withheld her piety. Every night had she refused reverence. She who was called to their protection as much as that of the pharaoh and his people.

I have sinned.

With a nervous flick of his tongue, Nabu lifted his stylus and marked condemnation on his tablet.

Shamesh raised his scepter and pronounced her doom. "Be condemned. Be reviled. Be utterly unmade." His arm fell, and the base of his scepter thudded dully on the stone.

The serpent, still waiting, still rearing, rose taller. Its coils on the floor thickened and lengthened. Its hood broadened. A pattern of dark gold appeared against its pale scales: Bastet's cartouche. And still the serpent grew, looming over the scale with her heart, looming over Bastet herself.

Shamesh on his throne disappeared behind the shifting coils.

Nabu dropped his stylus. *Tink, tink*—it rattled on the platform.

The serpent swung its vast and hooded head around, moving between Bastet and the scribe, then between her and Marduk. The coils of the snake surrounded her, their ophidian musk permeating the air, their tall and curving surfaces forming a circular maze.

The columns of the hall of judgment were gone. Only the snake remained, massive and moving, its muscular body forming living walls that confined her, directed her.

The snake's scales rustled as it advanced.

Bastet shivered, though she was not cold.

And then came another sound: a baby's cry, scared and angry.

My son! She began to run, following the curving channel formed by the serpent's coils. First around to the right, then redirected to the left, on and on through a spiraling passage, the scaled walls towering above her head.

The baby's cries turned to shrieks.

Bastet espied an opening in the snake's living maze and darted for it. Free for a moment, she raced across a golden plain under a black sky.

And then the serpent's tail rushed in from the side, knocking her to the ground, sweeping her back into the confines of its coils.

She scrambled to her feet just before her prison crushed her.

Amon-Ra, send me Ra—your warrior self!

It had always been he who fought the serpent, never she. She fought disease. She fought corruption. She fought the monsters of the *duat*. But Apophis belonged to Ra alone. And this *was* Apophis, she realized.

While Bastet held Ra's light—safe within her eyes—the sun god dueled Apophis every night. And won. Each time slaying the serpent of chaos and slicing its head from its body. And then he bathed in the waters of renewal. And received his light from her once more, ready to leap from the *duat* into the dawning.

The snake shifted abruptly and its massive flank slammed against Bastet's ribs. She leaped aside, still running, only to be smacked from the other side.

Ra is not here. Only I am here. I and my son.

For the baby still wailed.

I am here.

Another shifting coil struck her.

I am!

Then she pounced, raking the pale scales with her finger nails, which lengthened into claws even as they penetrated her enemy's flesh, drawing bloody ichor.

Whap, whap—right, left! Her womanly hands with their lioness claws did damage. And then the bite with her leonine head. Her fangs sunk deep, and the snake's ichor burned, searing her tongue, bursting from the scales to drench and scorch all her skin. It blackened as though brushed by flame, and she fell to her knees.

A baby lay before her, red-skinned and cloven-footed, with curving horns on its low brow. She scooped it into her burning arms.

My son! My son!

And she wept.

Where the tears touched her skin, the blackening char fell away, revealing red. She felt horns pressing out from her skull, breaking through the skin of her brow.

She wept harder.

Her feet ached, thickening, changing, becoming hooved.

My son! My son!

And he was. But the mothering of him could not be done as the protectress of Egypt. Ah, no. She must become—not forever, but for a time—protectress of Mios.

And she had.

From Bastet into Ishtar, the mother of war. An avatar. A reflection. A fourth form added to her three.

And with her transformation had come war. Between Egypt and the Hyksos, armies fought their battles, bloody and destructive, while Bastet's temples lay empty of her presence.

Egypt lost and lost. Until her people raised up a new protector: Mios, the cat-headed. Fierce like his absent mother and dedicated to fighting Egypt's enemies, he assumed his mother's role—the one she had failed.

When he reached his maturity, she reclaimed her duties, cat-headed once again. Together they drove the Hyksos out of Egypt, and the Egyptians rejoiced in their freedom.

Bastet looked now at her renewed reddened skin.

Mios had stopped crying. He hiccupped, and she put him to her breast. His baby hand—so small, so red—reached up to her lioness fangs, patted her whiskers, and clutched the fur of her neck. His baby mouth suckled her nourishment. And, as he nursed, his red skin faded to Egyptian coppery brown, as did her own.

She was Bastet once more. Herself.

A shadow passed across her face, and she looked up.

The hooded head of Apophis swayed above her, venom dripping from its fangs.

She stepped away, her arms shifting to cover her child.

The serpent tensed.

"Stay back from him!" she commanded. "He is mine, not yours!"

A hissing filled the air.

"Hhe iss mine!"

"Not now!"

"Yess, Isshtar promised him to me, and you were sshhe."

Bastet lifted her chin. "Only for a time. She existed before my borrowing. She continues after. But we are *not* the same."

She took another step back. "You *know* this, chaos-bringer!"

"Thhe sacrifice—sss—wass made, whether by shhe or by you."

"It matters, serpent."

"It matterss, yess, to you. Not to me."

And the serpent struck, its massive head bearing down upon her, its maw gaping, its fangs flared to deliver their poison.

She turned just in time to protect her baby. One fang broke on her skull, snapped by the force of the snake's thrust. The other pierced her neck, driving deep into her flesh, bringing agony and oblivion.

She managed to fall on her side, sparing Mios.

Fire scorched her again, flowing through her veins, searing her innards as thoroughly as Apophis' ichor—flowing from the wound she had inflicted—had seared her skin.

Within the blackness drowning her, images stirred.

Scaled and taloned legs burst from the body of a vast serpent, while scaled wings grew from its shoulders. Stars pricked out in the darkness and shone on the dragon's hide, turning it iridescent black. The beast leaped into the sky and flew away.

Someone sobbed.

The sound of water flowing—the chuckling of a rivulet—mingled with the woman's grief. Then the fresh smell of a breeze off a lake swept both away, and a man smiled tenderly down upon her.

He grew ram's horns, massive and curled and heavy. Weighty enough to anchor a nation, fairest Egypt. Spiraling, as wisdom spirals. A crown for deity, the god who ruled the living when they died, and the dead in the field of reeds.

Osiris.

His man's face became a ram's, noble and radiating compassion. His eyes shone darkly, deep wells of thought and mercy.

He bowed, dipping his immense ovine head—the ram, a symbol of sacrifice—and gazed at her. What did he see?

Then he changed again, returning his face to a man's form: steady of eye and firm of chin, a pharoah's beard below. Lord of the *duat*. His seeing would be true.

Osiris, forgive me.

"For what, cat-child?" His voice was warm.

For my pride. For my contempt. For all my sins.

"I need you strong, beloved."

Yet weakness does not erase all other virtues. She remembered Marduk's words.

"So you have learned, my cherished one. All is well."

Marduk spoke true.

"As did you, sweet cat. You are beautiful and fierce. You are all I would desire for you."

She wept again.

"Tell me your sorrow, my dear one."

At the beginning of my motherhood, when I first saved my son, could I not have nurtured Mios without failing Egypt?

Osiris' smile grew sad. "Egypt has learned with you, and not all ends are mine to choose, though my powers be great."

I am protectress of Egypt, protectress of the pharaoh, protectress of the gods themselves! Even amidst delirium, she felt her wrath. Self-wrath. *Egypt went down to defeat. The pharaoh fell beneath his enemies' blades. And the gods themselves felt my contempt.*

Egypt has risen again, but I am not all you desire.

"Oh?"

And then she knew. *I am not all I desire.*

"Yes, that is it. Now go free."

The darkness parted, and she awoke. To the dark eyes of the jackal, unwavering in their gaze.

He sat just as before, just the same, steadily meeting her regard. But she—she was different. Sprawled on the sandy floor in her womanly form, legs bloodied and bruised, her shift dripping venom, her tangled black hair a mane that strayed across her full lips.

She pushed up on one arm. Looked around.

Anubis was not alone in his witness.

Sobek had crawled from his lagoon to crouch at his barred gate, eyes beady and cold.

Thoth roosted on his leafless branch and watched.

The fox perched atop his hollow log, surveying her.

Maftet the cheetah had ceased her pacing to stand and stare.

All—all eleven of her compatriots—had emerged from their lairs or halted their accustomed activity to look upon Bastet. And behind the characteristics of their kind—the chill greed of the crocodile, the killing precision of the falcon—she saw something else.

They knew her.

They knew her faults. They knew her failures. They held a position to judge.

And judged not.

They might have condemned her contempt. Disdained her disdain. Pitied her lack of ruth.

And chose not to.

Their animal scents enveloped her—musky, musty, fetid and clean—the odors of fur and feather and scale.

She breathed them in. Welcomed them. Received them.

These are my natural essences too.

Strength and the power to yield.

Ferocity and the impulse toward nurturing.

Discernment and acceptance.

Just as this pantheon bore their animal traits, so did she. Just as they possessed divine gifts within their animality, so did she. She was beast. She was woman. She was goddess.

With her, they knew that too.

The proud lioness within her yet protested their compassion. The woman inside her wondered how it might feel to let it in. And the goddess in her said, "Yes."

Anubis' eyes, behind their flat obduracy, smiled.

Bastet would free him first of all. Dipping her finger into the muddy puddle formed by her dripping shift, she would write his name and encircle it to form his cartouche.

The jackal's ears dipped, and the smile behind his eyes strengthened.

She should free her fellow prisoners, oh, yes, but one other action must come first. Anubis knew it. And, now, so did she.

Bastet pushed herself up to sitting, fumbling at that remnant of battle caught in her hair.

Apophis' fang.

Lifting one tangled lock from another, her fingers probed the mass of her tresses. Bit by bit, the strands released their trophy: not a fang after all.

A reed pen.

Kneeling, the floor hard beneath her, she dipped this stylus in the puddled venom and wrote her name on the sandstone. Not Bastet, though that was she, but her more descriptive epithet.

Eye of Ra.

An eye might burn with anger. An eye might transmit the sun's light. But an eye could also see. As she saw now.

Somewhere beneath the threshold of sound, she felt more than heard her grown son's whisper: "O, mother mine, I salute you."

Her pen transcribed the last arc of the oval encircling her cartouche.

And the door of her cage swung open.

MORE BY THE AUTHORS

BRIDGET McKENNA
The Old Organ Trail
A Little Night Music
The Little Things
Hole in the Wall
The Little Book of Self-Editing for Writers

D.J. GELNER
Jesus Was a Time Traveler
Hack: The Complete Game
Rogue
Twilight of the Gods
The Big Book of Hobby Ideas

SARAH STEGALL
Chimera
Deadfall
Deadwater
Farside

A.C. SMYTH
Crowchanger
Stormweaver

S.E. BATT
Friend Ship
Baldwin's Bazaar of Curious Creatures
Martin Dripps, P.I.: The Lost Rainbow Case
Weapon of Choice
Short Story Omnibus

KEN FURIE
Artist Gods of Rock & Other Stories
Axis of Garg

SCOTT DYSON
14 Dark Windows
DIE 6
The Striker Files

JOHN HINDMARSH
Mark One
Mark Two
Glass Complex – Book One: Broken Glass
Shen Ark: Departure
An Accident on Church Street

R.S. McCOY
Sparks
Spirits

FRANCES STEWART
The Stonecatchers

J.M. NEY-GRIMM
Devouring Light
A Knot of Trolls
Sarvet's Wanderyar
Livli's Gift
Troll-magic

ABOUT *QUANTUM ZOO*

D.J. Gelner and J.M. Ney-Grimm—two indie authors with a yen for all the exhilarating work that goes into publishing books—decided that putting together an anthology would be great fun.

The indie community has some wonderfully talented writers. We sent out an open call for submissions and were amazed by both the quantity and the quality of the stories we received. Choosing the very best dozen for our anthology was tough. There were so many good ones!

We overcame our delighted indecision, selected the stories, edited them, and *Quantum Zoo* was born.

Here's a little bit about us.

D.J. GELNER

D.J. Gelner enjoys trying to surprise himself—and his readers—around every corner. Maybe that's why he has tried a number of professions on for size so far: attorney, radio personality, sports writer, entrepreneur, and now fiction writer. He also is a world traveler and wine enthusiast—in early 2014, he became a Certified Specialist of Wine. When he's not mentally exploring other worlds, D.J. lives in the suburbs of St. Louis, Missouri with his trusty dog, Sully.

J.M. NEY-GRIMM

J.M. Ney-Grimm lives with her husband and children in Virginia, just east of the Blue Ridge Mountains. She's learning about permaculture gardening and debunking popular myths about food. The rest of the time she reads Robin McKinley, Diana Wynne Jones, and Lois McMaster Bujold, plays boardgames like *Settlers of Catan*, rears her twins, and writes stories set in her troll-infested North-lands. Look for her novels and novellas at your favorite bookstore—online or on Main Street.

Made in the USA
Charleston, SC
22 November 2014